I AM A
MARTINICAN WOMAN

&

THE WHITE
NEGRESS

I AM A
MARTINICAN WOMAN

&

THE WHITE
NEGRESS

Two Novelettes by
Mayotte Capécia
(Lucette Ceranus)

Translated by Beatrice Stith Clark

Passeggiata Press
Pueblo Colorado

First English Language Edition by Passeggiata Press 1997
P.O. Box 636
Pueblo CO 81002

Library of Congress Cataloging-in-Publication Data

Capécia, Mayotte, 1916-1955
    [Je suis martiniquaise. English]
    I am a Martinican woman ; & The white negress : two
Novelettes / by Mayotte Capécia (Lucette Ceranus) ; translated by Beatrice Stith Clark
        p. cm.
    Includes bibliographical references.
    ISBN 1-57889-002-0 (cloth). — ISBN 1-57889-001-2 (pbk.)
    I. Clark, Beatrice Stith   II. Capécia, Mayotte, 1916-
1955. Négresse blanche. English. III. Title. IV. Title:
White negress.
    PQ3949.C28J413 1997
    843-dc21
                                                    97-14262
                                                       CIP

Photos of Lucette Ceranus (Mayotte Capécia) © by her son
Claude Combette.

Cover art © Passeggiata Press of drawing by Max K. Winkler.
Design by David Eaklor

To Nathan and Andrea, my grandchildren

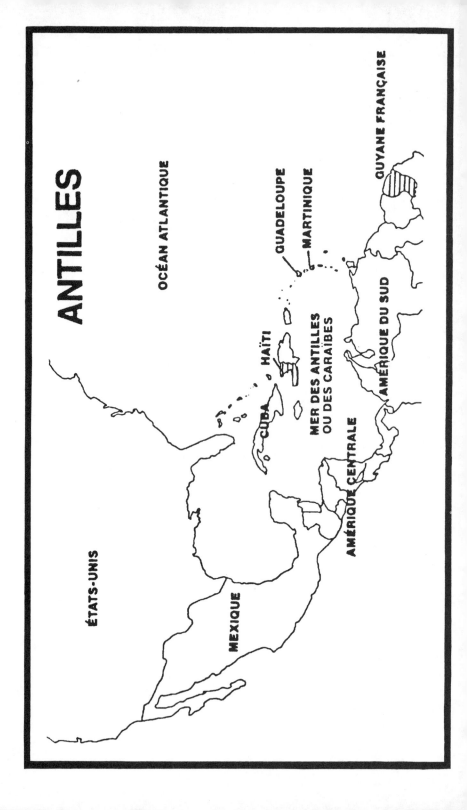

ANTILLES

ÉTATS-UNIS

OCÉAN ATLANTIQUE

MEXIQUE

CUBA

HAÏTI

QUADELOUPE

MARTINIQUE

MER DES ANTILLES
OU DES CARAÏBES

AMÉRIQUE CENTRALE

AMÉRIQUE DU SUD

GUYANE FRANÇAISE

Foreword

An Update on the Author

Since the summer of 1994, when I completed the final version of the *Introduction* to the English translation of Mayotte Capécia's two novels, *Je suis Martiniquaise* (1948) and *La Négresse blanche* (1950), I have gained access to significant biographical data on this pioneer Martinican writer. It is imperative that I share this information with readers because it casts new light, not only on her personal life story but on the criticism, both literary and social, which her works have generated since their publication in Paris.

In the Fall of 1994 as a result of discreet references[1] to the possibility that Capécia may have been a pseudonym, I began to probe my human resources in Martinique. Through persistent communication with professional resources arranged by a professor at the University of the Antilles and Guyana in Fort-de-France, I was informed that indeed this was the case, Capécia was the pseudonym for Combette and that the writer's year of birth was 1916. Challenged and inspired by this evidence, in the spring of 1995 I made arrangements to revisit my beloved Martinique which had become the focal point of my research during the past twenty-five years. Indeed, in 1973, I published an article on Capécia [2] and, as was typical of literary discourse during the early seventies, I adjoined the subtitle, "With Apologies to Frantz Fanon." The reference was to the influential revolutionary Martinican psychiatrist and author of *Peau noire, masques blancs* in which he excoriated his female literary compatriot.[3] Since the CLAJ publication, I have made several presentations on Capécia, denoting a more critical assessment of Fanon's scathing commentary and assigning to the Martinican woman writer a significant role in Francophone Caribbean literature. My article on Capécia's two novels, *Je suis Martiniquaise*[4] and *La Négresse blanche* was the first and has remained the only published study devoted exclusively to her.[5] Published as the autobiography of an Antillean woman of color, *Je suis Martiniquaise* was promoted as the first-time, intimate revelation of her mentality—superstitious, exotic and passionate. In the narration that follows, I describe the research accomplished while in Martinique, my mission being to seek answers to the question: "Who was the real Mayotte Capécia?" This sojourn in the "l'île aux fleurs" to probe further into the life of Capécia, produced notable results and proved to be quite an adventure for me.

The first few days were spent in Fort-de-France, confirming initial contacts with resource persons such as the head librarian at the Biblioteque Schoelcher whose courteous staff informed me about relevant holdings there. Having formed cordial bonds of camaraderie there some twenty years ago, I was welcomed by several friends with true Martinican hospitality. Among them was Josephe, a retired public executive, who lives in the commune of Schoelcher adjoining Fort-de-France, and who, when I made known that I was searching for biographical data on Capécia, offered to drive me to Carbet, which I knew to be the writer's birthplace. Early the next morning, we set out for this coastal town of around 3000 inhabitants, between Belle-Fontaine and St. Pierre. Upon arrival in Carbet, we drove directly to the City Hall where Josephe asked the clerk to locate records for Mayotte Combette, born in 1916. To our surprise, vital statistics records produced no such name.

As we exited the City Hall, we met two stately gentlemen, one of whom Josephe knew and recognized as the mayor of Carbet. They stopped to chat a moment and during the course of their conversation Josephe spoke of our mission. The mayor obligingly told her about a woman in Fond-Capot who knew the Combette family. Following his precise instructions, we arrived quickly in Fond-Capot, a short distance from Carbet. Josephe knocked on the door of a modest house which was opened by a slight, neatly dressed woman who listened patiently to Josephe as she explained our purpose, and we were invited to enter. Although she appeared somewhat dubious as to why we wanted to know more about Capécia, the soft-spoken matron made a valiant effort to recall the family that she had once known, but whose long absence from the region had dimmed her memory. She was certain, however, that Combette was the surname of Capécia's father, Eugène, who did not marry the mother; her surname was "Uranus." Our interviewee implied that the Capécia family she had known as a child, ranked in the lower strata of society in the community. As we departed, she pointed out a house across the road, the property of the son of Eugène Combette, who was in Paris at that time.

Josephe and I headed back to her home in Schoelcher where she called back to the City Hall in Carbet for a second search under the name "Uranus." Again, there was no record. Fortunately, Josephe had access to a local resource, a Mme. Mayotte Dauphite, who seemed to be well acquainted with Capécia's background. After a brief telephone conversation, we learned that Mayotte Capécia's name at birth was Ceranus, not Uranus. Once again, a call to Carbet where finally the official record verified that Lucette Ceranus, daughter of Clémencia Ceranus, was born February 17, 1916 in Carbet. She died of cancer in Paris, November 24, 1955, a death preceded by protracted treatment for about five years. She was buried in Montparnasse Cemetery.

According to the woman in Fond-Capot, Capécia's father,

Eugène Combette acknowledged Lucette and her twin sister, Reine, shortly before his death (1946). Soon after, the two sisters left for Paris where Lucette wrote *Je suis Martiniquaise.* Lucette returned briefly to the island in 1948 to get her three children, Claude, George and Annie, who now live in Paris in separate domiciles. Reine, who nurtured the children there after Lucette's death, still resides in Paris and has returned to Martinique for brief visits.

With the availability of this new data, we are enabled to conjecture with limited surety on certain facets of a life that have puzzled scholars and critics. In one instance, the author of "Three Martinican Novelists," a 1953 dissertation,[6] having requested bibliographical details from each of the subjects who were then in Paris, received cordial and informative answers from only two: Joseph Zobel and Clément Richer. The third, Mayotte Capécia, did not respond. Reportedly, the Martinican woman was in ill health during this period, but most likely, her silence was also prompted by the problematic fictionized version of her life as depicted in *Je suis Martiniquaise.*

It is difficult, however, to imagine that Frantz Fanon, Capécia's compatriot, was unaware of her true identity, since they were both in Paris during the same period. For even though she was his senior by almost ten years and of a different ilk, commonalities would have existed. To our knowledge, the only contemporary reference that signifies a fictional aspect of the autobiographical novel is Martinican Jenny Alpha's critique in *Présence Africaine*[7] in which she refers to Capécia's "bébé métis" (mixed-blood baby) as a "personnage fictif"(fictional character) intimating that Alpha knew of different circumstances. Thirty years later, Jack Corzani[8] narrates that "the most sundry and contradictory rumors spread about her and her life have left a disturbing mystery," and suggests that Capécia was "encouraged" and even "helped" to put pen to paper. Nonetheless, he analyzes her autobiographical novel in the smallest detail as if were factual. We are led to speculate on the reliability of Corzani's methodology and motives in not pursuing further the reports about the controversial Martinican writer.

Je suis Martiniquaise, therefore, is not an authentic autobiography as the reader will readily discern after contrasting it with the foregoing version of the writer's life. But more important is a just reappraisal of the fictive ability of the woman who adopted the nom de plume, "Mayotte Capécia." Character portrayal then enters the realm of imagination: the father-figure is omnipresent; the unwed mother is legitimized; the burden of departure from the island is lightened; the twin-sister relegated to a tranquil existence. The element of documentation, however, which we discuss in the *Introduction*, remains a valuable feature of both novels.

Now that previously unknown biographical facts are being disclosed, revisionist critics may choose to reinterpret Capécia's works. In fact, nebulous aspects of her life still linger: who were the fathers of her children? did she indeed have collaborators? who encouraged her to publish? how did she fare in Paris? Should we succumb to the lure of probing the factual existence of Lucette Combette née Ceranus or let Mayotte Capécia remain her fictional self? I recommend the latter.

Finally, on reviewing the areas of our research covering the process of translating Capécia's works, we noted that a significant amount was focused on the interpretation and documentation of socio-political conditions in Martinique during the Vichy Occupation of 1941-43. The second part of *Je suis Martiniquaise* and almost every chapter of *La Négresse blanche* revolved around this critical period of World War II on the island.

Earlier in our introductory remarks, we cited Corzani's somewhat diffident acknowledgement of this aspect of her novels, a factor which other critics and literary historians have ignored or avoided in deference to the more visceral themes of race, miscegenation and racial identity. A revisionist perspective of the works by this Martinican writer is long overdue, one which would create for her a niche among serious francophone Antillean literary figures and one to which we shall contribute.

Beatrice Stith Clark, Ph.D - May 1996

Notes

[1] In an unpublished article on Mayotte Capécia by Illona Johnson, she acknowledged my article as the first Capécia study and among other research notes, she mentions "nouvelles recherches" done by Christiane Makward which had revealed that the Martinican writer had used a pseudonym. Johnson and Makward (Ph.D candidate and professor respectively) were collaborating on an article "La Fémininité et la condition de l'Antillaise vues à travers Mayotte Capécia et Françoise Ega," Johnson writing on Capécia.

[2] Beatrice S. Clark, "The Works of Mayotte Capécia," (*College Language Association Journal* 16.4 (1973): 417-25.

[3] Frantz Fanon, *Peau noire, masques blancs,* (Paris: Editions du Seuil, 1952) 35-44. *Black Skin, White Masks,* trans. Charles Lam Markmann (New York Grove Press, Inc. 1967).

[4] Mayotte Capécia, *Je suis Martiniquaise* (Paris: Editions Corrêa, 1948), *La Négresse blanche* (Paris: Editions Corrêa, 1950).

[5] See Brenda Berrian. *Bibliography of Women Writers from the Caribbean* (Washington, D.C.:Three Continents Press, 1989) 199-200.

[6] Elizabeth Brooks, diss., Howard U. Washington, D.C., June 1953. Appendix i-vi.

[7] Jenny Alpha, "Chronique des Livres," *L'Echo des Antilles,* 2 février, 1949. (see *Introduction* for further reference)

[8] Jack Corzani, *Prosateurs des Antilles et de la Guyane françaises* (Fort-de-France: Désormeaux, 1971). 135.

Contents

I AM A MARTINICAN WOMAN

THE WHITE NEGRESS

Introduction

My acquaintance with Mayotte Capécia began in 1948, when a friend, residing in Europe at that time, sent me a copy of *Je suis Martiniquaise* from Paris. A young teacher of French, thoroughly steeped in traditional French literature and culture, I was fascinated by Capécia's autobiography which introduced me to the exotic island of Martinique. Indeed, some of the social complexities due to race and color that Capécia depicted in *JSM* resonated for me with uneasy familiarity (from the unique racial perspective of the USA, of course) because they had been an integral part of my societal background in Chicago, where I was born and raised.

I next encountered Capécia's name about 1970, while reading *Black Skin, White Masks*,[1] by Frantz Fanon, the fiery Martinican psychiatrist and theorist on revolutionary violence. Since the late sixties, the translation of his book about the assimilated psyche of his compatriots in the former colony of France, had become highly revered among young black American political activists and those caught up in liberation politics. In the second chapter, "The Woman of Color and the White Male," Fanon launches a scathing critique of Capécia's two works: *Je suis Martiniquaise* (*I Am a Martinican Woman*)[2] and *La Négresse blanche* (*The White Negress*)[3], berates his contemporary as a writer and vehemently psychoanalyzes passages that reveal Capécia's naive, but authentic sense of alienation in a color-conscious society:

1

> One day, a woman named Mayotte Capécia, whose underlying motivation was difficult to detect, wrote 202 pages—her life—in which the most ridiculous ideas are proliferated. *Je suis Martiniquaise* is cut-rate merchandise, a sermon in praise of corruption.[4]

During this period, duly impressed with Fanon's zealous, non-compromising ideas on the mentality of assimilated Antilleans, I published an article on Capécia's works, subtitled, "With Apologies to Frantz Fanon."[5]

Today, I would offer no apologies to Fanon. Indeed, I would challenge his sexist attacks on Capécia as, for instance, his regret that she "did not share her dreams with us..." for that, he says, would have "facilitated being in touch with her unconscious..."[6] In his analysis, Fanon, the psychiatrist, ignores the constantly expressed desire of the young Martinican woman for financial independence through her own labor, and for respectability as a woman of color in a racist society. He also chooses to overlook the psychological effects of her disillusionment with her profligate father. Further, he accuses the author and her protagonist in *Négresse* not only of a preference for white males, but of solving their problems by leaving Martinique for France. If Fanon was virtually unknown and unrecognized in his own country until about ten years ago, it was partially because he had chosen to remain in France after graduating from the Faculty of Medicine at Lyon (except for a brief period in the island) and had adopted the liberation cause of an alien Francophone culture in colonized Algeria. His marriage to a French woman from Lyon would appear to nullify his acerbic critical analysis made of Mayotte Capécia's penchant for white males in *Black Skin, White Masks.*[7]

Obviously, my appreciation for Mayotte Capécia and her literary output has undergone significant change. Although I was never antagonistic toward her writing, I had, nonetheless, succumbed to what, in present-day jargon, is known as the "politically correct." A closer reading of *Je suis Martiniquaise* and *La Négresse blanche* has led me to reevaluate these works, not as great literature, but as an inevitable expression of the realities of a marginal group, a buffer society, created by the dominant one to disseminate delusion and self-deception. During recent years, further travel and study in Martinique and Guadeloupe have allowed me to comprehend, ever so slightly, the complexities of their peoples and cultures. It is, therefore, my intent to share Capécia's "slice of life" with the growing number of American readers interested in the social history of these departments of France in the Caribbean.

The Publication

The original edition of *Je suis Martiniquaise* was enclosed in a wide band on which appeared a photograph of Mayotte Capécia who was obviously attractive, indeed beautiful. If we were to attempt a "look-alike" identification for our American readers, we would name the actress-singer Diane Carroll. It should be understood, however, that the notion of race differs from the "one drop theory" utilized in the States to distinguish between who is white and who is black; in the Caribbean, "whitening" is most often the equivalent of white. The announcement on the outside band read:

> *For the first time, a woman of color narrates her life, her childhood in a fishing village, midst a picturesque people, impassioned with politics and cock-fights, her adolescence in Fort-de-France and, with war-time Martinique as a backdrop, her love affair with a naval officer. A unique testimony that must be read in order to understand the mentality of the Antillean woman, in which Catholicism and sorcery are combined.*

In promoting the autobiography, the publishers, Corrêa Editions, adopted an obviously paternalistic and popular approach. An illustration on the front cover depicts a young, dark complexioned woman bedecked in a dress with a floral design, over which falls a madras smock. A matching headpiece with pointed ties and large hoop earrings complete this stereotypical sketch of female exoticism in the French Antilles. Ironically, in both works, Capécia gave detailed descriptions of the fashionable attire worn by herself and her heroine, Isaure.

Fanon intimates that *JSM* had a favorable reception in France by claiming that he felt compelled to analyze the book due to the enthusiastic acclaim by "certains milieux."

Our research has produced only one contemporary criticism of Capécia's first novel published in Martinique. On February 2, 1949, under the rubric "Chronique des livres," an excerpt from an article by Jenny Alpha, already published in 1948 by *Revue Présence Africaine* in Paris, appeared in a weekly Fort-de-France newspaper.[8] Alpha, also Martinican, upbraids her compatriot for not voicing "un beau cri de révolte" in sympathy for the working class to which she laid claim. Alpha condemns and ridicules Capécia's liaison with the white naval officer and like Fanon, she renders a diagnosis of color fixation based on an inferiority complex. Principally, Alpha's condescending and caustic commentary is directed toward Capécia's depiction of Martinican women. She addresses the novelist:

> You will perhaps think me harsh, Mayotte Capécia, but I wanted you to hear the voice of another Martinican woman.
> If I had not felt that the Creole woman had been implicated by the title you chose, I probably would have written only a few evasive lines, short but laudatory, 'for release to the press,' like an alm thrown for the burial of a neighbor that one has never met, even in passing on the stairway.

Alpha further chastises Capécia by stating that, unlike the other Martinican, her desire to affirm her love for Truth and her Africanity caused her to write the lengthy book review.

In the United States during that period, the reading public for *JSM* was, of course, very limited. Mercer Cook (1904-1987), a professor of French at Howard University, Washington, D.C.

and a distinguished scholar and writer on the black presence in French literature, did review the book in 1949.[9] He informs us that *JSM* had been awarded the Grand prix littéraire des Antilles in that year, describes the autobiography as "a revealing study of race relations in the French West Indies," and delineates universal phenomena in the themes of "love, poverty and religion" blended "with local customs, politics, superstitions and prejudices." Cook acknowledges Capécia's white complex as having governed her choice of life style and partners in romance, which lead to her eventual departure from Martinique. He discerns a structural weakness in the novel due to its uneven quality: in the second half, it appears rushed and incomplete, and does not sustain the "poignant beauty" of the first part. This American critic, well acquainted with the Francophone African Diaspora, praises the chapters in which Capécia presents the intimate scenes of her childhood in rural Martinique, those which are usually scorned by French critics, Metropolitan and Antillean alike, as devoid of literary substance.

Cook wisely points out that American "Negro" readers might resent Capécia's lack of "race consciousness" and cautions that her cultural background should be taken into account. We concur, and feel assured that the reader's response to both of Capécia's works will include recognition of the similitude to problems of race and color in this country, and also of essential differences in the racial legacies of our two cultures, neither to be praised.

Unpublished manuscripts featuring Mayotte Capécia are relatively few. Elizabeth Brooks' M.A. thesis, *Three Martinican Novelists* (Howard University, 1953) is undoubtedly the earliest. Capécia is the one woman among two male literary compatriots, Clément Richer and Joseph Zobel. In the *Appendix*, Brooks presents amicable letters from the other authors, having explained in the *Introduction* that Capécia had never responded to her request for biographical and other kinds of information.

There appears to have been a lull in Capécia studies until very recently. Of recent vintage, however, is a thirteen-page article by Ilona Johnson[1], currently ABD at Pennsylvania State University, entitled "La Fémininité et la condition de l'Antillaise vues à travers Mayotte Capécia et Françoise Ega." Johnson's manuscript contains a footnote relevant to biographical data about Capécia which warrants attention and which I translate:

> According to recent research by Christine Makward, we learn that she was born in 1916 and died in 1955. Moreover, the name that she used was a pseudonym. (p.6)

Makward has indeed uncovered significant data about Capécia's life.[10] She is diligently pursuing the research begun by Johnson on Capécia and her efforts have revealed that *Je suis Martiniquaise* is not entirely based on actuality. According to Makward, she obtained some pertinent, intimate details from Capécia's family: two sons, a daughter and the twin sister, all living in Paris. For example, she was told that Capécia died from cancer and lies buried in Montparnasse Cemetery in Paris. If we are to believe these accounts as related to Makward by at least one of the children, the grandmother (Mayotte's mother) was poor and single and the close family unit of her childhood depicted in *JSM* did not exist. The twin, "Reine," actually followed her sister to Paris and it was she who cared for the three children after Mayotte Capécia's death which was preceded by a lengthy illness. We can now surmise that Capécia's illness prevented her from answering Brook's letter.

Johnson also lists a dissertation in which Capécia's works are analyzed among three other Caribbean writers: "Spectral Analysis and Evolutionary Models in Caribbean Literature," by Maude Shambrook (University of California-Irvine, 1980) which this author has yet to examine.

Capécia and the Critics

Why are the works of Mayotte Capécia important enough to be translated? One indisputable fact is that she is discussed as a writer in all major anthologies, literary manuals and bibliographies on Francophone Caribbean literatures. Leonard Sainville (1910-), Martinican writer, included excerpts from *JSM* in his anthology of representative prose from the African Diaspora. His unfavorable assessment is not surprising considering his militant, leftist political leanings: "... *Je suis Martiniquaise* is a detestable book. If, however, we mentioned it, it is only because we wanted to give a literary sample of the sickness, incurable for some, that racism produces." [11]

Jack Corzani, metropolitan French scholar and critic, includes two excerpts from *JSM* in his anthology on prose writers of the Francophone Antilles.[12] One describes the first communion experience of the child Mayotte in which she expresses her inbred color inferiority complex; the other relates Mayotte's desperate struggle to join her French lover as the defeated Vichy naval forces depart from the Antilles in the aftermath of World War II. Corzani, while recognizing the originality of Capécia's work, characterizes her "acceptance" of alienation as "her desire to become white, her disdain for the 'black savage' which transcends reflection and becomes a simple transcription of a lived experience."[13] Corzani suggests that there are troubling, unanswered questions about the author's life, and offers the cryptic vital statistic that she died about 1955.

In the six-volume series on the literature of the French Antilles and Guiana, also edited by Corzani, Mayotte Capécia's name appears in four of them: once in volumes i and iii, on twelve pages in volumes iv and v, and on five in volume vi.

Again he notes her "honesty" and "naivete" which allow one to study "the process of alienation, its causes and serious consequences." Simultaneously, Corzani adds an important dimension to the literary contribution of the maligned writer:

> . . . the two works provide detailed information of historical
> and sociological import on Martinique during the war. They
> help us to better understand the racial problems in the political
> context of the moment in a period when the destiny of the
> island was to be redefined forever. . . . All in all, they are
> documents.[14]

In his appraisals throughout this series, Corzani presents Capécia as the progenitor of the "flood" of literature, mostly by women writers, which dealt with mixed-blood racial themes. Jacqueline Manicom, of East Indian and black heritage, falls into this category. In his view, she buries the real problems of Antillean society "under the psychological preoccupations inherited from Mayotte Capécia, under feminist and Maoist chatter, fashionable in Paris . . ."[15] and moreover, Manicom, is accused of ". . . resuming the theme formerly raised by Mayotte Capécia in *Je suis martiniquaise*"[16] in her novel *Mon examen de blanc* (*My Study of White*), whose heroine differs from Capécia's only in a more subtle degree of scorn for blacks, which "does not lessen the psychological imbalance."[17]

Capécia is again used as the literary gauge in Corzani's account of Guadeloupan Michèle Lacrosil's *Cajou*, a psychological study of a young mulatto woman's self-inflicted denigration. In his opinion, Lacrosil, while resuming the "theme cherished by Mayotte Capécia," projects a more serious intent and deeper insight as a novelist. Lacrosil found it expedient to:

> . . .rewrite *La Négresse blanche*, to cease presenting alienation
> as a creole adornment, a masochistic subtlety which graciously
> compliments the madras and gold jewelry, in order to show
> the relentless destruction of a being.[18]

A third woman writer, Claude Carbet, who, at one time, collaborated with the more talented Marie-Magdeleine Carbet, is chastised by Corzani for her collection of folkloric creole songs and poems published in *Musique noire* (*Black Music*) (1958). Although he cites lines that he admits reveal the poet's "new state of mind": "The too white body of the white/can suddenly awaken/a wild desire to bite black flesh," he chides Carbet:

> "Under a harmless facade, *Black Music* responds, in its way, to all the Mayottes Capécias, to all the Martinican white negresses."[19]

Maryse Condé, internationally acclaimed Guadeloupan novelist, playwright and critic, includes four excerpts from Capécia's *JSM*, in her textbook anthology on the Francophone West Indian novel,[20] two of which are under the rubric: "Color Prejudices." Condé observes that, in general, Antilleans consider color prejudice a blemish on their society and are uneasy about broaching the subject:

> ...This is one of the reasons why Mayotte Capécia has been criticized so much, why some would like to ban her from Antillean literature.

For Condé, however, this malaise seems unjustified "because color prejudice is but the tenacious reflection of the rapport of the dominant to the dominated.[21] Somewhat condescendingly, she finds it "absurd" to be ashamed of "this aspect of our personality and dangerous to view as criminals those who cannot cure themselves,[22] for Capécia incarnates the idolatry of whites as well as a desire to be white and, therefore, her feelings "can be considered as representative of what many other Antillean women felt, but were afraid to confess."[23]

The foregoing citations document the extent to which Mayotte Capécia's literary reputation has persisted under the dubious symbol of Antillean alienation. Certain excerpts from *JSM* have become classics; for example, the one cited by Condé,

Fanon and Corzani where young Mayotte marvels at being the descendant of a white grandmother. Another, on the occasion of her first communion when, dressed in white, she is dismayed by the contrast of her darker color with her vision of the traditional pink cheeked angel, to whom she had been compared in an innocent compliment. She follows this with a very ingenuous comment about the all-Negro cast in the American film, "Green Pastures," which she indignantly rejects as not in keeping with her version of a lactescent Heaven as taught by the Catholic church fathers, and attributes the idea to the ignorance of Americans. Capécia makes several anti-American references, seemingly based on reports of the lowly status of blacks in the States due to racial segregation.

The Phenomenon of Francophone Alienation

Edouard Glissant(1925-), Martinican poet, novelist and leading theoretician on the Francophone Antilles, identifies the unique legacy of French colonialism by comparing it with that left by the British to its former Anglophone colonies in the Caribbean. The cultural impact left by the British was involuntary rather than conscious, Glissant claims, since the British, believing themselves superior, never intended to produce black Englishmen. However, "One of the assumptions of French culture is to assimilate people, to have them all become like a transcendent French model." Consequently, Martinicans and Guadeloupans were subjected to a form of colonization by the French that has penetrated to the core, a lasting assimilation and one Glissant regards as a lingering malaise24[3]

In *Discours Antillais (Antillean Discourse)*[25], Glissant offers lucid theories on the French colonial policies of assimilation inculcated in the consciousness of ordinary Martinicans of all colors from the beginning of colonization. The French Antillean existed under the economic domination by France, says Glissant, but they co-existed under the assumption that they were French, in opposition to Africans or Indochinese who remained so. Antilleans were sent to Africa, where they were considered white and acted like whites, thus forming a "pseudo-elite" and ending in a "depersonalization" of their own identity: "Thus we saw in Martinique and Guadeloupe, people of African descent for whom the word "African" or "black" usually meant an insult."[26]

Aimé Césaire (1913-), eminent Martinican poet of negritude and statesman, has also probed the dilemma of the Antillean conscience. He considers the psychological effects of "a brutal uprooting" followed by three centuries of "depersonalization" and a repressed bitterness toward Africa the "fatherland" that had "betrayed its children." Césaire predicts that the slave trade will remain imbedded in the Antillean psyche.[27]

Self-imposed alienation from others existed among all groups in the Antilles. A native of Guadeloupe, Maryse Condé reveals another side of this intricate spectrum of color differentiation in the French Antilles. In an interview, she talks about her childhood in Guadeloupe where she was reared by parents who were "racists in their way," a well-to-do black family that remained aloof from "common blacks," from mulattos who were considered "bastards of the whites," and from whites, who were "the enemy. She admits that her personal experiences are reflected in those parts of her novel, *Heremakhonon,* which portray a proud, black upper middle-class family, unaware that "In the end, to be black is to be white."[28] Her revelations serve to situate the complex role of the literary mulatto heroine who was tolerated but denigrated by white society and scorned, perhaps envied, by blacks. Traditionally, these protagonists of mixed-blood, the métisses, the "tragic mulattoes," condemned by writers and critics, male or female, Antillean, African, French or American, have borne unfairly the burden of alienation.

11

An Historical Aperçu

At this point it would be useful to situate some of the major historical events that relate to Capécia's narrative frame of reference so that the reader might better understand the "peculiar" institution of alienation in these former colonies of France.

Martinique and Guadeloupe were acquired in 1635 through a royal act of possession by a commercial company organized for the purpose of settling French "colons" in these territories and converting the indigenous inhabitants to Catholicism. In 1633, French authorities had granted their merchants the right to begin a slave trade on the coast of Senegal. The enslavement of black Africans, who became the main source of labor, was given civil and religious sanction by the Black Code, promulgated in 1685 and entitled: "Edict of the King . . . concerning the discipline of the Church . . . and concerning the condition and Status of Blacks in the French West Indies. . ." These 60 articles defined the basic code of conduct for master and slave, ranging from instructions for the religious conversion of slaves to the punishment of fugitive slaves. The document remained the basic text on the subject until the abolition of slavery.[29]

The Code's message discouraged, even forbade marriage among the slaves for reasons always predicated to benefit the master, and couched under the guise of Christian morality. Marriage among blacks depended on the master's consent, many of whom found it against their interest to encourage conjugal union since the Code (art.47) prohibited the sale of a husband without his wife and young children. Immorality on the part of the white masters, condemned in article 9 of the Code, was forced on the slave women, who became their concubines.[30]

The Black Code, which instituted the legal sub-human status of the slave, also had implications for free people of color and whites. Under the early version of the Code (art.9), when a free black married a slave woman within the Church, she became free along with children of that union. Within certain conditions, they were granted "the same rights, privileges and immunities enjoyed by free-born persons." [31] These liberal rights allowed freedmen in the early code laws, and were later revised in favor of racist restrictions as stated in Article 9: "Let us prohibit our white subjects of both sexes to enter into marriage with blacks, under threat of corporal punishment and discretionary fines, and [prohibit] their parish priests, priests, secular or religious missionaries, and even ship chaplains, to marry them." [32]

Other measures, just as incisive, were coded into law, often by decree of a municipality, e.g., freed slaves, mulattoes, and other dependents, whatever their racial mixture, could not assume titles of "lady" or "sir," or appropriate the name of their master or any local white family (to protect whites from the suspicions of having "mixed-blood"); they were forbidden to mingle with whites in the theater, public walks or inns. Missionaries were required to maintain separate records of marriages baptism, grave sites, etc. for whites, mulattos and blacks. [33]

Since people of color were sometimes mistaken for white, they were subjected to a dress-code law which forbade them to wear apparel, headdress or jewelry that assimilated the attire of white men or women. [34] Gisler enumerates other laws affecting the lives of people of color from the seventeenth to mid-nineteenth century in the colonized French Antilles, all of which, he concludes, established "the class of color." [35] In the interest of stabilizing the colonial order for the French government, it was expedient to instill in the black slaves and all colored people the principle of their inferiority and, consequently, the superiority of the white master: "Thus color prejudice, resonating for so long, for the most part, had a political origin . . ." [36]

Since sugar and slaves formed the dynamics of the French economic system until the early 1800s, it became imperative to maintain the source of labor. As a means of limiting the number of free blacks, obstacles were placed in the way of manumission, for instance, making the verification of documents governing the free status of people of color increasingly difficult. "Color was wedded not to slavery but to sugar," states Eric Williams. His table, indicating the ratio of free coloreds to slaves, places Martinique (1.25) lower than Guadeloupe (1.61) and Saint-Domingue [Haiti] (1.35).[37] between 1776 and 1779.

Blacks and mulattoes were excluded from the professions of medicine and surgery; by 1771, these professional limitations were extended to law, pharmacy and public service.[38] Free mulattoes were also denied political equality with whites in the French colonies. As early as 1791, men of color from the educated elite bourgeoisie had begun to revolt against the intransigent racial prejudices of the white creoles by demanding equal civil and political rights of the Revolutionary governments. At the onset, there was slight concern for the abolition of slavery, only for the severe limitations placed on their own rights. To be sure, slave resistance had not been absent from Martinique, where there were serious uprisings in 1822, 1831 and 1833. The hesitations of the French government and the obduracy of the békés, the Martinican white masters, served to bring closer the interests of free people of color to those of the slaves as the former became more radical in their thinking.

From 1815 to 1848, the French colonial system of slavery was in a period of crisis which worsened from year to year and finally crumbled. The abolition of slavery was the climax of a long process, fomented by the fall of the Napoleonic empire (1815) and the intervening complex phenomena related to the economic and political situations in France and the colonies. The French policy of abolition had been gradual; it was finally effected, April 27, 1848, under the leadership of Vic-

tor Schoelcher, a French abolitionist.[39]
Even after 1848, the structure of the colonial slave society did not totally collapse. A labor shortage developed, due to the revived sugar industry and, in part, to the exodus of ex-slaves to the cities or to remote areas. Between 1852 and 1884, thousands of immigrants were recruited from British India as indentured workers for plantations in Guadeloupe and Martinique. There followed a period of transition in relative prosperity which continued to protect the economic interests of France and the former slave masters. The condition of blacks showed little improvement; they remained at the lowest level in the social scale. The békés, as before, controlled the land and the factories — in sum, the island's economy. Between the blacks and the whites were the mulattoes, composed of sub-groups: some, quite wealthy, owned land; the majority, however, were engaged in small commerce and skilled trades—tailoring, carpentry, leather working, and so forth—constituting the working class. Later, bourgeois mulattoes were allowed to enter the civil service as educators or bureaucrats.[40] After abolition in 1848, black adult males had the right to vote and all towns and cities had their mayor and local officials. These rights were later suppressed during a period of neo-colonialism lasting from 1851 until 1870, when universal suffrage was restored under the Third Republic. Signs of social and political unrest were frequent in the colonies: crises in the sugar industry, labor strikes and a growth in socialist tendencies among black politicians.

The period between post-World War I (1918) up to post-World War II (1940-1945) provides the historical backdrop for the Martinique depicted in Capécia's autobiographical novel and in *Négresse*. The defeat of France by Germany, the subsequent capitulation of the French under the leadership of collaborator Marshal Henri Pétain, who set up headquarters at Vichy in the south of France, were events that shook the confidence of the colonies in the "Mother Country." There followed a four-year blockade of the French fleet off the shores of Martinique and Guadeloupe and occupation by the Vichy government in Fort-de-France under the authoritarian rule of Admiral Robert. After 1940, the European French population increased by 10,000, most of them French sailors from the Vichy fleet. With painful disillusionment, Martinicans witnessed the manifestation of racist tendencies of the French and, in addition to tense race relations, the strained economy—insufficient housing and low food—was partially accountable for the amount of collaboration with the occupying French government by Martinicans of all classes and colors. This may be attributed to a "psychological loyalty" to the "Mother Country," says Burton, which during the Vichy period was transferred to the French State: "Collaboration is, in a sense, the logical climax of assimilation."[41] When, in the summer of 1943, Martinicans demonstrated against Robert and for liberation, it was, according to Fanon, the first time and simultaneously that the realities of Martinique's existence coincided with its political expediency.[42]

By the time Mayotte Capécia's *Je suis Martiniquaise* was published in France, Martinique, Guadeloupe and French Guiana had been voted the status of Overseas Departments (1946), assimilating them into full French citizenry. Another era had begun.

Institutional Alienation

Two official institutions of the State, the Catholic Church and the regimented French educational system, had a paramount role in legitimizing the supremacy of the culture of France. The influence of the Church on the Antillean family and communities, of course, had begun during slavery. After abolition in 1848, primary, lay education was decreed free and obligatory in the colonies, but up to the aftermath of the Second World War, elementary school facilities were not guaranteed, and secondary education was reserved for the privileged few.[43]

Families like the Capécias, typically, held the parish priest in high esteem; he was their intimate counselor, his word was the fount of morality. Mayotte's first communion, overseen by the mother, involved all members of her extended family. But it was the priest who guided the young girl and her comrades through the "rite of passage," to responsible adolescence. Mayotte's childish adoration of the blond, blue eyed parish priest was in harmony with the community's norm. In *Négresse*, however, a more perverse side of the priesthood is revealed when Isaure recalls the lewd gestures of her priest on learning that she, at the age of eighteen, is the mother of an illegitimate child.

Until recent years, under the French educational system, Martinican and Guadeloupan children were taught to revere their "ancestors, the Gauls." They learned only about the history, civilization and literature of France, along with the implied message that their black heritage existed in a historical vacuum, labeled "non-history" by Glissant. It is not surprising, then, that Mayotte Capécia as a young girl, was overcome with national pride on first viewing the statue of Empress Josephine in Fort-de-France. And had she known that Josephine Tascher de la Pagerie, the Martinican born creole who became the wife of Emperor Napoleon I, had encouraged her husband to restore slavery in 1802 after it had been abolished by the Revolutionary government in 1789, she probably would not have been greatly perturbed."

"Sub-Cultures"

Despite her unabashed admiration for European culture, Capécia wrote with considerable verve and knowledge about two "sub-cultures" of Martinican life: quimbois and Creole. In all Caribbean/Latin American societies where Catholicism is the dominant religion, there exists a corresponding, widely practiced, underground form of worship, having its roots in an African slave culture and syncretized with Catholicism. In

Martinique it is called *quimbois*. We would not presume to define or interpret this intimate reality of Martinican life, but rather would allow Martinicans, themselves, to address this matter within the limits of scholarly references available to us. It should be noted that the two works cited are written by persons in social medicine: psychiatrists and psychologists;[44] there are, of course, other perceptions of this phenomenon so deeply entrenched in the Antillean psyche.

Quimbois, it seems, attacks both the individual psyche and the body. But, first and foremost, quimbois is identified as the symbol of evil performed by the quimboiseur:

> To be "quimboised," is to undergo a feeling of powerlessness, of inferiority, . . . To be cured is to regain confidence, to lift the barrier to success. . . . When a Martinican wants to harm a rival, he goes and sets down something, a quimbois symbol, in front of his house (magic bottle, shroud, doll-like effigies, etc.)[45]

For those skeptics who would relegate these matters to superstition, irrationality and ignorance, we offer the observations of Martinican Gilbert Gratiant who includes within the supernatural beliefs: zombies, the three-footed horse, the guiablesse (devil woman), the werewolf, etc., all which appear in Capécia's works. For him, the propensity of Martinicans (of all classes and colors) toward such beliefs is not without its historical and religious connotation:

> The facility with which the Fathers and the priests brought about the fervent belief in a Catholic God in Trinity, in the cult of saints, has it counterpart in the unquestion-ing response to the exploits of the Evil Spirit, of the Devil, counterpart of the Christian God. The religious fervor of Antilleans has its source in the same regions of the soul as the belief in the quimboiseur, in their power, in their mysterious acts; Nature does the rest.[46]

Several incidents in Capécia's narratives dramatize the de-

gree to which belief in the supernatural, unhampered by faith
in the official religion, had become legendary in this society.
Not only does she describe with specificity the performance
of quimbois rituals, but she integrates other traditional folklore into the life of ordinary people, a tradition that many
Antilleans would deny or negate.

The Creole language is also an end product of the mixture
of ethnicities and cultures. Historically, it had been the means
of communication among the slave population, but it served
the interests of the white master to understand and speak it.
There are significant deviations in Creole as spoken by Hai-
tians, Guineans, Guadeloupans and Martinicans, although
some similarities exist. Until recent years, Creole was usually
referred to as "dialect," thus rendering it subordinate to the
language of the dominant culture. The French policy of assimilation in the Antilles was perhaps no more effective than
in the realm of linguistic imperialism. In some Antillean
middle and upper class families, parents forbade their children to use Creole, reserving its parlance for their private
conversation or banishing it completely. The ultimate goal of
the "coloreds" was, in the words of the poet, Leon Damas(1912-
1978), to speak: "the French of France, the French of the
French, French French."[47] Capécia demonstrates her aware-
ness of the importance of correctly spoken French by literally
spelling out the habitual, frowned-upon dropping of "rs" as
spoken by black Martinicans, an indicator of class or education according to the manner in which the "r" is dropped,
completely or slightly. She also observes that Martinicans sometimes affect a cultivated voice tone when talking with whites, in
contrast to a more guttural one used among in a familial setting.
These speech distinctions present a singular problem for the
translator who must decide how to interpret levels of communication for the American reader. One may either translate all
speech in "standard" English or attempt to relay the equivalent
of the American linguistic idiom. We have decided on the latter,
with the intention of lowering the barriers between cultures and

interpreting the writer's implied class distinctions.

Reflections

Je suis Martiniquaise and *La Négresse blanche* end in situations where the métisses are catapulted into a newly defined postwar society, one which extols the black self, its difference from that of Metropole France—in a word—Negritude. Mayotte and Isaure, incapable of internalizing this concept, silently protest the open hostility of their compatriots, who, collectively, oppose their way of life. Both women are ambivalent about their African heritage, neither in total denial nor acceptance.

Would they be more socially at ease in the present-day political culture in the Francophone Antilles? Would the current ideologies of antillanité (caribbeaness)—"the diversity of the Different"[48]—or métissage—affirmation of a racially mixed culture—offer them an identity through choice? Glissant and Condé have declared their disengagement from negritude, and along with Dépestre,[49] and other intellectuals, have bid "adieu" to the movement. Such opposition stems from the tendency of Negritude theories to substitute "one alienating definition for another," that is to oppose "a putative essence of blackness, or Africaness [to] the essence of Frenchness," thus continuing the European assumptions of a "reductive universalism" in which assimilation to French culture is deemed beneficial for Martinicans.[50]

On a non-theoretical level, Capécia, yearning to render legitimate her racial mixture, may be regarded as a precursor of sorts to these quasi-political theories. For she knew that even in France, acceptance would be marginal for her and her fictional character, Isaure. The latter defines the essence of her personal métissage when she recalls Caribbean folktales told to her and songs sung by a black mother, and others by a white grandmother, in which several races and religions were mingled: "All of this gave birth to a magic spectacle, like the mixture of races that had created this new race to which she

belonged, because, all things considered, it was stupid to identify only two races: black and white."

Beatrice Stith Clark
August 1996
Washington, D.C.

NOTES

[1] Frantz Fanon, P*eau noire, masques blancs* (Editions du Seuil,
    1952).
[2] Mayotte Capécia, *Je suis Martiniquaise* (Paris: Editions Corrêa,
    1948).
[3] Mayotte Capécia, *La Négresse blanche* (Paris: Editions Corrêa,
    1950).
[4] Frantz Fanon, *Black Skin, White Masks*, trans. by Charles L.
    Markham. (New York:Grove Press, 1967) 42.
[5] Beatrice Stith Clark, "The Works of Mayotte Capécia," *College
    Language Journal* 16 (1973): 415-25.
[6] *Peau noire, masques blancs* 39. (translation mine).
[7] See B. Marie Perinbam, *Holy Violence:The Revolutionary Thought
    of Frantz Fanon* (Washington DC: Three Continents Press,
    1982).
Perinbam's biography on Fanon reveals that he came from a
    large black petit bourgeois family of very modest means,
    which typically, thought itself "white" and stressed
    achievement, culture and refinement. Fanon's light
    complexioned mother, "daughter of an illegitimate union,"
    had broken social convention by marrying a dark skinned
    man. Fanon was the "blackest" of his parents' children, states
    Perinbam, and adds that Fanon, himself, observed that
    "Martinicans talk about who is blackest in the family, but
    they don't really mean that he is the blackest. What they

mean is that he is the least white." (31-34)

In 1961, Fanon died from leukemia in the United States at the age of 36. In the spring of 1982, homage was paid to him during Commemoration ceremonies in Fort-de-France, Martinique where an amphitheater also honors his name.

[8] Jenny Alpha. "Chronique de Livres", *L'Echo des Antilles* [Fort-de-France, Martinique 2 février, 1949].

[9] Mercer Cook, rev. of *Je suis Martiniquaise*, by Mayotte Capécia, *Journal of Negro History* Oct. 1949: 370-71.

[10] Johnson, on reading my article, sent me her paper prepared for publication in collaboration with Professor Christiane Makward (PA State U.) who is to contribute the Ega study.

[11] Leonard Sainville, *Anthologie:romanciers et conteurs négro-africains* vol.i (Paris: Présence Africaine, 1963) 248.

[12] Jack Corzani, *Prosateurs des Antilles et de la Guyane françaises* (Fort-de-France: Désormeaux, 1978).

[13] Corzani, *Prosateurs*, 135.

[14] Jack Corzani, ed., *La Littérature des Antilles-Guyane françaises* vol.iv (Fort-de-France Désormeaux, 1980) 200.

[15] Corzani, *Littérature* vol. vi, 196.

[16] Corzani does not capitalize "martiniquaise" as do other critics. Evidently, he interprets it as an adjective, not as a noun of nationality, as it appeared in the original edition.

[17] Corzani, *Littérature* vol. vi 208-209.

[18] Corzani, *Littérature* vol. v, 252-253.

[19] Corzani, *Littérature* vol. v, 336.

[20] *Classiques du Monde: Le Roman antillais* [*The Antilliean Novel*] (Paris: Fernand Nathan Editeur, 1977).

[21] Condé, *Roman* vol.i, 47.

[22] Condé, *Roman* vol.i, 97.

[23] Condé, *Roman* vol.i, 48.

[24] Edouard Glissant, interview, eds. Alain Brossat, Daniel Maragnes, *Les Antilles dans l'impasse?* (Paris: Editions Caribéennes, 1981) 97-98.

[25] Edouard Glissant, *Discours Antillais* (Paris: Editions du Seuil, 1981).

[26] *Discours* 16.

[27] Aimé Césaire, introduction, *Les Antilles décolonisées*, by Daniel Guérin (Paris:Présence Africaine, 1956) 13-14).

[28] Françoise Pfaff, *Entretiens avec Maryse Condé* (Paris: Editions Karthala, 1993)]

[29] *Entretiens* 14. By her second marriage, Maryse Condé, joined the ranks of the many Antillean literary personages and intellectuals of color who have married Europeans. She admits that she lived twelve years with her British husband, Richard Philcox, before marriage. In answer to a question concerning the presence of possible tension between the two, she answered: "I don't think about that anymore, because I realized that all this business about color makes no sense, after all, to marry a black or to marry a white means nothing. One should marry a man with whom one is compatible, whatever his color." (35)

[30] Antoine Gisler, C.S.SP. *L'Esclavage aux Antilles françaises (XVIIe-XIXe* (Suisse:Editions Universitaires, 1964) 20.

[31] *L'Esclavage* 61.

[32] *L'Esclavage* 91.

[33] *L'Esclavage* 92.

[34] *L'Esclavage* 94.

[35] *L'Esclavage* 94. Gisler cites an ordinance from the Governor of Guadeloupe in 1720 which " 'prescribes for them white cloth, Indian cotton fabrics and other materials of little value, with similar undergarments, with neither silk, gild, nor laces, unless very cheap in price. . . . hats, shoes and simple hair style'; and this is under penalty of prison, and 'even of losing their liberty in case of relapse.'"

[36] *L'Esclavage* 98.

[37] *L'Esclavage* 97-98. Gisler elaborates the steps of this political process: "l. to contain freedmen, descendants and slaves in one and the same group, all the while pretending to distinguish them from one another . . . 2. To keep this race in a constant 'state of humiliation' . . . to heap shame upon it, to make it believe that 'slavery is essential work'; to set up the "White" race as

'superior, sacred' . . . to create an abyss such that, in spite of misalliances, 'those who are of mixed-blood can never enter the class of Whites.' 3. To give credence to the belief that, in the colonies, two species of men of a different nature existed—the colored class, 'dedicated to servitude, destined forever for labor which defines it; for whom, freedom is precarious, easily revocable and a favor; and the white class, free and naturally predisposed by nature to command and dominate."

[38] Eric Williams, *From Columbus to Castro* (New York:Vintage Press, 1984) 189.

[39] *Columbus* 189.

[40] It is important to recognize that Martinican revisionist historians have challenged the traditional account of the exact date of abolition in 1848. Edouard de Lepine. a professor of history at the Lycée Schoelcher in Fort-de-France, notes in *Questions sur l'histoire* (Fort-de-France: Désormeaux, 1978). that, until 1971, April 27, 1848, (the date of the decree of abolition of slavery by the Provisional Government of France, brought to Martinique in June) had been the official date of commemoration for Martinicans and Guadeloupans. In 1971, the date was changed by legislative action in Martinique to May 22, in recognition of the slave rebellion in Saint-Pierre that had forced the local officials to decree slavery abolished. Generations of Antilleans, declares de Lépine, have supported the historical distortions: "They created the myth of a generously granted Abolition by an eternal France, above class and above all suspicion." (159)

[41] Perinbam, *Holy Violence* 38.

[42] Richard Burton, "Vichyisme et Vichyistes" *La Martinique sous l'Amiral Robert*, Les Cahiers du CERAG (Fort-de-France: Centre d'études régionales Antilles-Guyane, Feb, 1978) 39.

[43] Frantz Fanon, "Antillais et Africains," *Revue Esprit*, Feb. 1955.

[44] Viviann Duvioni, "La Martinique-Scolarité," *Atlas des D.O.M.* [Départements d'outre-mer (Overseas Departments)] n.d.

[45] [1] Bertrand Edouard, Germain Bouckson, *Les Antilles en*

question;Assimilation et conflits de Culture dans les DOM. (Kingston, Jamaïque: Féderation mondiale pour la Santé mentale, 1972).

[2] H. Perronnette, *9 Histoires de Quimbois: faits vécus de sorcellerie aux Antilles* [Actual deeds of sorcery] (Fort-de-France: Désormeaux,1982).

[46] Gilbert Gratiant (-Labadie), postface, *9 Histoires* 215-216.

[47] Leon Damas, "Hoquet" (Hiccups), *Pigments* (Paris: Présence Africaine, 1962).

[48] Richard D. E. Burton, "The Idea of Difference in Contemporary French West Indies Thought: Négritude, Antillanité, Créolité." *French and West Indian: Martinique, Guadeloupe and French Guiana Today,* New World Ser. 141 (Charlottesville: U of VA Press U., 1995). 146-147.

[49] René Dépestre, Haitian poet and author of *Bonjour et adieu à la Négritude* (Laffont, 1980).

[50] Burton 141.

MARTINIQUE

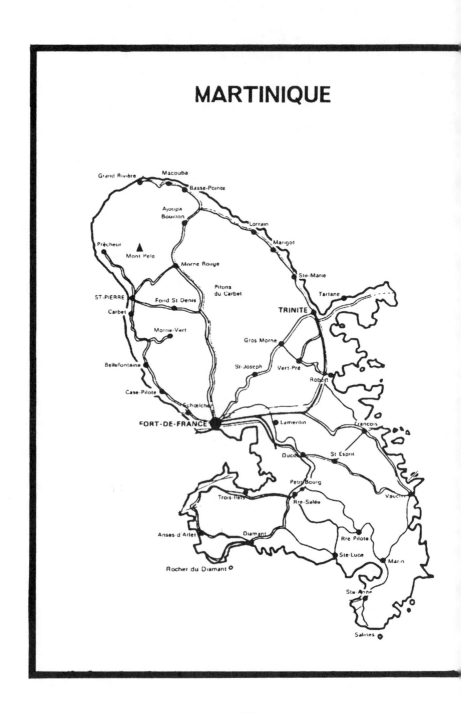

PART I

CHAPTER I

When we were little, my twin sister and I looked so much alike that our mother had to make us smile in order to recognize us. Nonetheless, we were quite different in tastes and personalities. I, for instance, not being very clever, began to walk much later than Francette. My mother would hold a bunch of bananas in front of my mouth which I grabbed because I loved them so. I really believe that it was through sheer gluttony that I learned to walk.

All that I remember about my early childhood is that I liked to fight Francette. We were separated rather early, my parents having given my sister over to the care of an aunt who was childless.

So, I alone remained at the family home, a wood structure with a thatched roof; a fisherman's house at the far end of the village of Carbet; a one-story house such as colored or poor white people lived in, both a cottage and a farmhouse because we had pigs, rabbits, chickens and even a horse. My father had enclosed a garden with a thin barbed wire fence where he grew mango trees, but even so, he had built a very decorative gateway which made us very proud.

At age seven, I had to go to school. This was the first event in my life. When I listened to my parents talk about it, the single word school was anguishing to me — the idea of submitting to discipline made me feel like an abandoned child — for I loved my freedom too much, I had too much zest for games, sports, and free-for-all play.

It was at school, nevertheless, where I had the opportunity to play games worthy of the tomboy that I was. This school was mixed and because Carbet, our village, had no religious institutions, all classes of whites and blacks mingled there. Only the rich creoles, more snobbish than the whites who had recently arrived on the island, sent their children to priests and to Fort-de-France or hired tutors as my aunt did for Francette.

Of course, at times there were incidents between the white and black children, but it wasn't like in the United States. I, a colored girl, didn't mind at all when I provoked them. In any case, when a classmate failed to respect me—treating me like a little "nigger," for instance—I took out my inkwell and threw it, showering his head. This was my way of changing whites into blacks. The ink ran down his shirt and that caused a ruckus which at the end of school, degenerated into a fight between my followers and those of the ink-spattered one, sniveling in the corner and thinking about the spanking he was yet to get at home.

Of course, I was punished and not just for these kinds of things. For me, arithmetic, grammar, and history were symbols of the enemy. I resisted them by refusing to let myself be overcome by them. In a word, they did not concern me for I had my mind on other things. I, whose ancestors had been slaves, had decided to be independent, and even today, although I have not always been able to enjoy it as I would have liked, I believe that there is nothing better in all the world than independence.

In spite of everything, I was very popular around my schoolmates, whites as well as blacks. I had no prejudices, only a dread of complicated people. Instinctively, I rejected all complication outside of myself, and once avenged, I held no grudge against anyone-such as the ink-spattered boy.

My authority was such that I had succeeded in forming a team, which obviously did not include the best students and which the envious had nicknamed "Weeds Team." Twenty or so youngsters made up this team of both sexes and all colors, from African black to white, going from yellow to red to the gamut of browns. There was among us a "chabine" and we were convinced that she would bring us good luck. Her father was black and her mother mixed, a métisse, but she and her kind had milky white skin that the hottest sun would not alter, and curly blond hair and blue eyes. Chabins[1] always roused the curiosity of the tourists who came to Martinique. Heavens, what a surprise it must be to have a child like that!

But if I had to describe all the races on this island of some sixty kilometers, I would never finish.

On Sundays and Mondays, I would lead the "Weeds" to the banks of the Cambeille River, a short distance from our village. That river, about eight meters wide, could change in a flash to a raging torrent, and as if a dike had broken, a flood of water would rush headlong rumbling like a volcano about to erupt, carrying along pell-mell rocks, trees, women's laundries and bathers, the strong and the feeble. The sky remained deep blue, but an unpredictable storm had petered out in the mountains. How I loved the violence of my country's storms, the huge waves brought by downpours from above, all laden with thunder!

Of course, we chose the wildest and most dangerous places, but as for me, my parents were always willing to let me undertake these expeditions which brought momentary tranquility for them. But luckily, there were no misfortunes other than a few broken arms and legs. A special children's God, no doubt, was watching over us.

On my team, groups were formed and even couples, all quite innocent. Like the other girls, I had a sweetheart, a little black boy, named Paul, who was about a year older than I. Every Thursday morning after catechism, I gathered my gang and we left. Again, we climbed along the Cambeille, passing by the spot where the washerwomen had long been at work. At a distance, we could hear them singing or calling out to one another in their sonorous voices from both sides of the river bank.

31

They greeted the newly arrived laundresses carrying their loads on their heads, as is the custom in this country:

Bonjou Fifi! Comment ou yé, ché?...
(Morning! How ya doin', dearie?)

Toute douce ché, et té, Youte?
(Fine, dearie, an' you?)

Tu vini pouend ou bain?...
(You come to take a bath?)

The boldest women went out on the rocks in the middle of the river, the more timid stayed on the river bank. Doing the laundry in Martinique isn't the same as in France. Here, no need to boil the linen, the sun takes care of everything. To whiten and scent it, women sprinkle it with warm water mixed with wood ashes and orange peelings.

After work, the youngest would bathe themselves unceremoniously in the river which naturally attracted the men who prowled about. When we passed by, they would call out jokingly to us and sometimes take a moment to chat.

Loulouze was the prettiest and the gayest among them and, in spite of the difference in our ages, we were good friends. Still a child, despite her seventeen years, she loved to laugh. After spreading her wash on the rocks, she would often join us while waiting for it to dry. When we had stretched a rope above the swift flowing waters, she would hold out her arms and walk, balancing herself as we did, but with her it was different. Loulouze's movements brought a new kind of feeling to me. At times, she also bathed with us. Her skin was soft and golden; her long black hair that she rolled in braids was not frizzy at the roots. Her nose was rather flat and her lips full, but the contours of her face showed that her white ancestry was not too far removed. I, who was quite flat-chested, observed her roundness with envy. When she was serious, her big black eyes that became brown when she was seen at close range, made her appear rather melancholy, but she was seldom serious and, at every turn, she displayed teeth which shone like the sun.

On arriving at our chosen destination, we undressed and bathed in the nude, boys and girls mixed, but with no thought of wrongdoing. In the distance, we could still hear the washerwomen beating their clothes against the rocks. Our spot was filled with moss, ferns and giant palms that rose like strange birds when the wind swirled them about. Each of us was armed with a knife, a rope and a whistle to signal alarm in case of danger. I always carried an inkwell, just in case.

At last, we had our picnic. Our menu was much simpler than the washerwomen's that consisted of manioc flour, red or green avocados with a pulp the color of butter, but mainly "féroce," which is roasted codfish, sprinkled with oil and vinegar and eaten with peppers, a dish that the women ate with their hands. We brought only things that were easy to carry: cans of sardines, bread, sausage, lemonade. For my part, I liked nothing as much as the natural drink of Providence— fresh water. The rocks scattered in the river were our tables. I had chosen for Paul and me the biggest one and I remember that, naively, I thought our setting resembled one in a Parisian restaurant.

In all seriousness, we discussed the expedition that we were going to take and after lunch, we started walking towards the mountain often traveling fifteen kilometers. Generally, the girls were not as lazy as the boys, but at times it happened that there were those who couldn't keep up, so I decided that they were not interested and had them banned from our group.

Young bamboo shoots adorned the mountain with a soft green velvet; palm trees beckoned to us, bending and undulating with the suppleness of a serpent as they danced among the giant ferns. We finally arrived in a forest where trees pierced the network of vines with extraordinary vigor. Luminous canaries and humming birds flew away as we approached. When the long, sweet melody of the mountain whistler burst forth, we stood motionless to listen to this wonderfully melancholy song.

At times, we met groups of young black girls carrying on their heads baskets laden with fruit, vegetables and meats and dressed in brightly colored blouses and short calico skirts. A scarf was wrapped around their hips, a kerchief tied around their heads, and a larger one called a tâche, serving as a cushion, rested on the tray. Shoulders immobile, torsos arched, they walked in long strides that made their lightweight skirts sway from right to left. In their movements there was a natural pride and grace, which did not keep one of them, at times, from stopping, spreading her legs and meeting a need right there on the path; after which, she would simply wipe herself with her skirt and go her way.

They traveled by day and never alone for fear of zombies[2] and moun-mos,[3] and also so as not to be attacked, for a lone woman in the mountains is suspect. The guiablesse[4] roams these paths and the isolated plantations, under the guise of a pretty young girl; the men who follow her are never seen again. But we were not afraid of the guiablesse.

One Sunday, when I had climbed in a tree in order to watch over the "Bad Weeds," I saw Loulouze coming and noticed something different in her bearing. She stopped at the water's edge, and glanced about. Perhaps she was looking for me.

"Hey there!" I shouted.

She raised her eyes and seeing me, laughed oddly.

"Come down out of that tree right away, Mayotte. Come see somethin'."

I slid down and went to her side. She held her left arm slightly away from her body, as if it were more cherished than the other.

"Oh!" I cried out. "Jesus, Mary, Joseph! Loulouze, what a beautiful bracelet! Where did you buy it? Did it cost a lot?"

"It didn't cost me a thing. I didn't buy it. I didn't pay nothin' for it."

"Your ma gave it to you?"

"No, not my ma."

"Your pa?"

"No, not my pa."

"Who, then?"

"You're too nosey, Mayotte. I hate to say so, but it's not your business."

"So why'd you show it to me?"

"It's gold, pure gold and it's heavy."

"Let's see."

Loulouze took the bracelet off her arm to put it on mine. It was, indeed, heavy.

"Who gave it to you? Tell me, Loulouze, I'm begging you."

"You really nosey, Mayotte. You always want to know an' you know nothin'. Ok, my sweetheart gave it to me, my fiancé, if you wanna know everything."

"Oh my! Oh my! You're engaged, Loulouze?"

"Yes, but nobody knows it yet. Not even my ma. Nobody but you."

"With who?"

"I can't tell you that, Mayotte. That's not your business. You'll know soon enough."

Loulouze's words had plunged me into deep thought.

"Fiances give rings," I insinuated. "They don't give bracelets."

"Bracelets are big rings, sweethearts give bracelets," Loulouze declared with great conviction.

I hurried to repeat these words to Paul.

"But where you want me to buy one?," he asked.

"I don't know, in a city store like in Fort-de-France."

"But I can't go to Fort-de-France, I'm too little and I don't have no money."

I looked at him with disdain, but he seemed so upset that I consoled myself by saying: "You're not a sweetheart fiancé."

A few days later, he came to me with great pride.

"Look, Mayotte, what I brought you . . ."

35

I had already noticed that his pocket was stuffed. He took out a bracelet made of pear wood that, I suppose, he had carved himself.

"You want me to douse you with ink?," I said indignantly.

Cautiously, he took a few steps backwards.

"How was I to know it would make you get mad, Mayotte?," he sniveled.

"Sweetheart-fiances give gold bracelets," I shouted.

I saw the tears in his eyes; he really was not a man.

A few days later, I asked him for the bracelet and I made up with him. I have never been calculating and am generally less vain than others, but I dared not show this wooden thing to Loulouze who strolled with hers that glistened in the sun on her arm that she kept away from her body as if it had been paralyzed from happiness. Loulouze did not dare show off in town where old women's tongues were caustic as could be. I imagine that she had hidden her fine bracelet near our river and that she put it on only to come walk with me. She was careful not to be noticed by the other children. One day, she confided to me that I was the only one who had seen it.

"Don't worry, Loulouze," I told her, "I know how to keep secrets. I already have a collection, this just makes one more."

For quite a while I didn't see Loulouze. First of all, on Thursday morning there was catechism which I couldn't miss often. For the priests, it was more important than school and they would punish me severely, forcing me to remain standing for hours while reciting endless prayers instead of taking walks. However, one day, I succeeded in getting away to the banks of my cherished river where I finally met my friend. She wasn't doing her laundry, but was seated on a stone and staring at the current which was hurtling wood as if after a storm. I don't know why my heart contracted. I sat down beside her, put my arm around her neck and forced her to turn her head. I noticed then that her eyes were red and that her beautiful orange color had become muddy.

"Somethin' bad's happen, Mayotte, a mouthful. My pa put

me out. He don't want me these days no more. I can't go back home."

"Why?"

"Can't tell you that, Mayotte. You're too nosey, I always tell you an', worse yet, you're still a little girl."

"That's not so. I'm not a little girl no more."

"My pa made a terrible ruckus and put me out," she repeated. "I got nobody in this world. I just oughta throw myself in the river right now."

"Loulouze!" I cried. "Loulouze!"

My heart was beating as never before and I couldn't do anything but call my friend by name—a cry for help—to hold her by her name. I would have liked to tie her with a rope, attach her to a tree to keep her from carrying out this horrible act, but that day, I didn't have a rope.

"I haven't betrayed you." I murmured.

"I know." She leaned against me.

"Do you still have your beautiful bracelet?"

She began to cry, she who was always laughing.

For the first time in my life, I knew pain on seeing someone cry, but also joy because I felt that without having said anything to her, not being able to say anything to her, I had won.

Loulouze's bosom heaved a deep sigh, that bosom that I envied so much.

"Life is hard for a woman, you'll see, Mayotte, above all for a colored woman."

There was no rebellion in her and I didn't protest that. I was like a mother who draws her child to her body. I was no longer a little girl.

Loulouze was seen no more in Carbet, but she was talked about. Many approved of her fathers's action. Our island is small and women's tongues are sharp. I learned that Loulouze had left for Fort-de-France and there, no doubt, in order to have a little money, she had sought to sell her beautiful bracelet. But the bracelet was not gold, it was worthless. It was then, that I started to like my wooden bracelet. At least it did not lie.

CHAPTER II

Why did I decide to write? I had just arrived in Paris. I had come to get married, but that is another story I don't want to talk about. It was cold and snowing and the gentle whiteness falling from the sky that I was seeing for the first time both fascinated and caused me pangs of homesickness. That is when I wrote down some of the childhood memories about my country. It stopped snowing and the streets of Paris were dirty again, but I had enjoyed writing, and now I continue, even though spring has come and the weather isn't as cold.

In spite of my laziness in studying, I did so-so in school, but catechism was a dismal failure. When the time came for me to be examined for the first communion, I had to be put back two years. I felt neither guilt nor shame, but a slight annoyance on thinking about my comrades who were going to leave me alone with the younger ones. As for my parents, they said that this decision was made from Above and they resigned themselves to it.

Nonetheless, a few months later, after long discussion about me, they let me know that they felt it useless to spend more money for a child who did not care to study. I don't know what they meant, since catechism didn't cost anything; I think it was about the cost of my shoes. The priest's house was, indeed, quite a distance from the village, and it was not proper to go there barefoot. I resented the idea which could not have come from my mother, always so good and sweet with me, but from my father who thought only about money and was very stingy. I was determined to take catechism, and actually took a liking to it, not only because I was with boys and girls who engaged in a lot of pranks, but because I had fallen in love with the new priest. Young, tall, very blond and handsome, he made a thousand little butterflies whirl around in my head. I no longer thought about Paul, no longer wore his wood bracelet. I made great progress in catechism to please my dear priest, but I would have liked to express to him my feelings in a more direct way. Finally, one day I dared to say to him, "Father, when you're dead, I'll carry flowers to your tomb." His smile caused a tumult within me and perhaps he understood me, for on every occasion he favored me in so many ways.

Being the oldest among the children he taught to love Our Lord, I was usually sent to look for the books needed for the lessons. I had to cross an immense courtyard where chickens, ducks, and rabbits roamed about. Father grew flowers there and had planted mango trees and a few vines. In passing, I would swipe a few unripened grapes while they were still hard to be used for our marble games at the end of catechism. Then we dispersed, each one returning to his paternal home where varied household chores awaited. For instance, there was wood to be gathered, but I preferred feeding the chickens because my father fed them chopped coconut which I loved and devoured as least as much as they did. Our village, Carbet, a part of Grande Anse district, stretched the length of the only road that ran along the sea. There, one could see beautiful stone houses in European style where the rich whites lived—but we also called "white" some of those who were mixed blood and who had money, providing their complexion was light enough—and the wooden shanties where peasants and fishermen lived. These dwellings, quite a distance from one another, were concealed under giant palm trees to which sunlight gave beautiful yellowish brown colors, and which, when shaken by the wind from the open seas, moved like live animals.

Each day for me was different, each day brought its own

revelation, each day was like a net that brought strange fish to the shores. But I think that my favorite moment was the evening when all the village children gathered on the endless beach. We rolled in the sand, still lukewarm, flecked with tiny stones, clear as glass in which the last rays danced, and which, I thought, were like dead stars fallen from the sky the night before. On our half naked bodies we felt the voluptuous caress of a fresh breeze. The sun set slowly and, minute by minute, the colors changed. The ocean horizon became yellow, then orange—I do not remember ever in my life having seen a more beautiful spectacle.

Later, the boats laden with fish came in view on the water, now lilac colored. Women and men came to wait for them on the beach. When the boats were near enough, everyone ran shouting into the sea. We children threw off our clothes and dashed after them. The smallest children clung to the others like puppies, but we got rid of them as best we could. I was already a good swimmer and I was soon first among those who charged the boat. "Ho! Ho!" yelled the fishermen, who then became fish vendors. In the water, the distribution of maqueriaux and colious began among quarrels and shouts. The poissons-coffres, so ugly but so good, were snatched first; flying fish were less valued.

Finally, when the boats were empty, we went back to shore, our meal held in our arms. Then, we had to find our clothes again which wasn't always easy because the children who stayed on the beach had fun in hiding them. We clowned a lot among ourselves and this had become a classic prank. Sometimes we would discover them in a thicket or on top of a palm tree.

One day, I didn't find mine at all. They had been carried away by the waves. What was I to do? Start crying? This wasn't like me. As best I could, I arranged some leaves around my body, and thus attired, I resigned myself, not without some misgivings, to return home.

I had been the last one on the beach. A blue darkness seemed to come out of the earth, like a mist. Night didn't fall,

41

it rose from the earth so forcefully that it finally made the sun tip over. To reassure myself, I spoke aloud, I said : "Mi la nuit ka ga'dé moin. Mache toujous dé'ié moin, lan mé!" ("Here's night looking at me. Oh sea, always walk behind me.")

Happily, my mother was the first one that I met. She raised her arms in the air.

"Jesus, Mary, Joseph — Mayotte what is this all about? What are people who saw you walking through town in that indecent get-up going to think"

"They'll think nothing, mama. Didn't the Good Lord think that it was right to send me into the world without covering?"

"Yes, you were little, but now you're a big girl. It's no longer right for you to walk around like a new-born baby. What are Mrs. Sarah and Mrs Josephine going to think? And the Father, who will soon know!"

At these words. I felt my heart beat faster. I surely hoped that the Father wouldn't hear about it. He, alone, could make me ashamed.

At last vacation time came. A childhood friend of my mother's was coming to spend it with us, along with her two children, a pretty fourteen year-old girl and a ten year-old boy. Well ahead of time, my mother gave me numerous warnings.

"These children are being taught by the nuns in Fort-de-France. They are well raised. I hope that you'll be on your best behavior."

"I'm not planning to do anything bad, mommy," I answered, "Am I ever bad?"

"Above all," she ordered in her most severe tone, "don't drag them in the hills or to the riverside. You must stay at home while they are here like a well-bred young lady."

I answered with a vague yes. I don't like to make promises; in my mind, I had no intention of making her a promise.

My mother went to meet her guests who arrived by boat and I accompanied her. They kissed profusely, my mother, her friend and the children, all smacked on one another like candy. I didn't like kissing, so I merely extended my hand graciously. The pretty lady leaned toward me:

"Well, aren't you going to kiss me, little one?"

I smiled as best I could, she didn't insist and went on with her daughter and mama. I trailed behind with the little boy. He was the only one in the family I found interesting, but he seemed very timid.

"What's your name?" I asked.

"Jacques."

I saw that I had to keep the conversation going.

"So, Jacques," I began, "What do you do for fun in Fort-de France?"

"I go to the movies."

"What do you go to see at the movies?"

"I go to see "The Sleeping Beauty," "Patachou" and "Double Patte.""

His prestige grew and, at the same time, his timidity was winning me over. I, who had never been to the movies and I didn't even know the names of these stories, wondered anxiously what would please him here.

"What are you going to do here at Carbet?"

"I'll do what you want," he answered.

I was absolutely obligated to get something together. The very next morning, I decided to take him cray fishing. I took advantage of my mother's absorption in her kitchen chores and scurried off with him bound for my dear river.

I had often gone cray fishing with the gang, "Wild Weeds," not in the traditional way, that is, at night by luring them with lanterns and manioc roots, but during the day and by hand. This was not without its danger because the crayfish of Martinique sometimes are the size of lobsters and can inflict serious wounds. But I knew how to catch them and I loved the sport. In any case, I thought that it was proper to please a little boy who went to the movies.

Unfortunately, on that day, the water was not as clear as usual. As if it were playing a trick on me, the river had put on its brown dress, which I should have predicted because that always happens in autumn. I felt angry toward it and myself. Nonetheless, we went in the water because I refused to have come for nothing, but the crayfish were hiding under a thick bed of leaves. Moreover, the corner that I had chosen was filled with leeches, which, tempted by our tender skin, clung to our legs.

Suddenly, Jacques let out a scream.

"I'm afraid!"

"You're afraid? Of what?"

"Wild beasts!"

"Beasts! They're no beasts here that can eat you."

The leg that he lifted out of the water was full of blisters. I couldn't keep from laughing, although I didn't want to hurt his feelings, but I was used to leeches.

"Wait" I said, "Just be patient, they'll go away by themselves."

In fact, ten minutes later, all the leeches having dined well had left. But since we had to think about returning home, my heart burst with pity for little Jacques. What was his mama going to say? Was she going to beat him? Heavens!

"Tell me, Jacques, are you mad at me for getting you bitten by those miserable leeches?"

"No. . ."

"What will your mama say?"

"Nothing."

"You believe that. . . Mamas always say something. And now, we've got to leave because it's getting late and my pa hates to wait. I'm going to try one more catch. I don't hold to being cheated from eating. Of course, for you it's not the same, my pa won't dare punish you."

"Of course." said Jacques.

Yet, after thinking a moment, he added:

"But he's my godfather and you know he can take the place of my father."

"Where did you learn that?

"At catechism."

"You've made your first communion already?"

"I'm sure it'll be this year"

"You're lucky."

"And you?"

"Oh, I don't know when. They put me back two years."

It was noon. Now we had to run.

"Would you like for me to play horse?"

I put a creeping vine around my neck, happy to make him forget his woes. H ied "Hee! Haw!" and I started off in fine gallop, taking the shortest route as I dashed through the woods. Branches caressed or scratched us; at times, the high bamboo stalks tried to block our path, but I was thin and quick enough to pass through. I finally emerged in a huge corn field and I glimpsed the sea between the golden tasseled ears. It sent a fresh and salty breeze to our open faces and I ran harder than ever against the wind, pulling poor Jacques who no longer was able to shout "Hee! Haw!" I thought no more about the punishment awaiting us.

Finally, I arrived in town, jumped over my father's garden door and, with one leap, landed on the veranda steps. I stopped short before father and mother and at the same time, I heard a cry. The nice lady guest had thrown herself on her little boy, showering him with kisses and shouting indignantly about the traces left by the leeches on his legs. Assuming that he had been bitten by the poisonous fer de lance, she saw him already dead.

"All this on account of that bad little girl, disobedient and badly brought up," she screamed, turning furiously toward me. My father, who until then, had said nothing, thought it his duty to intercede:

"You'll get nothing to eat," he said to me. "You can stay here to look at Jacques, but you'll eat nothing at all."

Despite his words, he didn't seem very angry.

Jacques sat down at the table surrounded by the noisy solicitude of his mother. They had kept a pile of sweets for him. I couldn't stand the sight of this and lost no time in leaving.

The fresh air and the race had made me ravenous with

45

hunger. I went to the pig's sty and devoured a good portion of their peelings. They grunted, furious, but I talked to them explaining what had happened, and I no longer thought much about the little boy who was stuffing himself with goodies.

Did he eat too much? In the evening, he was put to bed early because he was feverish. Naturally, his mother blamed me. My father, no doubt to anger her more, suggested sending for the quimboiseur.[5] Upon which, the lady called him a savage, old-fashioned, an enemy of science and progress.

The next day, she left with her family to the great relief of my parents. And this time, I didn't have to endure the bevy of kisses.

CHAPTER III

I think that it's time for me to speak about my father. He was a handsome man, tall and strong. He talked a lot and his deep voice served him well in his electoral speeches. He used to recall the time spent in the war in France which brought him great prestige, and he never missed the opportunity to talk about his adventurous life.

Having lost his parents very early, he was apprenticed to a cabinet maker. However, since the latter gave him no salary, it wasn't long before he left to go to a large fish business where he began by mending nets. He earned what was called a godrone of five francs per month, which evidently was not much for a young man who loved pleasure, and all the more so because he did not want to go to the public dances, seeing himself as worthy only of those dances where one had to pay an entrance fee. He loved to court young girls, and if he is to be believed, he was very successful at that. So it was that, from need as much as inclination, he began to play and became a cockfight expert which allowed him to infiltrate a class of men who handled large sums of money. Soon, he decided to leave the fisheries to undertake an orange and vanilla business between Fort-de France and Trinidad that brought him good earnings, but the money that he earned was quickly eaten up by gambling and women.

Possessed by a yearning for travel, one fine day he abandoned this business and left for America. According to his story, he didn't retain good memories of his trip over there:

"I never learned a serious trade. In America, work doesn't grow on trees and the Americans are not friendly toward a colored man. The little money that I brought with me was not long in slipping from my hands. Finally, after a number of applications, I managed to find a job in a store as a salesman and I picked up a little change to pay for my trip back to my native land. So, I came back to Carbet and with the bit of money that I earned, I bought this little white frame house."

Hired to keep books for City Hall, he soon became involved in politics. He belonged to the extreme left party and, having become elected mayor of our commune, he successfully led heated electoral campaigns which often degenerated into brawls. Once he was carried home half conscious, knocked out by huge conch shells that his adversaries had used as arms. At other times, we found him in front of our door with a burial notice addressed to him on which was drawn a skull and cross bones, all wrapped with a ribbon; or even the carcasses of baby lizards stuck with pins in whose mouths the ill-wishers had stuck a coin. My father, having been in many other countries, didn't believe in sorcery and hardly gave this a thought, but my mother, still very superstitious, picked up these things with nippers and washed them with sea water and with alkali. She would forbid me to go near the places where she put them, but when I could, I would take the pennies from the baby lizards' mouths to buy myself pink, green and blue coconut balls.

Once a year on election day, my father held a big feast that reunited his friends, at times over fifty of them. The members of his party were colored and white men, poor and uneducated. My mother, who was slender and delicate in health, dreaded these events but she could not do other than give in to my father's wishes. On that day, this man who usually kept account of every penny, paid no attention to expenses. My mother, thrifty without being stingy, disputed this matter, saying that her bill at the grocery store had not been paid, that she had children to rear and that household money must not

48

be wasted. But my father forcefully maintained that he had to do everything "to get people together and make them feel good. It's my duty," he said. I now know that his exceptional generosity meant that his finances had a stake in the success of his party.

I remember the first time that I helped with one of these banquets. It was on a Sunday. My mother had set up a large table on the porch. My sister, who was more dexterous than I, had been given the task of placing the white napkins and silver. Mama, shuddering, took out the beautiful Baccarat[6] crystal glasses from the buffet.

"I know they're going to break my beautiful glasses I love so much."

"Now, mother dear," I answered, "you bought them so they can be used."

"Of course, but to have these loud-mouth fellows who yell and perhaps have never drunk from a crystal glass in their life."

The guests arrived in small groups; they had donned their best suits and shoes—those shoes that most of them carried by hand up to the church entrance when they went to mass—which made them waddle like ducks. Standing in front of the table shining with trays and glassware, my father spoke softly and bowed low which made me want to laugh. He ordered me to serve the punch that I had prepared. In each glass I put a thimbleful of syrup, three of rum and a bit of lemon for the aroma and taste. I passed the tray as gracefully as possible, then stood at attention, a pitcher of water in my hand, ready to obey at the least sign. It is customary to drink a large glass of fresh water after each punch so as to neutralize the effects of alcohol.

Finally, the meal began with the traditional pâté en pot that my mother had worked hard to prepare. Pâté en pot is a soup made with pastes of tripes, hearts and livers of sheep, carrots, turnips, cabbage, potatoes, celery and leeks, all cooked over a low fire. When ready to serve, a few capers and white wine or vinegar are added. It is the local specialty and no good meal begins without it. Next came leg-of-lamb, a fish bouillon with rice, dishes of crayfish, fricassee rabbit and macaroni-au-gratin.

Bottles of Saint-Emilion and sauterne were no longer being counted. And these folk, all excited, clinked their glasses more and more. What an uproar! My father was keeping watch so that, as soon as glasses were emptied, they were filled again. At each clink, I saw my mother pale.

I was seated at the end of the table beside Francette, the odor of alcohol and sweat was going to my head and I looked at these men, black as crows, in their suits they wore only for baptisms, marriages and funerals, in their glossy shirts which were like water on their chests, where shadows played. Only the bow ties added bits of color and fantasy to this solemnity. With the help of the drinks and the commotion, the butterfly bows leaned to the left, at times to the right, or sometimes became half undone, hanging comically. In spite of this, my father continued to take a lot of trouble to be a man of the world. I didn't recognize his heavy, loud voice and the airs he put on made me burst out laughing.

"My dear colleagues," he would say, "you will give me great pleasure to accept this piece of chicken. My wife will be all the more pleased because she made it."

Not to be outdone, my mother would insist:

"Please do me the honor of tasting this dish that I took particular pains with."

To be polite the guests protested, then served themselves generously. The one I preferred was my godfather who was called "Solitary Tapeworm" because he was short and couldn't stand living alone. He had a mustache that he was proud of. A heavy drinker and eater, he liked to clown at such events. Warmed up by the drinks, he had opened wide his coat, uncovering pants that came up to his chest and were held up by canary yellow suspenders.

"Say," asked my father, "Why did you choose that color?

"Angela gave them to me for my birthday," he answered mischievously.

"So, you even wear it on your suspenders!..."

My godmother showed no embarrassment in affirming that yellow was her favorite color. But my father made a clumsy joke. "Say, Angela, do you change these suspenders every year? After all, if it's only every year, that still happens!"

And since he was tipsy, he burst into song: "If all men are cuckolds/Women are too."

At that moment, we heard an awful noise of broken glass; my mother got up and left the table. My godfather, who had drunk too much and who, perhaps, only slightly appreciated my father's jokes, did not delay in following her example in order to find a spot where he could lie down.

Francette and I, worn out by this lengthy meal and from the noise these men were making, left the table in turn. Father no longer paid us attention. We wanted to look for my godfather because, we always had fun with him, but we didn't know where he had hidden himself. At last, we found him in the pig pen, stretched out on a bundle of hay, his coat thrown back displaying the infamous yellow suspenders. He seemed to be in a deep sleep. At the sight of that head bent backward, offering its mustache, an unfortunate idea came to mind. I got some paper, rolled it like a cigar, stuck it in his open mouth and set fire to it. I didn't give thought to the mustache saturated with alcohol. It blazed up like punch and my godfather became clean-shaven in less time that it takes to tell about it. I fled, terrified. But Francette, who never could keep from tattling, went directly to father to inform him about my escapade. At first, he burst out laughing, then became angry and decided to have me stand at the garden door with rocks in each hand that I had to strike continuously one against the other, my arms stretched upwards. Soon, the neighborhood children came to form a circle around me. Francette also came to ask forgiveness, but I shrugged my shoulders, all the while bumping my stones. Has it ever been worthwhile to ask forgiveness?

CHAPTER IV

One day, the parish priest sent for me at the rectory. What did he want? I was very excited beforehand about this special meeting.

He ushered me in ceremoniously (how simple and gentle he was!) and pointed to a large armchair where I settled awkwardly.

"What do you want with me, Father?" I asked him, trembling with impatience.

"I want to talk to you like a big girl, Mayotte," he said. "Do you want to please me?"

"Why are you asking that, Father?"

He looked at me with his bright blue eyes. Oh, how I would have loved to be blond like him! Never had he seemed so handsome to me.

"Yes," I stammered, "I want to please you, Father."

"And please your parents?"

"Yes," I said, with less enthusiasm.

"Well," he said, "it will soon be time for you to know your catechism lesson and you must be able to answer all questions without fail. I know that you can if you want to. I want you to promise to double your efforts."

So that was why he had sent for me! To encourage me!

"What day is it , Father?"

"The test? Twelve days from now. You see you don't have much time left. Promise me to try, just to please me."

"If that can please you, I promise, Father."

"Good that's settled. I trust you. And now, come see pretty pictures that I ordered from France."

I went over to the table where about fifteen chromos were spread out: Parisian boys and girl in their first communion dress, the Three Wise Men, the Baby Jesus, the entry into Jerusalem with the mule and brightly colored flowers of all kinds.

"This is the one I intended for you," said the priest, showing me a picture apart from the others which portrayed the Virgin Mary. "I made it myself, just for you, with India ink."

"Why with India ink?"

The priest smiled. "All right," he said, "if you prefer another one, you may choose."

"No," I said precipitately, afraid of hurting him, "I really want the one thou did for me."

How did I come to use the thou [7] form? I was so ashamed that I dared not look at him.

"Oh! excuse me, Father, excuse me, I didn't say that on purpose, I swear."

He touched my head. "It doesn't matter. It doesn't matter."

"I have to go," I said.

"Wait a minute, little one. As a matter of fact, I must go see your mother. I'll go along with you."

"That's not possible, Father. I have errands to do and that would hold you up."

"All right, be quick about it and I'll come by the store for to get you."

I rushed outside and ran to town with all the strength my legs could muster, so as not to have him wait. I had finished my shopping, when I saw his carriage approaching. My heart was beating so fast that I remained glued to the spot, incapable of taking a step. The priest got out, took my basket and settled me on the seat. When he gave the word, the horse started forward. Everything obeyed the priest, men and beasts —why not the wind and clouds?— without his having to raise his voice. I gave myself over to this extraordinary force that I sensed beside me. Never had the sun appeared more glorious to me. No doubt, it was as he wanted it, the Father, as he wanted it to please me.

Passing through town was triumphant. The children formed a procession and since the old horse didn't go very fast, they had a good time circling the carriage.

"Good day, Father!," they shouted with in shrill voices.

"Good day, my children, how are you?"

At last, we arrived home. I was happy to be with Father and, nonetheless, I wished that the trip through town had been longer, much longer.

My mother was expecting this visit. She had dressed up, wearing the local dress which is made of a silk material decorated with huge floral bouquets, flared at the bottom, tight at the waist. She knew how to tuck it up elegantly so as to show the magnificent petticoat, itself covered by a satiny cloth, matching the pink scarf that she had gracefully placed on her shoulders in native fashion. Her blouse was close fitting. She was wearing her lovely Parisian shoes and her prettiest madras on her head which brought out the radiance of her black eyes. She had a very chic way of tying the madras with a knot that ended in two points allowing a third to come through. To me, she was charming and I was very happy.

She served the priest a delicious coconut cake and a sweet wine, knowing that conversation goes more smoothly when one is eating. My father soon arrived. He had left work early so that he could have a few words with Father.

Then mother withdrew to the kitchen to prepare dinner and to allow the men the tête-à-tète as was fitting. I joined her.

"Mama, are you going to have Father stay for dinner?"

"But dearie, that would be too much work because there's only one way to entertain Father. That would make us go to bed later, child. But of course, if your father invites him. . ."

"I'm sure that he'll invite him," I cried.

In a flash, I went back to the porch where my father and

the priest had begun a card game. I don't know how I did it, but finally Father was invited. He accepted.

I rushed into the kitchen.

"Mama, you know that Father really likes stuffed crab. . ."

Mama raised her hands high.

"But it takes four hours to fix them! And, furthermore they're not in season. That's a Pentecost dish. . . "

I was given permission to go get Francette. Father must have told them about the agreement that I had made. I ran all the way.

"Auntie," I shouted, "The Father is at our house! He's playing cards with papa. He said he would stay for dinner and mama is fixing a lot of good things. She told me to come get Francette."

"I don't know if I can let your sister leave. It's quite late and we have already eaten."

Finally and reluctantly, that incorrigible old maid let me take Francette away. And so the two of us left by the light of a moon that made people older than us dream. We began to gambol, to play with the beams and the shadows, appearing and disappearing by turns like two will-of-the wisps. Francette, whose life with old-maid-auntie must have been really boring, was laughing heartily. She was very affable. I should have been that way, because we resembled each other so much that when I looked at her, it was as if I saw myself in a mirror. I admired myself, in admiring her.

Then, when we were calmer, I told her about my conversation with the priest. I would have loved to talk about him, but I spoke mostly about the pictures he had shown me.

"He made one just for me." I proudly stated, "And it's the most beautiful one."

"But didn't you know that Father is going to be replaced by another priest?"

"Who told you that?"

"I heard auntie tell a neighbor so."

My heart stopped, the night faded away. I had no more joy.

55

"I think it's strange," I remarked, "that Father didn't say anything to mama."

But I was no longer able to mouth any words. I finally arrived home, deathly pale like the moon.

"What's wrong, Mayotte? Are you sick?," mother queried.

Without answering her, I threw myself onto her dress like a baby who needs to be cuddled.

"Francette," mother insisted, "tell me why your sister's crying."

"I told her that Father is going to be replaced. That's probably why she's upset."

Mother softly stroked my head. I loved having her hand on my hair; I drew closer to her.

"Well now," she said. "If it's true, he'll surely be nearby and you can go visit him, though not every day."

Francette, who had already eaten, served the dinner, then sat down to drink a glass of punch. My father asked for details on the replacement.

"He's an older man and quite charming," answered the priest.

"Perhaps, but we are used to you. You've been here for ten years."

"Fifteen."

Fifteen years! How old is Father, I wondered. Is he that old? Why, of course, he's not old. I didn't take my eyes from his blond head. I had never thought there could be a man as handsome as he.

"It will seem strange for us to meet a new priest." my father continued. "You are the nicest priest who ever came to our humble parish."

"I am very moved by your words," said the priest. "After all, I only did my duty and the years passed quickly at Carbet. To be sure, I have witnessed many changes. I have seen children grow up, become fine young men and women, who, in their turn, will have their own children. . .

His blue-eyed gaze, which was fixed on me, went back to my father.

"I have also seen death. At first, I had a lot of financial problems. But, ultimately, profits from local charities added to those of the Apostolate Guild and the Sacred Heart Guild, allowed me to support my church. To sum up, I had only minor worries, easy to bear when one has faith."

I listened in silence, for I loved the sound of his voice and could have listened to it all night, even if what it said didn't interest me.

Soon mother told me to see Francette home. That girl was always playful and thought only about having fun. Not being in a hurry to get back to auntie's, she suggested that we take the beach route and chase crabs. I agreed, first to please her, but I was soon carried away by the game.

"There's one," shrieked Francette. "There's another and still another."

We ran, we leaped midst the fireflies which were fluttering around us like little wild stars, and we kicked unmercifully the shells of the poor crabs. Then, when they were just about half crushed, we picked them up and put them in our pinafores.

At last, Francette remembered that she had to return home. When we arrived at auntie's, I noticed that my pinafore was quite dirty. Since our aunt had a mania about order and cleanliness, I didn't linger. Francette got along well with her, I told myself; she was used to her.

I took the road to return home, for I was not afraid. The queen of stars, the Southern Cross, shone brilliantly and the sea breeze kept me company.

Once again at home, I found mother telling her beads in front of the chappelle. This is a corner where, set on a shelf, are crosses, pictures of Jesus, statues of the Virgin and saints. A candle burns day and night and it is here, in front of this light, that we pray.

Father, as usual, had gone outside. He liked to smoke his pipe in the fresh air before going to bed. I knew where he was. He always sat on the same coconut tree that the wind had blown down, just to give him a seat.

As for me, I was still too upset, too enticed by the light of the full moon to be sleepy. I didn't want to end this day, so poignant with feeling, so I asked my mother to let me join my friends.

In the evenings, they were to be found on a narrow street lined with a high pavement. There the girls would be seated, the boys facing opposite them, or we formed a circle and began to play "flower language."

One boy asked the question:

"What does the rose say?"

"That my heart can love only once," a girl would answer.

Then it was our turn. One of us would ask:

"What does the pineapple leaf say?"

We didn't have to wait for an answer.

"I would walk on a razor blade to have a kiss from you," a boy declared. Then a girl, who looked like Loulouze, sang a folksong.[8]

> Knock, knock, knock! Who's knocking at my door?
> It is I, Love. Open your door.
> The rain awakened me, the sun warmed me.
> Open your door for me and give me a kiss.
> Give me one kiss, two kisses, three kisses, dear.
>
> Give me a kiss to console my heart
> So that my heart will pain me less. (bis)
> If I could be changed to a bird,
> Like the nightingale who takes flight.
> I would fly into the arms of my beloved
> To tell her all I am thinking.
> Give me, etc., etc.
>
> The flower is never without butterflies
> The sky never without stars
> The sea never without fish.
> I, alone, will mourn in the depths of the tomb.

We returned home in couples, playing at being lovers. But

that never went very far. The boy who accompanied me that evening didn't even kiss me. Without a doubt, love had not knocked at his door and, no doubt, he had not understood the language of flowers.

I got into bed, but couldn't fall asleep. The dogs barking at the moon, the muffled rumbling of the waves, the sharp cries of birds, dominated by the deafening bleating of the wild goats we called cra-cra, all those night sounds, those memories of that day, kept me awake. I heard my father come in. He forgot to close the door that connected my room to theirs. Soon strange whispers reached my ears, which mixed with the noise of all the animals, disturbed me even more.

CHAPTER V

I kept my word. I reported to the presbytery every day after school to learn the catechism and not only for the pleasure of seeing Father. He seemed more tired than I and he no longer smiled; perhaps, he too, found it painful to leave us. I dared not think to leave me, but nonetheless, I thought that, because it was good to think so.

Finally, the day of the test—that day I had waited two years for—arrived. Out of the three hundred-four children who had taken it, two hundred sixty-nine were successful and I was among them. My mother wept for joy. I, too, was happy, feeling that I could ask for anything.

"Now, mama, am I going to have a beautiful long dress like the ladies who get married?"

"Yes, darling, you'll have everything you want."

My imagination took off in leaps and bounds. I thought about a thousand gifts that relatives could give on that day. I ran to our aunt's house so that my sister would hear my news before anyone else.

"Say, Fancette, I have a surprise for you!"

"Oh no, I know about your surprise already."

"T'aint so . . ."

"You passed your first catechism test."

"Who told you?"

"Everybody knows it now."

Francette wasn't telling the truth. When I arrived at my godfather's, he knew nothing at all, and was so overjoyed by my announcement that he gave me ten francs.

I spent the evening alone with my mother. Her face—that face that I had so often seen filled with sadness and even anxiety—was aglow with joy.

"I'm so happy," she said, "that God allowed me to be near you until this day which must be the first day of your life. Ah! how I would like to be your age . . ."

"But didn't you have other happy days, mama dear?"

"It's not the same thing . . ."

"Why not?"

I saw her hesitate. The extraordinary glow on her face had disappeared. She continued softly:

"Very well, you see, you have a mother and I, I never was that fortunate."

I snuggled up to her.

"Forgive me, mommie, If I hurt you . . ."

"No child, I'm only sorry you don't have a grandmother."

"But I have one, that's enough," I said, while thinking about my father's mother whom I didn't like much.

Mother gave me a kiss that wrung my heart. I drew back and stared at her.

"Mama, tell me the story of my other grandma."

"It's so long and I'm afraid you'll be bored."

But I had already made up my mind and insisted so, that I finally convinced her to talk.

"Well," she said, "your grandmother came from an old French Canadian family. Her parents had visited Martinique and found Saint-Pierre such a lovely place that they settled there where your grandmother was born. She was brought up in a convent like all wealthy white children. Unfortunately for her, she met and fell in love with a young colored man. I don't know how that happened, but what I do know is that my own grandparents didn't want a marriage under any circumstances. They paid the young man a handsome sum to leave Saint-Pierre and he left, perhaps because he didn't love her enough. This probably hurt your grandmother deeply. A few years later she married another young man that her parents accepted and she had two daughters, your aunt and me. We were raised, 'under cover,' in the same boarding school for white children, but after all the suffering she had endured, my mother soon died. I hardly saw her and barely remember her. That's why I can say that I was unfortunate not to have a mother.

Your father and I were very young when we met. We had to wait a few years before getting married. Your father traveled but he wrote me every day. I struggled hard against everyone in my family to marry the one I loved. Finally, after waiting two years, we were married in the church where you are going to make your first communion. . . But it was war time and he was soon called to serve and he left for France. He had just been sent to the Front, when I gave birth to Francette and you. He was wounded soon after and when he returned he was not altogether the same."

"How was he before, mama?"

"War changes men a lot . . ."

Mother stopped. She had become sad but she forced a smile.

"You must take advantage of your first communion," she added, "to meditate and pray for your future life. Life is hard for a woman."

I remembered Loulouze who had said something similar: "above all for a colored woman."

And so it was that I found out that I had a white grandmother! I was proud of that. Surely, I was not the only one to have white blood, but a grandmother was less commonplace than a white grandfather. So then, my mother was a métisse?[9] I should have suspected this because of her pale complexion. I found her prettier than ever, more refined, more distinguished. If she had married a white man, would I, perhaps have been all white?...And would life have been less difficult for me? What did my mother mean, what did Loulouze mean? Life, to me, didn't seem very hard. I knew by looking at Francette and because boys told me so that I was pretty and attractive. Some even declared that I was beautiful, adorable and my godfather, for instance, said I was charming. He had said it again that very day, when he gave me ten francs . . .

I gave careful thought to this grandmother whom I had never known and who died because she loved a colored man, a Martinican. How could a Canadian woman have loved a Martinican? I, who was still thinking about the Father, decided that I could love only a white man, a blond with blue eyes, a Frenchman.

CHAPTER VI

Since it was required that I pray for the difficult life that lay ahead, a few days before my first communion, my mother sent me to a retreat at the priest's house. There, I was among a large group of children, white and black, rich and poor. According to their means, parents supplied the meals we ate together. All kinds of dishes were spread on the table, from the minced conch meat and stewed red crabs of the poor to the trays laden with fowl and all kinds of candies and sweets sent by the rich.

Greedy as I was, however, I was not concerned about eating. My heart was touched by something else—music. I sang with real fervor: "Good Mary/take my crown/I give it to thee/take my crown, I place it in thy hands." I was captivated by the melody of this hymn; it was as if I were an angel, all pink and white, taking flight. In the morning we returned to the church to memorize the vow to be taken the day of the ceremony. The church was beautifully decorated to receive us and transformed into a paradise by bountiful white flowers. The communion table, covered with a lace cloth was already prepared. Two by two, we came forward and when we got to this little table behind which stood Father, we uttered in a trembling voice the words of the ritual: "I renounce Satan, all his ways and works and I belong forever to Jesus Christ."

The first time, we were overcome by such fright that most of us couldn't open our mouths, or rather, when we did, no sounds came forth. Finally, we got in the habit of doing so.

After the rehearsal, Father spoke at length to us about communion and the preparation we must make to receive Our Lord. I didn't understand very well and Confession Day held a rather disagreeable surprise for me. I had always loathed admitting my faults, so Father's questions embarrassed me terribly. I had never asked them of myself, for I had never worried about one act being good and another bad. In the end, to please him, I confessed a few sins. But on leaving the confessional, I was most uneasy as I thought woefully that I would never again dare to look him in the face. That evening, I spoke to my mother about this confession, intending to tell her a bit of what had taken place with Father, but mother refused to hear anything.

"That's a secret confession," she said, "Father has to hear you. I don't have the right to know."

So I was alone with my shame.

For her part, mother was keeping her secret, no doubt in order not to disturb my meditation by talking about clothes. She said absolutely nothing about the dress that I was to wear on that solemn day. Her silence, however, aroused all the more my curiosity and my impatience.

At last, the eve of the big day, Saturday evening, July 11, mother came to get me, accompanied by my godmother who, although she didn't care about traveling, had taken the trouble just to come for this ceremony. On the way I asked them many questions and, since my godmother was talkative, I learned that mother had ordered a magnificent outfit at "Vide Poches," the largest store in Fort-de-France.

My bedroom door was kept locked, for, on my bed were the dresses I so much wanted to see. I had no desire to eat, for I was too impatient. When mother finally opened the door, I let out a cry of surprise. My room which, until then, had looked like a boy's room, had been changed to a young lady's chamber. Spread over the bed was a lovely light blue coverlet, and in a corner, I glimpsed a statuette of the Virgin upright on a shelf, and in front of it, an oil night lamp which I knew I was to keep lit night and day. It was an altar like the one in my parents room, like those owned by all respectable people. I rushed to open the armoire, but the dresses were not there.

Although tired, I slept badly that night, being both weary and curious. The next morning, at last I was able to gaze upon the wonderful things mama had bought for me: a long white dress, more beautiful than I had imagined; white shoes too, and a slender necklace that looked to me like gold (gold like Loulouze's!) on which hung a tiny cross. But I didn't have time to admire all that finery, for I had to get dressed—quite a large order. Mother seemed to find so much pleasure in this. She circled around me, talking, laughing, sticking a pin here, fixing a pleat there. As for me, my feelings and my joy were too mixed up for me to separate them. That morning, I couldn't really enjoy anything.

The carriage was already at the door. Mother and I got in and seated ourselves with the greatest care so that we didn't wrinkle our dresses. In his seat, the fat black coachman, laughing heartily, seemed quite happy to see us so elegantly dressed.

"Mayotte," he shouted, " You look like an angel!"

I was unable to respond. I knew that white was becoming to me, and I could have fancied myself a pink-cheeked angel, if I had not seen my hands that became even darker in contrast to the startling whiteness of my dress.

Since then, I have seen "Green Pastures"[10] where angels and God himself are black and that was a terrible shock for me. How can God be conceived with Negro features? That's not my idea of Paradise. But, after all, it's only an American film. We are more advanced in Martinique. Surely the God that Father Labat[11] preached about to our ancestors is also the colored people's God, but he is white.

We arrived at the church faster than I wanted. I alighted from the carriage and found my place among the children who were lined up two by two. An impressive silence held sway over this usually unruly group. Upon Father's command, we started walking. We passed through the main door, slowly marching forward toward the holy table, our small faces tense from so much gentleness and purity. I didn't recognize the girl at my side, so renewed were her features. But I wasn't astonished at this and told myself: "Her sins have been taken away." We felt the burden of the gaze of all the people of Carbet which heightened both our pride and our anguish. To accompany that triumphal entrée, the harmonium began to play. At that moment, the music covered me like a cloud. I saw nothing more; I was carried away to another world.

The ceremony seemed endless to me. At last, we left as solemnly as we had entered.

Suddenly, there I was in the plaza flooded with light. The mothers, lined up in a semi-circle waiting for their children, were so heavily bedecked in their jewelry that glistened in the sunlight, one would have thought they were wearing fireworks. As soon as I had recovered from my bewilderment, I looked for mine. Eventually, I spotted her red and yellow madras head scarf, the black crepe-de-chine dress adorned with large rose bouquets (transforming her, I thought, into a marquise), and the rose shawl that was so becoming to her. Thus, for me, she seemed to be the heart of those fireworks. But I didn't rush toward her as was my habit. Just to show her how much I had changed, I walked sedately to meet her, somewhat uncomfortable in my new dress, but aware of my new dignity.

CHAPTER VII

Two years after my first communion, my mother, who had suffered from heart trouble for a long time, died suddenly. I had kissed her; she had spoken to me ten minutes before she was no more. The anguish of solitude brought a lump to my throat, but I could not cry. I was like a body without a soul.

She was no longer on this earth, yet I could not believe it. There she was in the bed, lightly ringed eyelids closed over her large big black eyes, her half-opened lips held a ghost of a smile as if she were having a pleasant dream. But, I said to myself, she no longer breathes. I dared not touch her. For a long time, I remained motionless, standing at the foot of the bed, in order to fix her face in my memory. Already flowers surrounded her, their odor weighing down the dark room. The blinds were shut and the flame of the night lamp on the altar was as weak and fragile as my breath.

People, garbed in black, were coming and going in this room, where, I thought, everything should have been still and silent. They spoke in hushed voices; I even recognized my father's voice. Why didn't he let himself go? A woman came upon me and gave me a hug. Then, in order to be unnoticed, I withdrew to a corner in the room across from where the flame of the night-lamp burned, and I huddled there. My gaze was still fixed on my mother's face, but I could no longer detect her mysterious smile and no kind of peace or consolation remained. Perhaps I was thinking mostly about myself. I was afraid . . .

It must be true that misfortune never arrives alone. I don't want to give details about the funeral, of my father's noisy grief, of Francette's pointless convulsions. For me, everything happened as if in a dream.

I went to bed, at last, hoping to regain security through sleep and I believe that I soon fell asleep. Not long afterwards I woke up, my body drenched with perspiration. At first, I thought I was feverish, but the cries that I heard and the unwonted light coming through the blinds gave me a foreboding that something extraordinary was going on. I hastily put on a dress, opened the window and left.

An astonishing spectacle met my eyes. Torches of flames were spurting from the mountain, tragically lighting up our little town. The air was more stifling than in my room. The flat sea glistened like polished steel and the palm trees, dropping their leaves, looked like snuffed out candles. At first, there was the silence of catastrophe, even the roosters on their perches seemed to have lost their voices. I felt no sense of shock. This end-of-the-world sight, in my mind, was the inevitable consequence of my mother's death. Soon, in the frightening light of the flames, I viewed the tumult in the town. People were leaving their homes, running down the narrow streets or on the beach. I saw hunched-back or flattened silhouettes, deformed by the bundles carried on backs or heads, set out hurriedly for Fort-de-France. Finally, a group, in which I recognized my father, came running toward me. He was shouting more loudly than the others. I heard the words: "Mount . . . Pelée . . . eruption . . ." [12]

My father took me by the hand and tried to lead me towards town. But soon a cloud of ashes, coming with unbelievable speed in that broiling, scorching atmosphere that no wind could stir, surrounded us. We stopped on the beach in the midst of a gathering of children who were crying: "Nous caille mot, nous caille mot! We're going to die!" Old folks answered them back.

I had heard about the terrible eruption in 1902 that had

destroyed Saint-Pierre. Everyone died then, but I thought that a similar catastrophe would not happen again. Once again, the ill-fated city, only a few kilometers from us, was threatened. We could see the rocks hurled in full swing in its direction and huge balls of fire that were sliding towards it.

Its townspeople, terrorized, arrived in our town by car and by foot, adding to the congestion in the narrow street already swarming with crowds. They brought news which my father repeated. If what they said was to be believed, the city was nothing more than ruins and the number of dead was horrible. The governor had made a boat available for the poor who had no means of transportation, but they fought so hard to get seats that the onrush had degenerated into a brawl.

We came to my aunt's, who, completely bewildered and going in circles, was shrieking. Francette screamed to me: "Look! Look!" and she laughed as if watching a fireworks show. The rain of ashes, now thicker, kept us from seeing more that two meters before us. Just at that time, a commotion could be heard in the street teeming with people. Some cars that had tried to get away were moving back towards us; their passengers told my father that a bridge had just collapsed, making the road to Fort-de-France impassable. Panic had reached its climax. However, the most dangerous time had passed. Little by little, the temperature was becoming more bearable and soon, under lighter ashes, we were able to get back to our home.

The next day, the sun rose as it did every day in the same sky. I went to the village with my father where, naturally, all conversation was about the events of the night before. In Saint-Pierre, a few houses had been damaged, but happily, not the museum where the mementos of the last eruption were kept: carbonized objects, gold coins, lava fragments and burned clothing. I had visited it with my aunt and Francette as well as the ossuary which holds the bones of victims. They even display the skull of a Chinese, the only Chinese on the island at that time who had the ill-fortune to die in the catastrophe.

This time there were no deaths to mourn, although fields were destroyed, crops ruined and the priests's parish was still covered with ashes. Only my mother was dead and since the day before, buried. I walked to the cemetery before going home. I don't know why I had expected a miracle. The tomb was fresh and undisturbed. Mama was still dead. Mama was dead forever.

CHAPTER VIII

I was, henceforth (at twelve years of age), the mistress of the household. My aunt, who was already rearing Francette, had proposed to my father that she take me into her home, but he insisted that he could not do without me and I took advantage of this encouragement. I felt that my aunt did not love me. For her, I was a "weed" badly planted and grown, and she must have had misgivings about what she would do to curb my independence. As for me, I swore that she would not make me like Francette and that I would remain loyal to my cherished liberty.

In the beginning, the neighbors came to help me cook, do the laundry and clean house, but they soon tired of that, and I found myself alone in my life of a little housekeeper. Evidently, I was quite free. My father came home only for meals, for as long as they were ready and the house clean, he asked for nothing else. I have already said that he was stingy; he never gave me enough money and we quarreled continuously about that. At the local grocery, moreover, I was not allowed the same credit that my mother had been given. I told all of this to father, but he didn't bother to do the shopping himself. I asked him to let me have the small earnings that the sale of mangos from our garden would bring, but he refused. He wasn't mean to me, but controlled everything with an avarice that repulsed me. I remembered the conversation held with my mother at the time of my first communion, and I thought then that I understood the reason for her sadness.

Often I was tempted to ask father to let me live with my aunt, as had been suggested before, but stupid pride kept me from proposing this. On the other hand, I asked to have Francette come so that she could help me; that seemed natural to me, but he replied that one daughter sufficed to keep house for a man. I knew, however, that our aunt would not allow Francette to leave. She was strict with her, requiring her to go frequently to confession, not to miss mass, to be excessively clean, correct and orderly, but she loved her more than if she had been her own child.

It was at this stage of my life that a feeling was created within me, one that was hurtful to me: injustice. I was not jealous of Francette, but when I saw her so well dressed, so well taken care of, so carefree because she had no worries, I told myself that I was unlucky and would always be unlucky. I was not rebellious, I already accepted that injustice as do all colored girls.

During this period, my father did not bother with politics and didn't tend his garden at all. He had found a new and more profitable source of income: cock-fighting.

"That brings in more than the fruit business," he said.

He then began to raise fighting-cocks. A few months before the fight, he took special care of them, grooming the head and the legs of the cock, sharpening the spurs, rubbing it with an alcoholic lotion. Finally, the big day arrived. The fans poured in from every nook and cranny of the countryside, each one carrying an indignant cock inside a white sack. Sometimes, father asked me to accompany him to the pit where the cockfights took place. Under a roof covered with sugar cane stalks, tiered benches, surrounding the circular hard ground arena, held a noisy throng of people squeezed into this narrow space.

The cocks were first carefully examined by one of the referees who returned them to their owners. The latter, upon signal, threw them into the ring. Soon the betting took hold and mounted midst the yells uttered with gusto. The two cocks, still excited by all these cries, their feathers ruffled, went at each other using their beaks and spurs to attack or to fend off the other. At times, they let loose, and completely disconcerted, ran around the circle, one following the other. Suddenly, they made an about-face, leaped up in a flurry of feathers while the spectators shouted excitedly. Cocks rarely killed one another—this was not, moreover, the purpose of the fight—but the loser was always bloody and the winner itself rarely got away without injuries.

Perhaps it was because my father loved cock-fighting so very much, that I preferred the snake and mongoose fights. For although I was totally indifferent to cocks, I detested the snake and adored the mongoose. The snake was first presented in a large wire cage. It slithered about, then, as if it knew what awaited, writhed left then right, and finally took refuge in a corner. Then it stood erect on its tail and balanced itself while wickedly showing the flat head from which came the fangs of venom. But suddenly, it crumpled, folding like a spring that looses force. The cage door had just been opened in order to throw in the mongoose. At first, the little furry beast with its big tail seemed as scared as the snake. Without taking its eyes off the snake, it curled up making itself as small as possible in the opposite side of the cage. But after a while, as if it could not do otherwise, it drew near the snake, even near enough to pull the end of its tail.. The snake turned around abruptly, hissed and sprang forward to bite. The little mongoose then quickly recoiled and dodged its adversary, then attacked again, trying to seize from behind. After several feints, the mongoose finally succeeded with a wonderfully fast jump in biting the back of the snake's head. The snake writhed in pain and, by means of contortions and flips, managed to get loose of the mongoose. Enraged, it lunged towards the mongoose, fangs protruding, but the little animal, with incredible rapidity, dodged the attack and abruptly seized its enemy by the neck. They struggled, resuming a dance replete with lively, unpredictable and graceful movements. Excited by the cries of the spectators, the two beasts executed a joyous dance, seemingly finding pleasure in the fight.

What I liked best about these fights was that the nice mongoose always won over the evil snake who ended up by being dragged off, no longer defending itself. However, although obviously happy from having beaten the enemy, the mongoose was sometimes bloody and seemed exhausted when its owner took it out of the cage. Nonetheless, everybody was satisfied and my happy shouts were mingled with those of the others.

One Sunday, when I had not gone to the fights, towards evening, I saw a group of men approaching our house. I could see that they surrounded a person lying on a stretcher. What a shock I had on recognizing my father! He was bleeding, trembling, moaning and was so battered that he was incapable of taking a step. I had never seen him in that state, even after a political meeting. It was only the next day that I learned from neighbors what had happened. To be sure of winning, and moved by his love for the game and money, father had attached false spurs to his cock. The thing had been so cleverly made that the experts had not detected them at first. When, however, his cock killed its competitor, the owner demanded an official investigation and the trickery was discovered. Father had been severely booed and beaten to a pulp by those who had bet against his champion. Finally, his friends arrived to snatch him from their hands and to bring him back home. The story does not end there. The wrath of the owner of the dead cock didn't subside; not satisfied with the solution, he decided to file suit for losses. I should mention that his cock was the most famous champion of the village. But my father, who had recovered from his injuries, only scoffed when he heard the news. He had not been mayor for nothing; he still maintained good relations with the courts and knew ahead of time that he would win his case. In front of the judge, the two men squabbled in Creole like two rag-pickers. Father vehemently denied the deed. He had brought as many witnesses as the other and all of them, as noisy as the plaintiffs, gave exactly opposite testimonies. The judge, not knowing how to untangle the truth, dismissed the case. Anyway, that is how most law suits are settled among us.

Nonetheless, our enemy, ever more furious had left the Court House swearing to get even. The next day, I was told that he had paid a visit to the quimboiseur. When I informed father about this, he, not believing in magic or evil spirits, only laughed. A few days later, while doing a bit of leisurely gardening, he found a strange looking bottle. Through curiosity, he examined it closely and found that the bottle contained a little doll, tied up, painted black, and pierced with pins that spelled out my father's name. He had the nerve to take it in his hands and, of course, stuck himself. Since he had no faith in sorcerers, he paid no attention to this, but one month later, his arm began to swell and make him suffer terribly. He had to take to the bed and stayed there four months to the great joy of our enemy who never failed to laugh wickedly when I met him in town. Father's spirit was affected by this incident and I suffered the consequences. All the while demanding that I care for him and nurse him, he gave me less and less money.

So I learned the value of money. I learned that fruits from the garden, fish from the sea, cane sugar from cane, cow's milk did not belong to me; that men had forbidden their fellow men to enjoy the riches that nature offered so generously, that they had divided the land, enclosed gardens, that they sold everything and had consideration only for those who were able to buy a lot. It was my father who made me understand that, but he didn't give me enough money and it was his fault that, no matter how I tried, I was not considered. The innate feeling of injustice grew within me. Would I ever have any money? Would I get married? Would I be happy? Already, I answered these questions negatively. I was, however, becoming very pretty; everyone told me so. But then, I had only to look at Francette. We resembled each other so perfectly that, when we exchanged dresses, people mistook us for each other.

One day, we tried an experiment on George, one of our cousins, who had a crush on Francette. We agreed that I would take her place at their rendez-vous.

"Hello, George," I said tapping him on the back.

He looked at me in surprise.

"You are really lively today, Francette," he replied.

"I ate some Terrible* today."

I moderated all my movements, forcing myself to be delicate like my sister and George did not recognize me. This was positive proof that I was as pretty as Francette . . .

* A strong local dish

CHAPTER IX

All Saints Day arrived, a day of great festivity. Like everyone else, father and I spent the day and part of the night at the cemetery in honor of my mother, decorating her grave with flowers.

The vendors stationed at the cemetery entrance easily filled their coffers through the sale of flowers, candles and white sand. I looked with curiosity at the families gathered around their relatives' grave sites. From time to time, friends joined them, bringing flowers or candles as gifts. Dressed in black, people of all ages walked about in the narrow paths, some holding in their arms jars of paints and brushes, others with large black wooden crosses on which was inscribed the name of the deceased, sometimes in gold letters. The rich people's tombstones were magnificently and symmetrically decorated with pearl crowns, while around the smaller ones, flourished strange beds of conch horns like the ones found at the bottom of the sea.

The children were having a good time. Accustomed to death at an early age, as much by tales as by the sight of corpses preceded by townspeople walking in a procession, they were not at all impressed. They played hide-and-seek among the stones and their laughter joyfully answered the incessant prayers of their parents. To be sure, the latter had a lot of difficulty in maintaining the solemn state suitable for All Saints Day. The young people began chatting slyly; men and women arranged rendezvous.

Night fell. This was the moment these folk were waiting for. Over the tombstones, candles and tapers glowed like stars; it was a sign of joy and freedom. We could hear the shrill voices of the *machannes** walking through the pathways with their offerings of doughnuts and cakes. Couples, whose dark clothing made them almost invisible, took refuge behind tombstones, and the cemetery, which a few hours prior had been the temple of sadness and remembrances, changed into the temple of love and future hopes.

Because I was kept busy with so much housework and with school (my father insisted that I continue, for good or for bad), time slipped away imperceptibly. I was growing up and important changes accompanied this growth: I was no more the "tomboy" of by-gone days; I laughed less and became emotional. My breasts finally took shape, oh, still quite timidly. So, on the advice of a friend, every evening I rubbed my chest with garlic. At last, I began to love my father and to develop a great admiration for him. To be sure, he was much kinder than before and spoke to me as if I were a little woman. I was also more free because he left every evening and returned late at night. Sometimes, I took advantage of this to play the "Flower Game" with my friends. Other times, I would take solitary walks along the moonlit shore, for I was in love with the moon. I absorbed the core of its light which seemed to me both purer and more complex than sunlight. I shuddered at its touch, I spoke to it, offering my virgin heart and said:

"It's your turn to talk to me, tell me that you love me."

It was not long, however, before I learned from neighbors that father was seeing a young girl who, at sixteen, was scarcely older than I. This news shocked me terribly and, at first, I denied it. This was not possible, I told myself; it wasn't like him, for I couldn't admit to such wickedness. I thought about this matter for hours at a time. The fact that he could not remain faithful to the memory of my mother revealed to me a new aspect of life.

* Food Peddlers

Francette often came over to keep me company in the evening. During this period, I somewhat despised her because she led such a carefree life. She was very talkative but her conversation, in my opinion, was truly childish. I preferred by father's who could, at least, understand me, or so I thought. I usually kept most of my thoughts from Francette, but on this day, however, I could not help but speak to her about what weighed so heavily on my mind.

"Do you know the latest? You have a sixteen year-old stepmother."

Since Francette stood open-mouthed, I shouted:

"So how about that?"

"That's shameful," she finally said. "The only thing for him to do is get married."

"He doesn't have to get married, he can have a 'behind the door marriage', or as they say, 'get married by the devil.'"

"No, no," she cried with tear-filled eyes, "I don't want the devil to marry papa."

"Little fool," I said, "there's no devil. That just means they don't get married in the church."

"Would you do that, yourself?"

"Yes, if I found a man I liked. Why not? It would be cheaper and you wouldn't have to buy a wedding ring. Do you think Mr. Mayor and Mr. Priest are so necessary?"

"Of course," Francette responded scornfully, "they are absolutely necessary."

"Well not for me!," I shot back, "You make me sick with your devilish language . . ."

Francette didn't answer. Having turned towards the garden entrance, she suddenly cried: "Hey, here comes your father." I looked at her indignantly: "Isn't he your father too?"

But I didn't have time to say more about that. While Francette's eyes grew wide, father was approaching the house with heavy steps. I saw that his hobnail shoes were covered with mud. "Where you coming from?" I asked him.

"He smiled slightly.

"Don't worry, Mayotte. As I came through the marsh, I fell, that's all. Blame those youngsters who put traps out for crabs." There was no need for this explanation. I knew where the marsh was, for even though some distance from our town, lovers went there to be alone. I guessed what had happened on the shore of the small, dormant river with greenish waters banked by intertwined bamboo and vines that preserved hidden love nests, where only the sounds of twittering, chirping birds could be heard. But the lovers would not hear these songs.

Francette left. Her anxiety did not cause her to forget about the late hour. I went to the kitchen to look after the dinner and when I returned, I found father slouched in a chair. In the light I noticed the pallor of his face.

"Are you sick?" I asked.

"No, only a few heart flutters."

"Rest for a few days. All you do is run around every which way, walking in the rain and sun."

"You know I can't stay in one place. Anyway, walking is good for you health."

My suggestion went in one ear and out the other. My father was too excited over his young conquest. He had no appetite and had lost so much weight that I noticed his pants were hanging down lower than usual.

When we spent the evening together, he often enjoyed telling his fortune with cards. Watching him, I became interested too. One evening, I vowed to spring a surprise on him so that he would know that I was on to his shenanigans. So I offered to deal the cards and he gladly accepted. First, I predicted with the ace of clubs that he was going to win a large sum of money in cock-fighting, then by the might of the nine of diamonds that he was going to take an unexpected trip. Satisfied, he wiped his hand over his greying head and a smug grin softened his face. But suddenly, I slapped down a queen of clubs:

"You're in love!" I shouted, "Head-over-heels in love!"

81

He gave me a severe look and abruptly picked up the cards. Then going towards the shelf that he called his library, he took a down a book of romances and ended the evening alone.

I, also alone, went outside to rest my elbows on the veranda and gaze upon the stars which were casting their twinkling lights in the shades of night. But I didn't feel the satisfaction that I had expected. And soon, I was no longer watching the stars but the cats running silently, with all the agility their legs could muster, to get to their nocturnal rendezvous. The wind wafted towards me the odors of leaves and flowers and I heard the deep breathing of the sea, accompanied by the sound of the old market clock as it slowly struck eleven.

I then slipped away into the night arriving at the sea rendered silver in the moonlight. For quite a while, I had been in the habit of talking to the moon, sending my prayers to it, letting it fill me with its disquieting light. I felt it quiver in my heart as I begged it: "Speak to me, tell me that you love me too . . ."

It didn't speak, but as if it wished to send me an answer, there appeared a small boat gliding silently on the waves, a boat like the fishing boats of Martinique called pirogue, pointed at both ends and built from the trunks of the gum-tree. A sail was hoisted in front. A young woman, who to me appeared beautiful, was stretched out on the knees of the man who was steering the boat. I assumed that they were on their honeymoon, but even though her face was not revealed, in the light of the moon I could see that she didn't come from our town.

My first instinct was to leave, but my curiosity took over. I hid behind a coconut tree so as to hear what they were confiding to the moon. But I heard only a song that the boat was leaving on the silvery waves in its wake—a song that I knew.

Adieu! foula', (Good-by headscarf)
Adieu! madras (Good-by madras scarf)
Adieu g'ain d'o' (Good-by gold beads)

Adieu! colliers doux (Good-by lovely necklaces)
Doudou a moin qui ka pati (My sweetie is going to leave)
Hèlas! Hèlas! C'est pou' toujou' (Alas, it's forever). (bis)

The skiff moved on, the song died down and I neither saw
nor heard anything more. I stood up and also moved away,
humming:

Bonjou'! Monsieur le Colonel! (Good morning, Colonel)
Mais non, Madame, il est t'op ta'd (No, madam, it's too
late)
La consigne dèjà levè (The order is already signed)
C'est pas la peine (It's not worth the trouble)
Doudou a moin, etc.... (refrain) [13]

I didn't know where my steps would lead. All of a sudden,
there I was in town where I found the girls and boys seated in
a circle under the mysterious rays of the moon playing the
game of "Flowers." Invitations and messages flew all about me:
"Yellow lime, write me . . ."
"Cane peel, you are too vulgar."
"Ivy, I die where I cling."
"Coal, you are too black for my 'bedroom.'"
"Campeach flower, I am the Wood Fairy"
"Camwood tree, I am the demon of the forest!"
"Pepper flower, I mourn your absence."
"Coco flower, I'll wait for you this evening."
It was on that night, I believe, that Horace fell in love with
me.

CHAPTER X

My father wasted no time in settling his young conquest in our house. Henceforth, Rènelise shared our meals and joined in our conversations. I envied her bust which was like Loulouze's and surely she had beautiful eyes, but the ardor that they showed was so intense that she left me no chance to admire them; I never succeeded in making out their color. Moreover, I never could learn her favorite color, for the gaudy dresses that she got my father to buy for her and wore with a lot of style, were all multi-colored.

At first, I was quite distant with Rènelise. I didn't know whether I liked her or hated her, but I was good-natured and I tried to be agreeable. Unaware of the conflict taking place within me, from time to time, she took me into her confidence. Father took a dim view of this and during our conversations he looked at us in a way that was odious to me. Of course, people were gossiping about his behavior and when I went to town I was the target of curious or piteous glances that made me uneasy. Without a doubt, my father was the butt of some heckling. For instance, I knew that neighbors were saying that he had bewitched Rènelise.

One fine day he decided to move inland with her; I had to follow them. I said good-by to Francette without tears, but with a heavy heart. I was amazed and a little disappointed to leave Horace with less anguish. For wasn't he my sweetheart?

Father had located a house in open country that an old black man by the name of Papa Amboise had rented to him.

Papa Amboise was well-off and he liked to make the most of it. To show off his wealth, he had all his teeth pulled and replaced with pure gold teeth. He had a dazzling smile, a smile like the sun, and I was struck dumb with admiration before him.

As for the house, it was a shanty with a straw roof. Bamboos cut in half, on which hung a number of wasps' nest, were used as eaves. There was, however, a huge dining room with a mahogany floor and a porch that encircled it. Behind the house there was an orchard and, in an out-of-the-way place, an arbor of apple creeping vines. When she saw this place, Rènelise let out shouts of joys and I, myself, was moved by her happiness all the more because Papa Amboise smiled as he looked at us and lit us all up. But the days that followed were dull. The interior of the island was rainy, and I already missed our sunny village. I better understood why Papa Amboise had decided to wear the sun in his mouth, but I needed to feel it on my skin, to feel myself bathed by it. I no longer heard the songs of the sea-birds who returned, happy to walk along the blue waters. The cries of the mountain birds frightened me, above all at night, their dismal sounds carrying a bad omen. Finally, life took shape: I did the housework and cooking and spent the afternoons taking long walks with Rènelise, who like me, loved animals and flowers. Often, the two of us were alone at the house because father had taken up cock-fighting again and when he returned home, it was quite late in the evening. Rènelise then showered him with lavish attention which troubled me, for it seemed to me that he cared only for her. My outlook hardened and I wanted to hurt her as she had hurt me. I suspected her of evil intentions and when she got a new dress or a new necklace, in my own mind, I accused her of ruining my father, for I was dying from jealousy.

One evening while we were alone, I decided to speak to her. I could no longer restrain this hate I was nurturing against her. So giving her a mean look, I yelled:

"I can't stand looking at you any more."

"Because of my age and beauty?" she answered in an insolent tone.

I felt myself becoming angrier; I was besides myself. I lost
the last bit of respect that I should have had for the woman
my father had chosen.

"It's much worse than that," I fired back, "I hate you 'cause
you got no morals."

She didn't deny this and said no more than:

"What business's that of yours? At your age, those things
ain't important."

"You're only a short-term drifter," I muttered.

"Who cares about tomorow? I ain't immortal and you
oughta learn we can't order what's already done."

"What's done," I repeated with scorn, "ain't you ashamed
to talk like that?"

"I can't be ashamed . . . and you", she shouted, "ain't you
doing the same things with Horace?"

I was greatly disturbed by what she might be assuming.

"No, mam'm," I exclaimed, "our love is pure and shame-
less. He's young and even if we're apart, our two hearts are
one. As for you . . . don't tell me you love my pa, you only here
to gain from what he can give you. . . . Do you think he's
going to marry you?"

I saw that finally tears were clouding her face; she could say
nothing in answer to my insulting remarks. Perhaps, now she
understood the harm done to me by her presence. After that,
I withdrew to my room.

Horace's name, that she had uttered, resonated in my heart
and rose in my head like a prayer. Yes, our love was pure. If we
had played together, if our bodies sought out each other, both
of us were unaware of the acts of love. As for me, I had always
avoided the secrets that my older comrades would have confided to me, for in spite of my curiosity, it would have been
unpleasant for me to listen to them, and asking Rènelise was
repugnant to me. I went to the window and gazed intently at
the star that was to watch over my Horace, and I pledged my

vow to it: I would marry Horace, I would keep house for him, we would have children, we would be happy, and together, we would learn the wonderful gestures of love, we would be united forever . . .

I was so overcome by an intense yearning for Horace, for Francette, for my town, for the sea, that one day, I announced to my father that I could no longer cook because the heat made me dizzy. I proposed that he put me in charge of running the errands in town instead of Rènelise. Also, I missed Francette, I told him. At first, he looked at me in a peculiar way and then agreed.

On a fine September day, I mounted my horse to go to Saint-Pierre. Behind me, a dark storm threatened the mountains, but before me, the sky was an unblemished blue. Soon, from the road I was following, I could view the ocean sparkling in the sunlight, and the fishing boats as they were cradled lazily by waves that seemed weighed down by the heat. I slowed the horse to a slow trot wishing to prolong my wonder as long as possible.

After completing my errands, I took the road to Carbet. It was strange that I was not more anxious to see Horace. I first went to my aunt's to hug Francette and I was so happy to see her again that I spent quite a while chatting with her. She told me her troubles which were mostly about the severity and the pettiness of our old aunt. In turn, I described life in the mountains as being delightful. I don't know why I had this urge to embellish the saddest period of my life, perhaps it was the need to show off. I felt Francette becoming more and more unhappy about not sharing my good life. Our aunt, who disapproved of father's behavior, would never allow Francette visit us. That left me free to invent and I did so light-heartedly.

But even so, while talking, I was admiring Francette. She wore no make-up (our aunt would not permit her to), but she had changed her coiffure so as to lengthen it. A spiral of her very black hair lined her forehead vertically and fell behind in a delicate contour. Her smile, her countenance seemed more intent than before; and last of all, I saw her firm, small breasts, just like mine, showing under her thin dress. I resolved that as soon as I was back home, I would carefully examine myself in Rènelise's mirror to see if I still resembled Francette. I would style my hair the same way.

After so much chit-chat, hours had passed, and there was not much time left for Horace. I was able only to say hello and make a date for the next week, but on the way back, he alone was in my thoughts.

CHAPTER XI

Horace was waiting for me on the beach where we had agreed to meet. He, too, wore a happy smile on his lips. We joined these smiles when he kissed me and then gave me an abrupt hug. We sat under a coconut tree and I set about contemplating the object of my dreams.

Horace was the most handsome specimen of what is considered Martinican. His dark skin set off enameled white teeth; shining black eyes held glints of precious stones; lips were full and sensuous. He was tall and the legs displayed beneath his shorts were straight and muscular.

I never tired of admiring them, for I loved to run my hands over his thighs covered with curly, knotted hair. He would squeeze my waist and kiss me impetuously. As his hands wandered over my body and under my thin dress, I felt the warmth of his flesh. "Will you always love me as much?" I asked in a hushed voice. One hand clasped my left shoulder while the other caressed my bare legs. His passionate look went to the depths of my heart and at the same time, he answered: "Don't you trust me?"

I, happy at that moment, in turn, began to kiss him. We lay down on the warm sand, he stretched himself over me. I didn't know what he was going to do and probably he didn't either, but finally, he did it. Not a sound came to us except that of the ocean which played gently and then forcefully at our feet. I was swept away to an unknown world and would have remained forever in Horace's arms who seemed overcome with bliss and almost scared. Already, the sun was sinking in the horizon, the breeze lessening, so I had to think about my return.

I managed to rearrange my hair and slipped among the coconut trees where I had left my horse. My whole body hurt and I had difficulty getting back up on the blanket that I used as a saddle. I went along at a slow pace, frequently turning to look at the ocean and that beach where I had just been loved. Under the oblique rays of the sun, the countryside came alive. I saw no more than a patch of the sea whose horizon seemed suspended, a bit of the sea whose mixtures of blue, purple and red were blended in deep tones, changing from one minute to the other in a slow rhythm that seemed accented by the gait of my horse. Above this patch, the sky was losing its color as I drew near the darkening golden ball. In front of me, a purple mass raised three mounds on that sky, and from time to time, I saw, on first one or the other, a little white or rose round hat that disappeared an instant after.

At last, as I entered the forest, dark as night, around me I heard the birds calling one another. Overcome with fatigue, I had let go of the horse's reins, but now and then, I lifted my head, seeking, in the narrow strip of sky framed by huge trees, the star that was to guide my Horace. Suddenly, the horse jumped aside almost throwing me to the ground. I had barely grabbed the reins, when I saw what had startled my mount. An enormous dog barred my path and I distinctly saw flames come out of its eyes and open mouth. There was no time to be afraid. Firmly taking hold of the reins with one hand, with the other I struck the horse sharply and it galloped away. We sped by the horrible beast which disappeared. Now, no longer able to keep up that pace, out of breath and sore, I slowed the horse. A moment after, I heard voices and went towards them. I was heartened on recognizing the market women on the way back from town, trays on their heads, and I noticed that one of them wore her head scarf backwards to chase away the zombies. We exchanged a few words, and to my surprise, because I was still wondering if I had dreamt, I learned that they too had just seen the terrifying dog. Reluctantly, I took leave of them because I was now afraid. I had yet to cross a small river bordered by bamboos among which, it had been reported, black maroons and former escaped convicts from Guiana hid and preyed upon passers-by, then fled into the forest. The moon had disappeared and under the great trees there was not the least glimmer of light.

My heart was beating loudly. Yet, while crossing the river, I heard only the sound of leaves rustled by the evening breeze. At last, in sight of our house, I came upon Papa Amboise. He had gone there to get fire. In one hand, he held a small sheath of metal on which Rènelise had put a few pieces of warm coals, and in the other a pair of tongs. Seeing me, he smiled, but on that night his gold teeth could not be seen and his mouth was no more than a black hole.

"Where you come from, girl?" he asked me.

"Hey, old Papa, can't you guess?"

"You coming back from seeing your Horace. Ain't you 'fraid to go alone in the woods at night?"

I answered with just a smile. I did not wish to tell him about what had happened between me and Horace. I now had two secrets: in a single evening, I had known love and seen the zombie. I no longer envied Rènelise, she could do whatever she wanted with my father. And I was still smiling as I pushed the little arbor gate to put my horse in the stable.

CHAPTER XII

We learned a few weeks later that my aunt was ill. I had noticed something amiss the first time I went down to Carbet, but to tell the truth, I had given my attention mostly to Francette. Father left to find out more about her. When he returned, he announced to me that our aunt was losing her mind, that he was going to have her committed to an asylum in Guadeloupe and that Francette would come home. I was overjoyed at the latter development, but I also was greatly concerned about how my aunt could bear the separation from my sister, whom she had reared and loved so much.

A few days later, I went with my father on another trip to Carbet. This time, I looked closely at my aunt and was struck by her appearance. Her face, always so smooth, was now full of wrinkles and her eyes were sunken like pebbles in the sand. She moved about in a trembling, disoriented manner. I heard father speak to her in his most gentle voice as if to a child:

"How would you like to take a nice trip to Fort-de-France? It would be good for you."

It didn't take much to persuade her because my aunt, heretofore so authoritative, seemed to have lost her tendency toward contrariness. As for father, he hadn't lost his head, for always thinking about money, he never missed an opportunity to make some.

"Before leaving for Carbet," he said, "why don't you make a will on Francette's behalf? Isn't she your daughter? Traveling in these times is still dangerous. You never know what might happen . . ."

Once again the poor woman didn't resist.

The notary, summoned beforehand, arrived promptly. He was a métis,[14] a man who for a long time had done business with my father. Very calmly, auntie signed the papers put before her. I watched in a kind of terror, however, as two huge tears slowly rolled down her emaciated cheeks. But the notary, who must have seen them too, quickly drew nearer auntie and firmly clasped her hand: "Now, everything is in order," he said and then left.

I took my leave of auntie who reacted indifferently. Then, father and Francette having to leave from Fort-de-France for Guadeloupe, after a short visit with Horace I returned home. There, I spent several miserable days sulking with Rènelise. Early every morning, carrying a pail and stool, I made my way to the barn to milk the cows. Then I took the milk to the road where a market lady on her way to town picked it up. After that, I prepared dinner because, in my father's absence, Rènelise did absolutely nothing. I missed Carbet and the ocean; the stillness of the countryside lay moribund in my heart. It was then that I made plans to leave that house, so detestable to me. I think that I would have carried out this plan without fail, if father and Francette hadn't returned. Her lively presence somewhat comforted me. She claimed that she was delighted not to be under our aunt's guardianship and, while father busied himself with Rènelise, we spent hours chatting together.

"Tell me about your trip," I said to her.

"You know, it was my first time on a boat."

"Yeah, I know. What I want to know is what you think of Fort-de-France . . ."

"Fort-de-France is marvelous. There's a lot of elegant folk, cars, houses, fine stores. . ."

Her descriptions were endless, so I interrupted her.

"Say, tell me what papa did. That's what I wanna know."

"I don't know what he did. I'm not his boss."

"But on the boat. . ."

"Well, you know papa. As soon as we took off, he couldn't keep away from the coconut juice, from morning to afternoon."

"Were you sea-sick at all?"

"Not a bit, in fact, I even met the ship's captain. He was terrific!"

"Did you eat anything at all?"

"You bet. At the back of the boat, there was a big kettle full of oil that was smoking like a volcano. That's where the passengers and crew filled up on codfish."

"Not interested in that, talk about something else . . ."

Soon after, father returned to Fort-de-France for about ten days. I could no longer restrain myself. I, too, wanted to see this city that I had listened to Francette talk so much about: those elegant people, those fine stores, and those beautiful women in bathing suits lying on the beach. One lovely morning before Rènelise and Francette were awake, I left, having taken my savings because I wanted to do some shopping.

Fort-de-France was not a very large city, but even when I compare it to Paris, I think that the sunlight and warm breezes that roam its street gave it a unique charm. First, I walked from one end to the other of Liberty Street, the main street—it could have been named Hotel Street. As I went by, I read their names: "le Coq Hardi, la Coupole . . ." and I was as astonished by their number as by their appearance. Of course, they would no longer seem as luxurious to me now, but I had just come from a small town and had never seen the like. On the right, the library, overladen with sculpture and decoration, to me looked magnificent. Facing it, on top of the large white edifice which was the seat of the government of Martinique, waved the tri-colored flag. I viewed it with respect.

Continuing my walk, I turned right, toward a large plaza whose paved lanes led to the middle of a circle where the statue of Empress Josephine stood majestically. My heart beat faster. Father had often spoken about the wife to the great Napoleon; she was the pride of our island. We gloried in the fact that a Martinican had succeeded in becoming Empress of all of France, of the whole French empire, that she had become the wife of the greatest sovereign in the world. We venerated her, and I, like all young girls there, had often dreamt about a similar destiny. I walked closer. The statue was in marble, graciously shaded by tall palm trees and I mused on it for a long time. At a later period, when I arrived in Paris, my first accomplishment was to visit the Invalides to admire the tomb of Josephines's great husband, then to Malmaison where she lived. But I have never relived the feeling that came over me, standing before that statue, both alive and majestic.

After a while, I went on my way, following a path that led to the "Monument to the War Dead." Father, who had been wounded in France, had also told me about it with great reverence, but to me, it was ugly. It was backed up against a small woods, that I later learned was called the "Bois de Boulogne" by people in Fort-de-France.

I next took a cross-street that seemed especially busy. Store windows bountiful with goods, one more beautiful than the other, enticed me. On both sides of the street there were candy stores, carpet shops, beauty salons, shoes stores, such as I had never seen. But I could never make up my mind to enter one of them. It seemed to me that I would not come out again, that I would be forced to buy, that I would inevitably be robbed. Tirelessly, I kept going from one side of the street to the other, I didn't want to miss one shop window. The movement in the street added to my excitement. The cries of children and women burst upon a muffled and continuous hubbub; horse-buggies and automobiles rolled by thunderously on the paved streets and this motley, teeming crowd was rushing toward who knows what. Even the dogs didn't seem to want to lose time. The only flaw in my happiness was the sight of those wretched beggars holding out their cups to passers-by, pleading in guttural tones and in the name of the Holy Virgin, to put a few pennies therein. Without them, I would have believed myself in Heaven.

I left there quite giddy from the noise and commotion. Then I came to Lavassor Canal, a small river spanned by a hog-backed bridge that pedestrians were crossing incessantly. I did so in my turn, then retraced my steps because the center of town had already cast its spell over me. I couldn't tear myself away from it.

I thought about my father. What was he doing in the city? Did he really have to abandon us for ten days? Suddenly, as I cut across a street, there I was face to face with him. He was holding a woman by the arm, almost as young as Rènelise and even prettier. On seeing me, he uttered an exclamation of stupefaction. I stood nailed to the walk, my legs astride to keep from falling. First, I had to explain my presence, so I said that Rènelise had sent me to run errands. He shrugged his shoulders, for, evidently, he didn't believe me. Then I became furious and made a terrible scene, stomping my foot, evoking my mother's memory, trying to make his ashamed. He made a crude answer, swearing at me in front of this unknown woman. Our shouts mingled, we no longer were listening to each other. A crowd gathered around us; people were smiling, even laughing. Abruptly, father stopped and I, trembling, also stopped. We looked at each other; then in a steady, calm voice he commanded:

"You are to go home immediately."

Without waiting for an answer and taking the woman's arm, he walked away. I did too, astonished that my legs could still support me and talking to myself, I kept repeating:

"I won't go back, I won't go back . . ."

At last, having arrived at the dock, I sat on a wall and, little by little, I calmed down. But I remained firm in my decision.

CHAPTER XIII

Towards evening, I made up my mind to go see Loulouze whose address, luckily, I had. She, majestic in a light blue dress, opened the door in response to my timid knock. She had aged and had put on weight, but I, too, had also changed because she didn't recognize me right away.

"I'm Mayotte," I said.

"Mayotte," she exclaimed, "how ya doin'?"

She drew me to her ample bosom, but her movements were not the same as before, they also appeared heavier. Immediately, I felt more lighthearted and gay.

"What you doing in Fort-de-France?"

I explained what had just happened and although, still upset, I really had to try hard to regain my anger.

"So," Loulouze said, incredulous, "You don't want to go back to your Pa's because he's playing around on Rènelise."

"It's not that . . . "

"It seems to me you don't like Rènelise and what's worse, I'd say it's none of your business. . . "

"It is too my business . . ."

"You not your pa's wife, the way it looks to me . . ."

"No, but I can't stand it when he chases after those gals."

"Oh," Loulouze answered, "All men's jerks . . ."

"You're not married?" I asked.

"I wouldn't get married for nothin' in this world," Loulouze declared. "Why get married when I got kids."

Loulouze showed me her children, already asleep. The oldest, a little boy, was white; the little girl, banana-colored like her mother, was truly pretty.

"They don't have the same pa," she informed me, "but that don't make no difference, they brother and sister just the same."

I spent the night in her bed. She had a sizable bosom and I took pleasure in comparing my small breasts to hers. The next morning, I awoke to the sounds of trucks on their way to market. From the street, rose the voices of women cleaning the gutters. Loulouze, accustomed to this racket, was still asleep, but I, lying next to her, was again visualizing our house, Carbet, hearing the ocean breeze and the cries of the birds. Would I ever see papa again, I wondered. Perhaps I had been stupid and, as Loulouze had said, what concern was it of mine if he chased girls. Nonetheless, I couldn't put up with that.

I figured that I needed money to live in Fort-de-France, and I was troubled. I thought about selling my gold necklace and earrings, but letting them go would be unbearable. Then Loulouze, who was really a good old girl, succeeded in arranging for me to be called for the next day's shift at the workroom where she was employed. I could have stayed with her, but I refused because I felt that I was a hindrance to her. So I set out to look for lodging and several days later, I moved to a small room located in a quiet neighborhood. The room was dark with unpainted walls, no electricity; in the evening, I had to use an oil lamp for lighting. My furniture consisted of a bed, two chairs and a little white wood table. My life as a city-dweller began modestly, but I was happy that I no longer depended on my father, nor even Loulouze. I would have liked never again to ask anything of anyone.

CHAPTER XIV

Life in the workroom soon lost its attraction. I didn't like the gossiping nor the back-biting done by my fellow workers. I was becoming unsociable and often had yearnings for my father, Francette and my old life. I earned only enough to feed myself. Now, I would have liked a business of my own, to be altogether independent with the prospect of earning more and more. I was, and still am, ambitious. Maybe that's a weakness, but I if couldn't change the color of my skin, I had the determination to better my condition.

I decided to sell the few jewels that I wore the day I arrived in Fort-de-France and which I had inherited from my mother: earrings, a few medallions and a small gold chain. One evening, I went to Loulouze's. She hadn't come home and while waiting, I admired her fine furnishings and wondered what she had done to earn so much money. Suddenly, there she was before me. I was so deep in thought that I had not heard her coming. She hugged me and noticing my worried look, no doubt, she was compelled to ask me:

"Hi, dearie, what's the matter?"

Gathering my courage, I cried out:

"Oh, Loulouze, I'm so miserable . . . I need money . . . I want you to buy this from me . . ."

I took out my bag of jewelery and held it out to her. Did she remember her bracelet? She seemed touched instantly.

"Poor little child," she said to me, "Why not go back home? You'll have a hard time here."

Her words hurt my pride and I exclaimed:

"Why you want me to go back to pa? Won't I be able to get along like you?"

"Get along like me? You call this gettin' along?"

In the end, she took me to a goldsmith, and this kindhearted man examined my jewelry and bought them on the spot.

I opened a little shop, happy to be rid of the prattle at the workroom, for the adventures of my former workers were of no interest to me. I had not taken up with any of them, and I think we had a mutual dislike for one another. They considered me a naive country girl; my pride separated me from them. I didn't want to settle for their pleasures and, in a word, for their fate.

CHAPTER XV

Loulouze had talked a lot about Carnival, but I never could have imagined anything so wonderful. Immersed from one day to the next in a world made up of tricks and adventure, I was unusually excited. I dreamt about the prince charming whom I would discover under a pierrot or a clown costume. I didn't yet know that, most often, it's the reverse that happens and that men, who are only clowns, disguise themselves as prince charmings, in order to abuse us.

From early morning, the city assumed a different look. On street corners, young men agreed to meet and plan for their pranks; young girls questioned one another about their pending masquerade. Everywhere it was the same story.

At last Mardi Gras day arrived. From three o'clock in the afternoon, young Martinican women in costumes of their own creation walked about in the street. Many, like myself, were cross-dressed, for I indeed had procured a man's suit. I wore a black velvet half-mask over my eyes and gloves so that even my hands wouldn't be recognizable. I had stuffed the coat to give me square shoulders and affected a more strident walk. Soon, I noticed that a masked woman was following me. Every so often I would turn around to verify that she was still there. She had to be an older woman because her gait was not at all graceful.

About four o'clock, two floats passed by with great fanfare, one representing the sugar cane harvest, the other the rum trade. They stopped in the middle of the Savanne[15] and the

101

performance began. The barefooted women cane cutters, in madras head-scarves, flowered dresses tucked at the waist by a sash, holding in one hand a tall stalk of cane and a cutlass in the other, were dancing to the beat of a drum, swaying their hips wantonly from side to side. They began to sing a biguine[16] tune. But suddenly someone, the guiablesse* or the zombie, threw a toy snake on their legs and there they were shouting in fear, running away then coming back to kill the snake, brandishing their knives while the drum tirelessly pounded out the same rhythms.

I was so intrigued by this spectacle (the first I had seen, because I had never been to the theater) that I had forgotten the woman following me. I saw her again that evening at the big costume ball at "Select Tango."[17] Midst the young girls in short skirts and low-cut blouses that revealed necklaces dangling on their bosoms, midst all these painted faces sprinkled with flecks of vanilla in place of beauty spots, she did not appear to me to be very chic. But, even so, I invited her to dance. She accepted with a big smile and I held her waist—which, gracious me, was rather wide—as firmly as I could. We said not one word during the first biguine. Moreover, I was quite concerned that I had to lead. But as we began the second one, my partner could no longer hold her tongue. Imagine my amazement on hearing a man's voice come from behind the velvet mask. At once, I recognized it as that of the métis, Yvon, a neighbor, an unbearable gabber, who made advances to me whenever he could. No doubt, he had already identified me. At first, I was annoyed; he was nothing like the prince charming of my daydreams. But, in the end, I didn't want to spoil his Carnival, so I accepted another dance which I performed like a woman.

* On Ash Wednesday, the revelers costumed in black and white form a funeral procession for Varal (King Carnival), an especially strong tradition in Fort-de-France. The Guiablesse is a she-devil who lures men to their death and loss of their souls.

The festivities ended about five o'clock in the morning; I went home and was soon fast asleep. Around one o'clock, I was awakened by voices mounting from the street. Renewing my enthusiasm of the day before, I ran to the window. At first, I wondered if I still were still dreaming, for the street was filled with little black imps[18] who were shouting, one trying to outdo the other. They were announcing that the death of Carnival would be celebrated that evening or, as they said, the death of Vaval.[19]

Indeed, the day after Mardi Gras is our day of the guiablesse. On that day, everybody dons a black robe tied at the waist with a white sash. Heads are enveloped in white cloths, and other cloths cover the shoulders. Masks set off faces so evenly powdered, that it is no longer possible to know a Black from a White. Some people fasten a long cord to their waists at the end of which a metal box emits a ghastly noise as it strikes the pavement. Musicians, leading the way for these revelers, roam the streets, singing howling, running and dancing. At seven, the noisy crowd disperses into dance halls. At midnight, everything is over; Vaval is dead and buried. Young and old, exhausted, fall into a deep sleep.

I did the same, all the while dreaming that the little black imps who had roused me with their clamor were chasing me and I could not get rid of them.

PART II

CHAPTER I

I stepped out on to the balcony. I needed to be alone for a moment because I was too happy.

We were late in getting up and the sun was already high. André's house looked down on the vast roadstead[20] of Fort-de-France. At my feet, across the rustling foliage of an uneven hedge, I discerned the slender silhouette of the *Emile Bertin* which had brought gold from the Bank of France to Martinique.[21] On the other side of Tourelles Bay, stretched a marsh bordered by a row of coconut trees; the airplane hangar there cast a dark mass on the glaring surface of the strip of asphalt. Farther to the left, the cliff of Pointe des Carrières speckled its white topped houses on the deep green vegetation and, farther still, there was a vast sugar cane field reaching out to the sea where hulks of old ships, resembling little piles of sweepings, lay forgotten in a corner. Lastly, in front of the mango trees that blotted out the view to the left, appeared Pointe de Sables where trees and cows made black and brown spots on dull green fields.

But mostly, I was looking at the deep blue roadstead where yachts with their white sails glided on what appeared to be an immense lake closed in by hills. I gazed at all of this as if it were the image of my happiness.

I was thinking about André. I sensed him behind me in that room, seated on the unmade bed, but I didn't want to turn around.

I thought about that wonderful night. I had a wonderful

lover! A white man! An officer! In my mind's eye, I went over every day of the past two months—we had known each other for two months. However, I had not fallen in love with him right away, for men much better looking than he had courted me and I had turned them down. I wasn't a frivolous woman and, after Horace, I had stayed away from men for a long time, despite the temptations that life in Fort-de-France offered me.

As for Horace, I saw him only once more shortly after the declaration of war. He came to my door in uniform, for like so many young Martinican men, he was leaving to take up arms for France, which didn't impress me at all. He stood facing me for a moment, awkward in his uniform, then he said:

"Mayotte, why did you quit me?"

"I'm no longer the little girl you thought you loved," I murmured. And that's how I separated from my first love.

Memories of my father caused me to spurn what my heart craved—physical love. Moreover, I was proud. No more would I touch those colored men, those skirt chasers, and I knew that white men do not marry black women. Yes, indeed, over and again I had occasion to convince myself that Loulouze's words held the truth . . . So to maintain that freedom that I valued so before, I first started to work in a sewing workroom, then I hired some young girls in order to set up a laundry service. I charged more than others but I did better work and, since Fort-de-France liked clean linen, they patronized me. In the end, they were proud to have their linens become whiter at Mayotte's.

At that point in my life, I was glad to earn more money and to buy myself pretty dresses, lingerie, shoes and those straw sailor hats that became me so well! I owned jewels, a lot of gold jewelry that had belonged to my mother, who perhaps had inherited them from her mother . . . from her grandmother: gold earrings like Martinican women, not necessarily wealthy, possess. I wore them to please André and also to impress him. I thought only of him; his words, his gestures, had turned my world topsy-turvy. At first, he had not said that he loved me. To the contrary, he had spoken about his love for another woman, a young girl. But on that morning, he had told me that I was his first mistress, although he had known women before me, which I did not doubt. What did he mean? At times, he was strange.

Oh! I'll always remember that Easter Day! . . . He had just been appointed Chief of Aviation at the base to replace the officer who had been in an accident. We had eaten lunch together in the countryside. The weather was glorious and I was wearing my pale blue silk dress in which I had never been happier. A few days later, after going to the movies, he offered to see me home. We walked along side by side, close to the walls, laughing when we had to jump over the gutters at each street crossing so as not to break our necks in the poorly lighted city. In front of my door, he drew me to him saying:

"Good-by."

Then he added:

"If you're not in a hurry, we could take a little walk by the seashore! It's so nice this evening!"

I accepted. The wharf was scarcely one hundred meters from us. All was quiet, there was no one around. The waterway, dimly lighted under a moon intermittently covered by clouds, shimmered gently under the light breeze. In the distance, the hills were outlined in black against a slightly luminous sky, and from time to time, we felt a chilling wind that made us shiver and draw closer to each other. Having arrived at the end of the path, we retraced our steps, and it seemed to me that the fifteen minutes I had just lived had been for always. Life for me was nothing more than that endless stroll!

And so it was that he told me about the young girl, almost a child, whom he had met at a dance given in honor of the visiting naval fleet at Algiers[22], about how she disappeared after a few dances, how he had dreamed of her without ever seeing her again, how he tried to pursue a correspondence which her suspicious parents forbade. He related to me the complicity of a girl friend, his letters to the father, the repeated return-mail deliveries after which each letter became more urgent. He lived this dream for three years with an unknown, but the war, the armistice put an end to this long romance. Finally, he spoke of the last letter that he had just received from her in answer to a farewell note sent before his departure from Africa.[23]

While listening to him, I drew a little closer as if he had confessed his love for me. Then, we decided to sit down and since there were no benches, we thought it romantic to settle down on the sidewalk curb. I leaned my head against his shoulder and soon was in his arms. We remained quiet, breathing in the night. Our lips drew nearer, he was now inhaling my breath, and then he gently raised his arm where my head rested. My lips were about to touch his, and then I don't know why, I stiffened. Perhaps I was afraid. Why he didn't insist, I don't know, but I was disappointed.

A cloud was passing over us, a few raindrops began to fall and we rose to go find shelter. A few steps ahead in the middle of the garden, set up on the wharf, was the Tourist Pavilion. A porch encircled the farthest rounded end of the house, bordered on the outside by a low hedge; it was there we waited for the shower to end. But the rain persisted, so we sat in the shadows. Since the cement was hard and cold, I followed his suggestion to sit on his knees. He held me firmly against him to help me keep my balance and it was then that I felt a tremor. Without realizing what I was doing, I put my left arm around his neck and slowly kissed him; he responded with a thoughtful kiss. At that moment, the uneasiness that had until then kept us apart, disappeared. I snuggled in André's arms, happy to feel his hands wander over my arms, legs, thighs, and back, shuddering with bliss and impatience. But he did nothing more than caress me. Was it because he was afraid of the custom patrollers who were walking behind the bushes in their heavy shoes?

To our surprise, the cathedral clock struck four. We thought it best to leave and took the wide street bordering the Savane. Unmindful of the first vendors going to market, we walked in the middle of the street, hand-in-hand. He was no longer fearful of being seen with a colored woman.

A few days later, I wanted to go dancing. André agreed, but he danced poorly and I was disappointed because he was slightly shorter than I. Nonetheless, I had a need to express my joy through dance, and it was only when one of his friends, a navy officer like him, asked me to dance that I was able to liberate my exuberance. This man, who was my height, danced well and I was so happy that I indulged myself to my heart's content. Once the dance was over, I looked for André, but in vain. His friend wanted to continue dancing, but I no longer felt like it since the one I loved was no longer there. So, I left. Where would I find him? I didn't know then where he lived and I had to go home.

The next day when I saw him, his facial expression was stern, but he soon explained why:

"When I saw you dancing as you did last evening, I began to doubt you, that exuberance, that wild shaking and jerking. . . Maybe I'm being unfair but . . ."

"That's just what I was afraid of, without believing so," I told him. "All night I was trying to imagine what could have made you angry. I wondered if someone had told you something about me that you took the wrong way. Then I said to myself that you were sorry about the other evening or, that all of a sudden, you thought about your young girl . . . Can't you understand that it was for you I was dancing, for you I was laughing and that it was you that I pulled so hard against me. It was the first time since I've known you that I could let my happiness burst out. I did see you in the corner, but I was sure that, for your part, since you didn't want to dance with me, you were reliving our kisses from the other evening like I was reliving them myself."

I believe he understood at last. After all, I had not been

angry about his jealousy. Suddenly, as I felt his arm around my waist, I trembled with joy. I was so engrossed in thinking about him, that I had forgotten his presence. I loved nothing more than to feel his hands on my body. He followed my gaze, and while the breeze fanned our faces with the scent of the warm earth, he began to explain every detail of the scenery, going from his Airforce base and the Bearn,²⁴ which lay like a huge beast in the roadstead, to the Régale Mountain and on to the gorge of François.

"That's the steeple at Petit Bourg," he said, "and that silver stream yonder is Salée River. The huge peak is Diamond Mountain, that bight is the cove at Ane, and over there, behind the moving bougainvillea tree higher than the gate, you can see the waterway of Trois Islets. That's where I'll land by plane when the trade winds make the waves lap too high."

It seemed to me that everything he named belonged to me. I laughed and drew nearer to him saying: "You seem to know my island better than me!"

"I have flown over it so often!" he answered. He was silent and looking down into my eyes, he then resumed:

"My little Mayotte, up to now we believed we loved each other; now we are sure. There is nothing to bind us, neither my country, nor our races, our origins, our education, but today, in spite of everything, what ought to have kept us apart,in spite of what they think, those who are already gossiping about our liaison, today was born between us a love on par with the purest of them. God used us to give life on earth to a great emotion, so as to bring together, every now and then, a man and a woman, whosoever, to give birth to a spirit."

"On the terrestrial level," he continued, "our union must remain fleeting. One day, tomorrow perhaps, the wind that blew me here will take me away again and I'll continue my wandering existence in other places. We'll be quite able to live on the exact opposite sides of the earth, each of us even bound to a husband or wife, but our love will not be an obstacle, for it will live in the depths of our hearts, locked in a secret hideaway from where it will cast invisible beams on our new found happiness and on our trials to come. Because, like the meteor, our love is not of this earth; it emerged from the vastness of nothingness. But unlike those miraculous rocks, it will one day return from whence it came, to descend, perhaps, a few centuries later on another couple. Men are nothing, Mayotte, they are born, live, mate and die. But ideas survive, feelings, everything we don't see. We can live and die separated, to forget our selves and the color of our skin. Our love is beyond all time and space!"

I think that is what he said, or nearly that. His words filled me with wonder and, at same time, saddened me. Abruptly, I turned against the wall and, in spite of myself, I began to sob. Surprised, he stopped and tried to take me once more in his arms, but I pushed him away. I had nothing against him but I felt that I couldn't be with him in the those lofty heights where his mind had wandered. He was speaking to me, perhaps, as he had spoken to the lady he had loved, but I was not educated enough, maybe not even civilized enough to be able to understand him. I wondered if all whites were as complicated. Why hadn't he simply kept on explaining the scenery to me? Was it because I loved André and because my love couldn't live elsewhere than on earth that I felt unworthy of him and desperate!

I explained my thoughts to him as best I could and begged him not to talk to me like that again. Didn't the memory of our first night suffice? Smilingly, he promised me. Then I was overcome with misgiving: from now on, wouldn't he treat me like a child, like other white men who have affairs with colored girls? I didn't want that; I would have preferred to try to understand him, and maybe I already understood him a little. I felt myself becoming another person; everything was so different with him than with Horace.

CHAPTER II

Quite naturally, I moved into the house that André had rented from the widow of a black civil servant. The house was located about two kilometers from the city on a hill that looked over the docks of the port. The road that led to it had the unfortunate feature of first cutting across one of the filthiest sections of Fort-de-France, where love is sold at unsavory prices in infected shanties. Except for the last 500 meters, it followed the edge of a kind of plateau that dropped sharply onto a flat land covered with sugar cane stretching from Pointe des Carrières to Pointe des Sables and where the straight road of Lamentin and the sinuous Monsieur river crossed. Not a house, not a tree cut the sea breeze that blew over the top of the grassy slopes. A few isolated shanties leaned together under the wind as if to enclose their foul odors so that the fresh air would not chase them away. From the plateau, the road ascended to other slopes toward Fontaine Moutte which, however, a branch-road took, by way of the Entr'aide district, going toward the steeple of Redoute. At that point, some really beautiful houses came into view. For the Navy had indeed bought land and built houses for the officers. André's house, on the corner of two roads, was at the foot of a hill. In back, facing a piece of vacant land meant for a garden, was the garage, the bathroom and kitchen. In front, stood the main house in which a hallway separated two rooms with connecting dressing-rooms. Last of all, across the full length of the facade was an immense room. A veranda encircled all sides of the house and a narrow strip of land filled with greenery distanced it from the two roads. At the junction of these, there was a statue of the Virgin, as is customary on our island.

André had a maid, a young, jet black negress, named Ophelia. I sensed right away that my dealings with her would not be easy and that I would have to use diplomacy, which was not my forte. To be truly in charge of that house which would be mine, I intended first to transform it according to my taste. I put on an old house dress, dressed André in his old khaki outfit, and then gave orders to Ophelia. Soon, parts of the bed littered the ground, plates and dishes were dismounted, the armoire went out by way of the window, crossing paths with the mattress. The owner's family, the "Dragons of Annam,"²⁵ the plaster statues of "Diana at the Bath" and "Spring" were packed into one of the dressing rooms along with the bed posts. I climbed on André's shoulders to nail the mosquito net to the ceiling, set up the buffet, kicked out the desk, set up the wash-basin in the other dressing room. Two hours later, dead tired, covered with cobwebs, hair full of dust, with my hand clasping the broom handle like that of a general on his sabre the eve of battle, I stopped to contemplate my work.

In the bedroom space, we had piled the pretentious dining room furniture. The walls of the big room were bare; only the squares of blackened paint showed where the grotesque photographs had been. The living room, divested of some of its chairs, was now clean, thus allowing space for air to circulate. Our bedroom had a new location in the other half of the room and, in the rear, against the wall of the former bedroom stood the bedsprings and its two mattresses. I was already planning for the bedspread that I would make with pieces of madras. André, who seemed overjoyed, promised that we would shop for them the next day, if they could still be found in the empty stores.²⁶ In another corner, between the door and a window, the armoire was discretely placed; nearby, a dressing-table lent a cozy touch; lastly, a night-stand supported a vase containing a few roses from the garden.

And so, a wonderful life began for me. I was living with a white man, an officer, who treated me like his wife, I was happy to show him how well I knew how to keep house. Although, at times, Ophelia looked askance at me, I paid no attention to that.

André, who gave in to all my whims, had bought rabbits and chickens. Aside from the edible animals, I soon had quite a menagerie. There was Grema, a Dane puppy given to us by the captain of the *Emile-Bertin*, the cat, Houla and the tomcat, Zombi, the most rascally of all and my favorite. André's duties took only a few hours of the day, but when he was away, I busied myself with the animals and weeded the garden (where I planted yams), always shaded from the sun by my big straw hat. The evenings with André passed even more quickly. From the radio broadcasts we heard the echoes of that far-off war, which, nonetheless, touched us. Then he read a poem from his country to me:"Mireille." We went to bed early. I could have lived that way forever. He was gentle, patient and I felt protected by his love.

I, alas, still had my bad disposition. One evening André took out an object from his pocket and, before I could see what it was, he slid a ring on my finger—a stunning, gold ring with diamonds. In a flash, I remembered Loulouze's bracelet. I snatched the ring off my hand and gave it back to him. Then distraught, feeling like bursting into tears, I turned and leaned against the wall. He drew near, trying to calm me.

"You treat me like a prostitute!" I sobbed. "You think I'm in this for the money . . ."

"My little Mayotte," he said, " you are hurting me, not by refusing this ring, but by making such an error in judgement. You gave me your love as I have given mine. Besides, you were the first to give me a present . . ."

He was referring to a small medallion that, indeed, I had given him after having it blessed.

"But my gift was nothing much. If you had offered me a trivial thing, I could have thought you unprejudiced, but the ring is so expensive . . ."

"That ring has no other value than my love for you. It's my love that I just put on your finger, my love, clear like the diamond. Do me the kindness of accepting it, even if you don't want to wear it. If you don't, you let me believe that you think poorly of me."

"No, André, I don't think poorly of you," I answered.

And with an instinctive movement, I snatched the ring Horace had given me from my left hand and extended my bare finger. André placed the ring, then his lips on the jewel and the hand that carried it. Since that moment, I have never worn any other.

CHAPTER III

Was André handsome? All I know is that he had blue eyes, blond hair, a pale complexion and I loved him. Standing, he was a little shorter than I and that bothered him, but when we were seated he liked to say that he was slightly taller. The fact was, my legs were unbelievably long, while his were rather short. I had taken charge of the household because André truly had no talent for domesticity. I had to dismiss Ophelia, who became insolent toward me and who could not get it into her head that her accounts would be checked, and hired an older negress named Elvire.

One morning, I found a few unexpected bills in my pocketbook. For the first time, I became violently angry with André.

"I put them back in your drawer. I don't sell my love or services."

He was very gentle and very patient.

"I don't want to sponge off you. You pay for the maid, the laundry, the food. You'd like to pay for my rent too? I don't see how your false modesty is proved by my providing for my own upkeep."

In the end, I let myself be convinced, and after going back and forth several times, the bills stayed in my pocketbook. I accepted the monthly sum, since Andre had persuaded me that he would not have done otherwise had I been his legitimate wife.

One night, we were awakened by loud knocks at the garage door. André went to see what was going on and soon returned, looking serious.

"I have to get dressed right away to go to the flight deck."

"What happened, honey?"

"Caravelle's signal station has picked up a distress signal from the *Winnepeg*. I have to pair up with another plane to see what it's all about."

"You're not going to fly in this weather!"

There was a gusty wind; it was raining in the pitch black night. I, who was never afraid, began to tremble, for I was not used to being brave for him.

"It has to be done," he said, hugging me. "But don't worry, no doubt, I'll be leaving before dawn and be back in two hours."

I buried my head in the pillow, forcing myself not to cry. André came back for lunch. He told me, with some indignation, that the *Winnepeg* which came from Morocco, had been stopped and searched less than twenty miles off the coast of Martinique, that is to say, in the security zone that the United States, not yet in the war, had guaranteed to Admiral Robert. André's mission had been difficult in the heavy rains that covered the island and a part of the sea. He had flown for over two hours, exhausting the supply of gasoline. Finally, he had to fly close to the water, the wind at his back, in order to recognize the flag of the examining ship. But the latter, so as to accomplish its degrading task, didn't even have the pride or the courage to hoist its colors.

After this alarm, our life resumed, even more happily. André took me to the movies or to concerts at the Municipal Theater. He explained classical music to me, for he had undertaken my artistic, even literary education, and I must say that I was a much more attentive student than at school. But he struggled in vain to make me pronounce the "r"; I never succeeded in losing my accent.

Some evenings, alas, he had to leave me to fulfill mundane duties. He went to Didier, the elegant section of Fort-de-France, where the "Martinican Békés"[27] who, perhaps, were not pure white, but often very rich (it is accepted that one is white if one has a certain amount of money), and the "French Békés" for the most part, officials and officers.

Among André's comrades, who like him were blockaded in the Antilles by the war, some had managed to have their wives come over. I understood that André could not remain apart; I also accepted not being admitted to this group, since I was a colored woman, but I couldn't help being jealous. It was useless for him to explain to me that his private life was something that belonged to him and that his social and military another, over which he had no control. I insisted so much that, one day, he took me to Didier. We spent the evening in one of the villas that I had admired since childhood with two officers and their wives. These women treated me with a forbearance that was insupportable for me. I felt two heavily made-up, inappropriately dressed and that I didn't do justice to André, perhaps simply due to the color of my skin. Indeed, I spent such an unpleasant evening that I decided never again to ask André to accompany him again.

All the same, I was delighted when he suggested that I go with him to a gala at the Municipal Theater. To affirm the union of the colonies the day after the drama of Syria,[28] the French government had decided upon a fortnight which was to be displayed in Martinique by a number of demonstrations of national propaganda. In particular, the Navy had decided to organize a gala performance at the Municipal Theater where major events from our history would be represented, all which would be followed by a great ball.

This was the first opportunity that I had to dress to go out with André, and I spent just about all afternoon doing so. I had chosen a short-sleeved white silk dress with long pleats that fell gracefully from the waist. Following André's suggestion that I not wear too much make-up and jewelry, I selected a simple necklace and pin to match my gold earrings. My hair, curled that very day, was held by a net; I settled for a touch of powder and a bit of rouge, to combat the light. André, made nervous by this lengthy preparation, was urging me to hurry.

At last, I declared myself ready. When I reached the door, however, I realized that I had forgotten my bag and rushed to my room to get it. On coming out, I caught my right sleeve on a nail sticking out from the partition, and tears sprang to my eyes. André didn't want me to mend the small hole, insisting that we were late and assuring me that it would not be noticed.

When we made our entry into the theater, the curtain had already been raised. On the stage, an enormous Père Labat[30], his robe lifted, was blowing up the ships of His British Majesty with canon fire. The room was glittering; all Martinicans society was there and, in a box seat in the center, was Admiral Robert,[31] in person. All heads turned toward us and I saw in the eyes of men and women that I was beautiful.

At the ball, I was asked to dance by several officers, one an admiral. Each time, I asked André's permission and forced myself to dance decorously as possible. I saw only André's eyes that were beaming with happiness and pride. This time, he knew I belonged only to him.

CHAPTER IV

Toward the end of summer, André had a few days furlough. He decided to use the time to acquaint me with the joys of camping, which as a former boy scout, he dearly loved.

One fine day, after having loaded the car with supplies, a tent and its accessories, we left for the Côte du Vent.[32] While going up to the François gorge, as we went alongside the oriental palace of the Aubéry family, I related to him anecdotes which made him laugh — about that old, very rich fellow who upon dying had bequeathed gifts to seventy-two people from two to thirty-five years old, whom he considered his children.

"Were they really his?"

"Some of them had no trace of white blood. But here, a lord and master prefers to give to a darkie that he didn't help make, and forgets a mulatto that he spawned."

In François, André went to the priest, who, upon his inquiry about a suitable place to camp, recommended the Frégate. André had already sighted this place from the heights of his airplane. Seen close-up, the shore was full of mud, rotten shells, slimy from seaweed piled by the winds, and was hardly inviting. However, since it was late, we set up the tent.

I had scarcely begun to prepare the evening meal when the first visitors arrived. From who knows where, darkies, seemingly endless numbers of them, ran over to see the spectacle that we presented for them. In vain, we tried to keep them at a distance, but they were bursting into laughter, jabbering and refusing to leave. Our camping had a bad beginning. The night was most unpleasant because the blacks, now hostile, did not let us sleep and we were devoured by mosquitos. The next day, there was nothing more pressing for us than to re-load our things and get on the road again.

At Robert, we hailed a policeman who suggested Mr. Hayot's property at Pointe Royale. The Hayots are to the Côte du Vent what the Aubérys are to the plains of Lamentin: absolute master and filthy rich. They owned the cane fields, the facto-ries, the pastures, the herds, the land, the people. They have bought everything with their millions, and the more they buy, the more millions they have.

On this long and rough peninsula that separates the Hâvre du Robert from the bay at François, a road spiraled across the fields of sugarcane ending at a cove where flowed a stream. A magnificent campeachy tree[33] sheltered a strip of flat ground where André decided to pitch camp. The first day was dedi-cated to organizing the camp and exploring the environs. We were located on the banks of a large pasture, which, rising suddenly over the hills, rejoined the last sugarcane fields. On the hilltop soared the watchtower, but the overseer's house was hidden from view. We were really to ourselves.

At some distance lay a wooden pier which seemed to invite us to swim in the clean, deep water, which we did without delay. On the beach, a shelter made of cane stalks covered several boats. Close to the other side of the tent began the forest, not a true forest like those that blanketed the hills of the interior, because perhaps ten times less water falls on these protruding lands than on the slopes of Pelée or the Carbets and the breeze there is salty, but it is a kind of savanna where pebbles, minuscule grasslands and spiny shrubs alternate, for the most part, from camwood trees to formidable thorns.

Hordes of cattle roamed freely through the prairies and forests. The oxen worked only four months a year during the sugar cane harvest. The remainder of the time, they regained their strength by resuming the wild life and, while the cows

preferred the fields and stables, the bulls and oxen disappeared for several days in the bush. André was afraid in this
area, but I, with memories of my childhood in the country,
tried to reassure him.

The night was wonderful. The next day we enjoyed sailing
a boat, for the trade wind was gentle, the sun splendid, and
the swell of the open sea broken by the small islands. I wore a
one-piece outfit: a sort of playsuit in navy blue set off by bright
red buttons that formed a double row, vertical between my
breasts and horizontal at the waist. A huge straw hat, adorned
with blue velvet ribbons, protected me from the intense sunlight.

"You look like a little girl!" André told me.

I felt that I pleased him and I was happy. We stopped at
Ranville island (he knew the names of every place) in a small
cove where the water seemed deep blue against the very white
bottom of coral sand. After our swim, I set about preparing
the canari[34] by mixing the vegetables and fish. Following the
siesta, I insisted on going to town to do a bit of shopping,
where I bought a few yards of English lace that would have
been impossible to find in the stores of Fort-de France. Finally, filled with fruits, vegetables and laces, our boat set out
again on the water. We felt that we were truly on vacation.

When we arrived at the camp, the little black boy, hired the
day before, had already prepared dinner under the campeachy
tree whose low branches had been cut down to set up the
kitchen there, sheltered from the wind. We spread out a blanket to eat on, and later we retired to the tent protected by the
tree and the car.

Nights, to be sure, were not always calm. The herds left
their grasslands and, with heavy steps, headed toward the
watering holes in the plains, going past the dried-up bed of
the stream. But, from time to time, a brief dispute, or quite
simply a beast's fantasy, threw it off course, causing him to
follow a wandering route. Woe unto the tent in his path.

On that evening, the commotion of the oxen seemed especially unruly and our little cook had recognized the foreboding signs of a major fight. In the evening, he had seen Cosaque snorting through both nostrils heading toward the swamps of the unplowed land in the East, and Ramon, followed by his heifer, reaching the rising ground of the South. At nightfall, the first bellowing reverberated in the depths of the savanna. For a long time we heard the two beasts insult each other across the valleys and the hills; they were bellowing about love and vengeance, jealousy, death. I knew what that meant: that night, perhaps tomorrow at the latest, in an isolated clearing, the battle of the bulls would occur, and when the weakest would flee into the woods, the other one would pursue him, sweeping away everything in his path. From a distance, the horde would watch the feats of the great males. Then at last, the victor, bleeding, would reappear at the head of the herd. No one is disturbed when the other returns a few days later, covered with wounds and with a broken horn.

Sunburned and exhausted by our day in the fresh air, we went to bed early. This was the first time we found the tent readied, still warm from the night before. Nonetheless, in spite of our fatigue, we could not fall asleep. The nearby woods resounded with the bellowing of warriors. I couldn't tell whether they were near or far. Those howls seemed to be a part of the air, coming from nowhere, and the emotional atmosphere created by those powerful cries of love and hate exasperated me and awakened within me inexplicable primitive instincts.

Didn't André understand? At the very moment I was going to ask him to hold me, the ground shook under our bodies. We heard deafening roars along with the mounting wild puffing and blowing. The gallop of one passing animal made us shiver; then came another and still another. Branches crackled all around our frail canvas house. The herd burst from the thickets and rushed toward the watering hole, and we were caught in the swirling cloud of that mad migration.

I flung myself into André's arms, for now fear more than

desire caused me to tremble. And wasn't it also fear that made me snuggle so tightly in those arms? Ah! How I loved that fright that thrust us one upon the other, that overwhelmed us and so abruptly rekindled desire!

When at last the galloping faded away and the wild bellowing died down, once again we were overcome with fatigue. I placed my head against my lover's shoulder and with our bodies clinging one to the other, we slept like children. I fell asleep dreaming that, yonder, near the water hole, the bloody Cosaque was inhaling the nocturnal wind with his mighty nostrils while the heifers gazed upon him, admiring the prowess of their new master.

CHAPTER V

We often repeated those kinds of excursions. One day, when we had been to Morne Rouge where we had located horses owned by an old Indian peasant couple that I knew, I asked Andre to be so kind as to return by way of Saint Pierre and Carbet.

From the road cut into the massive slope, one could look down on vertiginous cliffs which plunged into deep crevices. I rediscovered each setting and greeted the houses that I knew with joyous shouts. It was a Sunday and everything was festive as young girls' songs mingled with the birds' calls.

At one of the coves in the bay, I asked Andre to stop where old Mr. Martin, a painter who had come from France some twenty years ago, lived in a crude shack at the water's edge. Surrounded by old junk, he led a serene life among his canvases, his rum and his servants who were all quite pretty. I had known him during my childhood and we had retained our friendship. Prior to my affair with Andre, he never failed to come see me in his rickety buggy drawn painfully by an old horse. He would bring me his clothes to mend, for his servants were on better terms with punch and such things than with needlework. I changed collars, cut off sleeves and patched enormous holes, but I had never been able to persuade him to buy new clothes. After having sipped punch with him, listened to his tales and admired his collection of pebbles and shells, we started out again.

We had scant time to stop at Saint-Pierre. It so happened

that the boat was arriving laden with young people, the young ladies wearing large straw hats and short colorful dresses that blazed in the sun. Mr. Martin's punch was causing my head to spin. I showed Andre the Deliverance Convent, then we set out on the flat road to Carbet and soon I saw my little town pressed between the mountain and the sea. It seemed so tiny that I felt a kind of pity for it. Perhaps it was I who had grown.

Suddenly, I had a crazy idea. We had just passed by my father's house. I didn't show it to Andre, but about a kilometer farther on I asked him to stop for a moment and wait for me.

"Where are you going?" he asked.

"I'm going to see my father! . . ."

I ran to the house, but as I was about to push open the door, I hesitated, for although I had not stopped corresponding with Francette, I had never received any sign of life from my father since that explosive street scene in Fort-de-France. How was he going to receive me? It wasn't just the walk that was making my heart beat faster. Then, all of a sudden, I saw my sister coming out with a bucket in her hand. As she went slowly toward the pond, I noticed that she had become thinner and that her gait was weary. I called to her softly:

"Francette, Francette."

She startled, raised her head and finally saw me. Having put down the bucket, she came over to me in a leap, both joyful and frightened.

"Mayotte, what brings you here?"

"I wanted to see you and papa."

"He isn't here now, he's always running every which way. But our new step-mother's here, still bedridden, although it has been a month since she had her baby. Do you want to meet her?"

"No," I said, shuddering.

We were silent for a moment, then I asked:

"How is he?"

"He's well enough to run after women. But he has no more

money; he can't even take part in the cock-fights, after all the troubles he had. To think that he's been mayor of this town! No one respects him! He had to sell all his land."

"You don't mean it!"

"Yes," Francette said. "And now, there are two babies in the house and I have to take care of everything."

"Say, does papa speak of me sometimes?"

"Never."

I was quiet once more. I no longer knew what to say to my sister. It was she who resumed with the gaiety that she knew how to affect instantaneously:

"And you? . . . How pretty you are. I love that hair style. And your handsome lieutenant? He still loves you?"

"Yes. He isn't so handsome, but he still loves me. He brought me here."

"Where is he?" asked Francette, with sudden curiosity.

"A bit farther down the road. . ."

"I want to see him!"

"Ok, come on."

En route, we passed several people who looked at us side-long. I presented my sister to Andre who was very kind to her, then I walked back with her.

"You're lucky," she told me, "you're happy."

'Yes," I answered sadly, "I'm happy."

CHAPTER VI

There were increasing hardships with food supplies and André, on my advice, bought a little pig. This new guest of our menagerie was named Julius. In the course of our outings, we never forgot to gather young bamboo shoots for him.

Andre spoke less about God and more about politics, but the echo of events that were disrupting the world were muddled when they reached us. The campaigns of Syria, the Balkans and Russia unfolded for me on the radio midst the beguines of Tino Rosso. Andre, however, was obviously uneasy. Roosevelt had just had the lend-lease voted which brought him nearer to the war.

"He would like to take possession of the Antilles," said Andre, "particularly the roadstead of Fort-de-France which could harbor massive squadrons."

Several times already the United States had attempted an audacious coup more or less shielded by England and the Free French Gaullists. In June 1940, the cruiser *Fidji* had entered the roadstead with a menacing posture. A few months later, the *Cuba* had been taken to Freetown.[35] In May 1941, the *Winnepeg* and *Arica* affairs had occurred. Each time, Admiral Robert, whom Andre much admired, made concessions: he had to accept an "observer" of Fort-de-France, a permanently stationed foreign destroyer facing the port; to promise not to allow a French warship leave without a seven-day advance notice; lastly, to agree to the daily visit of a bombardier,

130

with an interchange of communication between the "observer" and the American authorities.

One morning, we saw an unidentified bombardier in the harbor. It was carrying the American admiral from Puerto-Rico who was coming to present his new claims. On the horizon, four warships — one of which was an aircraft carrier — were cruising threateningly. Our sailors were put on alert. The American admiral departed, then returned. Andre spent half of his nights on a cot in the Office of Aviation. He told me how each morning before dawn the engines were kept running, the machine-guns in position along with the bombs. They would have liked to fight even without hope. But fortunately, Admiral Robert conceded once again and the Americans allowed us a new deferment.

After the alert, life went back to normal, but I was no longer content or happy. I understood that I was not everything to Andre, that his military duties came before me. Moreover, I was not feeling very well; I suffered from dizziness and nausea. The visit to Carbet had saddened me or perhaps I was exhausted.

I had to dismiss Elvire, who in her turn, had become impossible. The scene occurred on Ash Wednesday as a long line of people filed past the cross in front of our house, lighting candles and praying to Our Lord to watch over their health and to grant them a good life. That cross, erected by a good missionary for the salvation of the souls of a few lost sheep, was at a road crossing. It was also used for witchcraft and the sorcerers never failed to go there to chant Satan's litanies. About three o'clock in the afternoon, when with candle in hand, I, myself, was busy saying the prayer that the fortune teller had prescribed for me to charm Andre, I saw my Elvire appear. Carrying a package in her hand, she went up to the cross, kneeled, unwrapped her package, took out a sheepskin (that I figured was covered with evil signs), then waited in silence until the second bell sounded. Next, she placed a small doll wrapped in black string in front of her, then a second one in wax, wrapped in black ribbon, with its eyes gouged out. She arranged the two dolls so that they were back to back, uncorked a flask and carefully sprinkled them with a liquid which smell choked me. She lighted a lamp enclosed in a small tin of preserves (I wondered if it didn't contain something else) bowed down to the ground and began to chant in her shrill voice the prayer of Gaspard, Melchoir and Balthazar.

Having ended my prayer, I walked toward her cautiously; she was too absorbed to notice my presence. My conscience bothered me for being indiscreet, but I was curious and didn't want to be fearful of her antics. While continuing to pray, she wrapped the two dolls in the sheepskin and abruptly, violently threw them on to the pavilion. Then she bowed to the ground, arms held upward and stayed for a short while in that position. At last she raised up. Her quimbois had lasted more than an hour. My anger burst forth:

"Wretched woman, possessed by the demon!" I shouted. "I'm not afraid of your scents and your wax dolls. My quimbois is stronger than yours. It gave me the power to charm men. Yes! I have charmed my lover and I'm not afraid. And you, you're going to leave right away and not come back. I don't want to see you anymore. Go tend to your filthy business."

After sending her away, I breathed more easily; I had won the game. The ill-luck that she intended to cast upon me turned against her. Her quimboiseur must have been mistaken in the recipe. She sought to take her revenge by spreading the rumor that I had bewitched Andre by evil means in such a way that I soon had the reputation of being the greatest of sorceresses. Now, does one need fortune to allure men? Martinican women, daughters of the sun and love, are, as everyone knows, the most beautiful in the Antilles. Indeed! How can a Guadeloupan woman be compared to a Martincan woman? Elvire had been forgotten by the sun; she was an odorless flower and all the quimbois in the world were useless. Nonetheless, I wondered if I owed my health problems to her and Ophelia, who had spread gossip everywhere that I had bewitched an officer.

After a while, I no longer doubted that I was pregnant. I didn't worry about myself, for with my people there is no shame in having a child out of wedlock; it happens frequently. But how was Andre, whose education and ideas were so different from mine, going to react? I pondered over this and resolved to make the announcement delicately. And so one evening I told him as awkwardly as possible, and then, my eyes fastened on him, I stopped, terrified. His face had become very solemn, and at last he spoke:

"I want it to be born," he said. "I want it to be born because there is the possibility of its being the only human being in the world who will bear the survival of my body. The war is long, Mayotte, surprising and murderous. If I have been able to escape its devastation up to now, nothing guarantees that it will be so until the end."

"Andre . . ." I cried. But he kept on:

"I don't deny the selfish aspect of the question as I am putting it. But if I am to be killed, at least somewhere on earth there will be a being born of me who will be able to transmit to others the qualities that I inherited. And you, you will have a remnant of our flesh and of our love. You will keep him and love him as you have loved me."

"If you die, Andre, I'll die too!"

"You won't die because of that child," he said.

I clung to him to protect him from that death he spoke of, and I wept. I had been weeping a lot since being in love — I, who as a child detested tears. I wept because all of this made our love too grave for me to bear.

CHAPTER VII

On the afternoon of May 8, 1942, a late model bomber again landed in the roadstead and, almost as soon, a state of alarm was ordered. This time, the United States was at war. The truth is, for a long time Andre had spoken to me about a probable overthrow of the government. The officers were talking a lot about it, and some who thought it impossible to defend Martinique had even suggested taking the Bank of France gold aboard the *Emile-Bertin.*

Andre was recalled immediately. The next morning, he sent word by a civilian driver to ask me to send his clothes from Moute. He said, briefly, that he was either going to fight or leave. I didn't cry while packing his things in suitcases, for I didn't believe in the war, and as beautiful as the weather was, I couldn't believe in it. Through the window I could still see the silhouette of the *Emile-Bertin,* and not a trace of smoke came from its smoke-stacks.

On Monday, nevertheless, I was awakened by unusual sounds. On the road I could see an endless and noisy procession: blacks shouting, children squalling, most all laden with balluchons, sacks and suitcases. Some of them had already settled down on the nearby field. I went up to an old negress who was crying and asked her what was going on.

"It's the war!" she shouted. "Admiral Robert call up the reserves. My two sons has to go. Soldiers's all over town telling folk to leave Fort-de-France, that it's gonna be bombed. It's worse than Europe," she whimpered.

I dressed quickly, and going against the flow of the mounting human river I walked down to the city as fast as possible.
People were hailing me and at times tried to stop me. "You're
mad, girl," one man yelled, "and you're making things worse."
But I didn't listen. Indeed, perhaps I was mad, for I was
thinking only about getting closer to Andre who was going
off to fight, which now I no longer doubted. At last I reached
Fort-de-France; it was lifeless. I met up with a squad of the
new Martinican army made up — or so it seemed to me — of
the lowest kind of blacks. Most were barefoot and unarmed; a
few carried sticks in place of guns. I wanted to get nearer to
the port, but I was stopped by soldiers who were keeping watch.
I realized that I could not see Andre, that he no longer belonged to me and that I had no right to him. All day I wandered in desperation through that city without life. When night
came at last, it found me huddled like a wounded animal
under the Tourist Pavilion porch roof where I had kissed
Andre for the first time. The night brought me a new terror,
its very calm seeming suspect. I felt all kinds of hostile spirits
circling around me.

So I was less surprised than startled when, towards midnight from the loudspeakers on the boats anchored in the
harbor, the alarm bell resounded giving the call to take up
combat stations.

I knew this because I used to hear it every week when I was
living in the city, although then it was only meant for drills. I
waited a few minutes, my heart pounding; the silence had
returned, heavier and more menacing. I heard one o'clock
then two o'clock strike, and I began to get cold and sleepy.
Nothing was happening. I didn't even hear the noise of the
airplanes that had so alarmed me during the day.

Finally the sun appeared, reassuring. Exhausted, I slowly
went back up to Moute where I found people encamped all
around our house. They came to ask me for water and fire, all
the while bringing me a lot of misinformation. I kept watching the roadstead where the huge ships still lay quietly. To-

wards evening, I noticed two fires rising behind the Pointe des Sables where the airplanes were stationed. Had there been a bombing? Of course not, I told myself right away, I would have heard it! I learned later, however, that planes really had been burned, because during the general panic, fire had been set there following a misunderstood command.

Things were going from bad to worse! And so it was that the next night a loud noise went off near the headquarters entrance. This was the deep hole dug out for an extension to the dry dock, which filled up right away after the break in the embankment. It is still thought to have been a desperate act or sabotage, but it was only happenstance that chose a night, already in turmoil, to break a poorly conceived dam. Alarm bells on the ships sounded repeatedly, but since nothing happened, people began to be reassured. Several families who had camped out around our house folded their belongings and went back to the city. An American bomber flew over the porti again, left, came back and turned around. Discussion had been resumed.

It was on the following night that my mother appeared to me. For several minutes there had been a creaking on the porch, then a sound of light steps could be heard. And finally, the door opened and a shadow was outlined. I guessed that, in the half-light, she was wearing her rose scarf and that she was as pretty as the day she died. She slowly walked toward my bed, leaned over me and put her hands on my chest. I could no longer breathe. My heart stopped beating. . . . Was I going to die in turn? . . . Was she going to take me with her? I was not afraid despite my unbearable discomfort. Then mama stood up and slowly went away without turning her head. I distinctly heard the sound of the door that she carefully closed again. For her to have come to me on a night other than Moun-Mos[36] she must have had something important to say to me. However she had not opened her mouth. The dead are hard to understand.

It took me a long time to fall asleep. I woke up early, but I was still worried, for all these happenings were mingled in my head and I didn't know how to interpret them.

It was just about evening when Andre arrived home. Elated, I rushed to meet him overjoyed, but on seeing his sad expression, I paused because I understood that he bore on his heart the burden of a shameful capitulation. I, too, bent my head. Soon we were in our room. I had started sewing in order to keep my bearing; he, as he smoked his pipe, was looking at me. I didn't tell him about my mother's apparition. I read both joy and sadness in his eyes and I dared not seem to be too happy.

CHAPTER VIII

The date of my confinement drawing near, I kept busy making the layette while wondering whether our baby would be a boy or girl. And so it was that on the evening of January 4th Andre informed me that he had just received orders to leave in two days for Guadeloupe where he was would be assigned to the *Jeanne d'Arc.*[37] Such news was a shock for me, but Andre assured me that he would immediately start looking for a house to rent where our love would be sheltered. He was certain to have me settled there soon after my giving birth. So, when two days later I accompanied him to the *Saint-Domingue* which ran from Guiana to Martinique, our farewell was sorrowful, to be sure, but confident. And so it was that during his absence I gave birth to a fine little boy whom I named François, as Andre desired.

I telegraphed the good news to him and he answered with a long letter, saying that, to be sure, he was happy to have a son, but he seemed very depressed by events. There had been an uprising on board and the officers were in a difficult situation. Under those conditions he scarcely had time to look for housing. But he suggested that I take the necessary steps to get to Guadeloupe. Once again, he spoke about God, which was not a good sign.

Far from being recovered, I undertook these tasks: I went to headquarters where the National Security was located. There, not having the least idea of what to expect, I presented my identification papers to the lieutenant on duty. When he learned what I wanted, the officer went to get a file on which, I noticed with great apprehension, my name was written in huge letters and underlined in red pencil. He read a few papers, turned toward me and simply said:

"I can't give you authorization to sail to Guadeloupe."

"Why not?"

"That's just the way it is," he said, giving me a stern look.

I insisted on knowing the reason for this refusal. He was silent for a moment, then said in an ironic tone of voice:

"Passports are no longer being issued, Miss."

"I don't understand you, lieutenant, sir. I know that, as of yesterday, you issued some. I'm French like anybody else."

"Don't insist, Miss, or I'll have you taken out by force."

"Force me to leave . . .!" I screamed indignantly. "I'm claiming my rights and I just want to know the reason for your refusal."

As he was getting up, I left, saying:

"That's all right . . . I'm going to see the Commanding Officer at Headquarters."

I was upset by this encounter. How could I, a colored woman, go see the Commanding Officer? After a lot of thought, I decided to go to his mistress, a métisse I knew. She was amicable toward me and promised to do her utmost to arrange for an appointment.

A few days later, I received a summons from the Commanding Officer. Again, I went to headquarters where the same lieutenant who had treated me so badly ushered me to the waiting room. A few minutes later, a young man came to ask me if I was Miss Capécia.

"Yes sir," I answered.

"Very well, follow me."

He led me across an immense corridor where the infernal noise of typewriters sputtered. Then he opened a door and there I was facing a man who resembled a lion.

"Have a seat, Miss," he said, without even looking at me. "I'm listening."

"I would like to go to Guadeloupe," I began.

He interrupted me:

"Are you a business woman?"

"No, sir."

"Then why do you want to go to Guadeloupe? Passports are issued only to business people."

"That's not true," I said. "You have other reasons for refusing me a passport. I haven't committed a crime. Tell me the truth, sir," I entreated.

"And if you should choose to go over to the other side?" he asked smilingly.

So that was it! . . . I had heard that the authorities distrusted the colored people who were becoming more and more Gaullist. An incident had even flared up a few days ago, because several blacks at a football game had shouted: "Vive le goal!"[38]—"Long live the goal!" The police heard "Long live de Gaulle!"

"Sir," I said haltingly, "I think you are aware of my relations with Lieutenant C . . .?"

I handed him Andre's last letter.

"I beg you, sir. Look at it."

He grabbed the letter and lowered his huge head as if to sniff it. Soon he started to smile and I thought that my cause had won. But, abruptly, grimacing as he rose from his chair, he began to walk to and fro in his office. Then, halting before me, he said:

"Since you have shown confidence in me, I don't want to leave you any longer in doubt. I count for nothing in this business. I've had orders from the Admiralty"

"I've nothing to do with the Admiralty," I stammered.

"You are forgetting that you are a colored woman and that an officer must follow his career. I am here only to carry out orders. I'm sorry to hurt you . . . "

Not withstanding the stripes on my interlocutor's uniform, I ceased speaking to him as an officer, but as a man. I tried to describe my love for Andre, to show him how deep our love

was, sacred for him and me. Finally, I mentioned little François.

"But that's it exactly," he said "It's because its getting too serious that the Admiralty is so concerned." He wasted no time in ending our meeting and I had to leave.

For a while I was in despair. I wrote to Andre, then I telegraphed him and he answered by saying that my letter and telegram had worsened his sorrow. But, he said, I must not be discouraged, for it was only a matter of getting over a bad time, and, in any event, he would never forget those two years that he had lived with me, for which he thanked God. I didn't like that last sentence. What did it mean? Was Andre being pressured by his superiors? Was he giving in so easily? Had he enough of me, despite his noble words? I had never yet suffered to that degree. I no longer ate, nor slept and, to my deepest regret, I had to stop nursing little François.

In another letter from Andre, he quoted and commented on a sentence which the Maréchal,[39] whom he still admired, had delivered: "In adversity itself, you will find the meaning and the path to greatness." This brought me another blow, but under the intensity of this new suffering I found the strength to take action. I wrote to Francette that I absolutely needed to see her. She came to Fort-de-France and I persuaded her to request a passport for herself, which she obtained with the utmost ease. I had resolved, for once, to make use of our striking resemblance. Since I didn't want to leave my baby in Martinique, I hired a maid, a Guadeloupan, not too black, who could pass for the mother. Finally, I boarded the Saint-Domingue. On the gangway, two policemen were verifying passports. They carefully compared me with the photograph, but having modified my coiffure to look like hers, I resembled her all the more. One hour later, the boat departed.

It must have taken one night to make the crossing which, it appeared, was not without danger. The captain, very nervous, constantly shouted: "Be careful! By Damm!" No one was permitted to smoke cigarettes and the port holes were covered with a layer of blue paint so that the German submarines, prowling off the Antillean shores, wouldn't be able to see the lights. Every hour, a sailor came through our cabin to see if all was in order.

At six in the morning, the boat arrived in Pointe-à-Pitre. I was on deck and, abandoning all caution, I held François in my arms. To my utter dismay, I saw the *Jeanne-d'Arc*, where I knew Andre was, getting underway. The huge ship, with its single chimney stack smoking, was gliding slowly away from the dock, then slipped farther way. The slowness itself was agony. If I could have fainted, I would have; I would have even . . . This time I felt that a fate stronger than I, stronger than Andre, even stronger than the Admiralty itself, separated us. It was as if my life's breath had been snatched from my body.

I had to disembark with the other passengers. A crowd of mostly black people was stirring about, howling, raising their fists menacingly where the *Jeanne-d'Arc* had been on the dock. I stepped forward to ask for information about Andre, but the women near me turned around, looking spitefully at François who was still in my arms. I didn't catch much of what they were saying, but I understood that I could expect nothing from them.

So, I went to a hotel and spoke to the owner. A negress, she looked at me, then at François's pale face, and finally told me in a guttural voice:

"I ain't got a room."

"I'm sick. I have to stay someplace."

"I don't give a damn! I won't put you up with yo' old white man in yo' arms."

"He's not an old white man's child," I murmured, for I no longer had strength to shout. "My husband is an official and I must go to Basse-Terre tomorrow."

"Yo' husband an official? We don't want no mo' officials!"

Once outside, I noticed that the city was decorated with tricolor flags and that placards were stuck on the walls. I struggled to read one about the historic days that Guadeloupe had just lived through. At last, a man was willing to give me some information: Guadeloupe had just liberated itself, but the tumult was at its peak. The night before, brawls had broken out in the port area; sailors had intervened and a black man had been wounded. Hostility against the officials, the officers, whites in general, was still very acute.

I wondered, in my anguish, if I would be able to return to Fort-de-France. I thought about my baby. What would become of us in this place where no one wanted to keep us? . . . And since I had money to last only a few days . . . I rushed over to headquarters office. Luckily, the run to Martinique was still operating, so I boarded the next boat.

A letter from Andre arrived in Fort-de-France almost as soon as I. When I opened it, a check fell from the envelope. I shuddered, hardly able to read, but finally, I did: "This is the solemn hour of the great departure . . ." He spoke a lot about God, trying to persuade me that our love would now pass on to "the realm of ideas." Then he spoke about our little François:

"You will raise him; you will tell him about me. You will say to him: he was a superior man; you must strive to be worthy of him. One day, he left on his boat, and since then it is as if he were dead. But you are here, my little man. You will become like him and later you will, in your turn, make a woman happy."

I felt an explosion of rebellion. Did Andre think he had made me happy forever? Did he think that I would be able to live solely on memories? Did he believe that, by sending me a check he was free in regard to this child he didn't know, but who was his? Ah! if I had been alone, how much pleasure I would have had in tearing up that check. I hated him already for obligating me to pick it up.

CHAPTER IX

Two years passed. Through one of his friends, I was able to locate Andre's address, but the letters I sent were returned unopened. I learned, again from the same officer, that he had married in France. For my part, I tried to forget him, but to no avail, for little François, whom I loved more and more, resembled him too much. I had not cashed my check; I couldn't have. I preferred to go back to work because it kept me from thinking and also guaranteed my independence.

One day, to my great surprise, I received a letter from my father. I was corresponding with Francette and saw her from time to time, but he had never written me. How joyful I was on reading that he wanted to see me again and that he proposed my return to Carbet with my son whom Francette had told him about. I made up my mind quickly, liquidated my business and, in a few days, I took the vedette-boat to Carbet. It took three hours to make the trip, going along that coast that I had explored so often with Andre. But now I thought only about my father.

At last, the vedette-boat came alongside the small landing of my town. Francette was there holding by the arm an old man, feeble, bent over and unsteady on his legs. I was so shocked that I let go my child to throw myself into my father's arms and sobbing, we hugged each other. My joy hurt me as much as his feebleness. But, since I didn't want to show him the grief I felt on finding him so changed, I took his arm and urged him to start walking. At that moment, François, whom

I had forgotten, in his turn burst into tears. "Look," I said to him, "he's your grandpa. Kiss him and be nice." But the child recoiled. He, whose skin was so white, surely couldn't understand why his grandfather was black.

Slowly, we set out to go through the town. As we went by, people turned around to look at us, and on seeing that I had a white child, did not fail to comment. I heard one woman say that I had betrayed my race. Well, yes! Perhaps I had betrayed our race, but I was proud of it. And I was grateful to my father, who, no doubt to allay the back-biting, took François by the hand.

We finally reached home. I was painfully struck to find a house more dilapidated than when I had seen it on my last visit. The garden, quite small now because my father had sold most of the land from our beautiful orchard, lay fallow. Father, on seeing my distress, explained to me that he was no longer able to work in it, and that Francette, by devoting all her time to household chores and not being physically able, could not handle the hoe.

Looking around inside, I could see that my father had sold much of the furniture; all that was left were the beds, a table and a few chairs. I felt very sad entering this house, so bare and poor, as I remembered the joy and well-being that I had seen prevail there during my childhood. I thought about my son and wondered if, in the end, I would be capable of living in that ambiance after the comfortable life I had enjoyed in Fort-de-France.

But in the days that followed, the love I always had for my father made me forget the comforts of my former life. I was happy to live, at last, in my native surroundings near him and with my son, happy that he was alone, abandoned by the successive women who had fleeced him. An intimacy we had never had before was created between us: we spent hours conversing, he talking to me about politics and claiming to have been Gaullist from the very beginning. In my turn, I told him about the life I had led, far from him, my love, my happiness, then the birth of François and Andre's departure. He listened to me attentively and one day I saw two big tears sprouting in the corners of his eyes. I was distressed because I would never have imagined that he could cry.

"Why are you crying?" I asked him. "You're ashamed of me?"

He drew near me and, after kissing me solemnly on the forehead, he said with that pompousness he liked to assume on important occasions:

"I have to admit to you that I haven't lived an exemplary life either. You betrayed your race, that may be so. You're an unwed mother, that too, may be so. But I want to forgive you everything and I'm ready to cherish my grandson."

In those words there was a pride that gave me pleasure.

All the while, huddled in a corner, my sister Francette listened to us in silence. To be frank, she had taken a dim view of my son's presence at our father's. More and more devout, she spent her time at the priest's. She never embraced François and seemed to consider my poor child a curse. We slept in the same room and every night I had to listen to her pray at length in order to atone for my sin.

I soon had to take charge of all the housework and the care required by my father's worsening health. It was then that I noticed the mysterious, hushed tête-à-têtes between him and Francette. They would speak in voices so low that I could not understand, but I knew, from the expression on my sister's face, that all was not well. As for my father, he was suffering without saying anything to me.

I understood, after a while, that François and I were the principal subjects of these conversations. Francette claimed that people were talking about me because of my white child and that she felt the affront of this slander. She felt that she could not tolerate this state of affairs much longer.

The war had changed many things; people had become arrogant. I don't believe that just a few years earlier they would have accused me of betraying my race. But blacks were holding their heads high, no longer satisfied with their numerical strength. They had turned out to be especially touchy. My father, who had always been ahead of his time, was delighted at this trend toward emancipation.

"The békés don't have more rights than us," he said repeatedly, "and they have the same duties!"

I had no response. My father, unlike me, had not lived with a white man. In spite of everything, I could not think of myself as their equal. I had sensed this keenly since my return to Carbet.

Father had urged me to file a law suit against Andre in order to force him to recognize his son, or at least to pay for support. I didn't answer. I could detest Andre, even hate him with the same passion with which I loved him, but I could not bring a law suit against him. Obviously, as my father observed, François would be a heavy burden for me, but on the other hand, I was proud and almost happy that he depended on me alone. "I'll not share him with any man," I said to myself. I had confidence in the future; François gave me that confidence.

Whenever possible, I would take walks with him. I rediscovered the Cambeille River with its rough swellings like fits of anger, the cries of the sea gulls, the wind in the palm trees, the high breezes from the waves on the beach. On one extremely hot day I went as far as the marshes, so cherished by lovers. In the surrounding trees, birds fluttered their wings so as to gain a bit of the cool air, and their many-colored down gently landed on the still water; midst the leaves, stark white ducks, half asleep, were nodding. I taught François to touch the zhèbe-moin-misé, asking him "Ess moin amusé moin?" ("Am I having fun?") The little plant never failed to fold over right away and answer, "Yes, you're having fun." I would open zanolis eggs before the lizard came out wriggling. I taught him to be wary of the poisonous snake, fer-de-lance, and not to look too closely at the thousand-legs.

I enjoyed walking alone on the beach as I did before. The huge fishing nets were stretched over the bamboo frames,

lightly stuck in the sand. One day, as I was approaching a group
of youngsters playing by the shore, one of them, a small black
boy, cried out: "It's Miss Mayotte!"

I did not recognize him. He must have been a baby when I
left Carbet. He had grown like the young palm trees that were
now stretched out under the sun.

"What's your name?" I asked him.

"Maurice."

"And how come you know my name?"

"I've heard about you. They say you were terrible. I wanted
to see you, but mama wouldn't let me."

"And why didn't she want you to?"

"The grown-ups say that you have a white child," he said,
opening his eyes wide.

My only answer was to stroke his black face, covered with
sand. Why did they want to make me ashamed of little François
when I wanted to be proud of him?

Despite all this, life was taking shape. I regained my position between my father and my sister. After dinner, Francette
would withdraw to feed the animals. On her head she carried
a baille, filled with fish-mush and meal. We could hear the
little ducklings quacking, while the hens pecked their feed
off the hard ground and the cocks, beating their wings, loudly
hurled their cock-a-doodle-dos. Father would get up from the
table, Francette would join me in the kitchen. Carrying eggs
in a large straw hat and holding a few cocoa-nuts under her
arms, she would never fail to complain:

"I have too much to do," she'd say. "It's making me ill."

"You're a weakling . . . "

These words always made her angry.

"I'm surely stronger than you! . . ."

"'Til now, I haven't told you how much I admire your
spunk." "My spunk! While you were having a good time in the
city, I was climbing coconut trees like a little monkey. I even
cut down trees for firewood."

"Oh my! So the war really changed you!"

But we didn't always quarrel. Often, she would question me closely about my life in Fort-de-France. I told her about Loulouze, the stores, the laundry business, and about how hard it was for me to keep orderly accounts.

"You must have made money." she said.

"A little, not much."

One day, I showed her my photo album. She looked at it with great curiosity, then suddenly, she pointed to Andre among a group of officers. "That's him?"

Abruptly, she ended her chatter, closed the album and with a curt gesture, placed it on the small table. That silence hurt me. Slowly, she put her hands on my shoulders, then, still without a word, she rose and went into her room. In a few minutes, I saw her come out, holding my little François by the hand. I was shocked, for indeed, she had never been willing to take walks with him.

In the evening, Francette and the little one having gone to bed, I was alone with father. I recalled the conversation with Francette and wondered what she was thinking. Why had she rejected the album on seeing Andre's picture? Why had she gone out with François? Why had she said nothing to me on returning? Why had she gone to bed early? Father, who must have noticed my distress, asked me:

"Are you happy now, Mayotte?"

I gave him a grateful look.

"Yes, papa," I responded, "I'm happy to be back."

"This is your home, my daughter."

Then taking my hands, he questioned me about Andre, asking me if I was receiving letters from him. I didn't give a direct answer because I didn't want him to know to what extent I had been forsaken:

"I wrote him and told him how you've welcomed me."

My father's voice became deeper and more serious:

"Mayotte, I must talk to you. Since you came here, little François has given me a lot of joy and happiness. You were quite young to know about men, my child. I hope you are not grieving."

"Ah! Papa, my happiness is to live here near you. I don't ask for more. The only thing that spoils it is how Francette acts. Is it such a terrible sin to have had a white child?"

"Francette is always close-mouthed, even with me. But, perhaps she's getting used to François's being here. Didn't she go out with him this very day?"

"Yes, but why does she pay attention to everything they say in town? I haven't killed anybody; I'm not a criminal."

"Calm down, Mayotte. You could hope for nothing better than a child like François. And now you have him."

I looked at father tenderly. Never, it seemed to me, had there been such understanding between Andre and me.

The next day, Francette's face looked more peaceful and happy than usual. She asked me nicely if I had slept well.

"Yes, and you?"

"I've thought a lot about you. You've been here two months. Wouldn't you like to have a little party this evening? You can do the cooking and I'll make a delicious cake with my eggs."

I knew that this was my sister's obsession. No one had the right to touch her poultry-yard or its products.

"That's a good idea," I said. "I'll try some recipes that I learned in Fort-de-France to surprise papa."

When he returned, the table had been set and decorated with flowers. He gave me a glance as if to say: "You see, Francette came back with a better attitude." Then he hugged both of us and put François on his knees. In good spirits, we all sat down to the table. The dinner was quite festive, at least until the dessert, at which time, I noticed my sister's disquiet. Taking advantage of a brief silence, she lifted her head, her eyes larger that usual.

"Father," she said, "what I'm going to say will hurt you, but since Mayotte is here, I won't feel as bad saying it to you."

Right away, I understood what Francette was up to, but I shared her anguish and an irresistible fear kept my mouth shut. I could not interrupt the little speech that, no doubt, she had prepared and that she continued to recite in a serene and sweet voice:

"I've given this deep thought and I want to say that my place is no longer here. There is another place where my duty calls and to fulfil it I must leave you. Mayotte will take my place near you. Only promise me not to hold it against him who called me and showed me the way of happiness."

She stopped and lowered her eyes to her plate. I looked at father. Huge tears were running down his cheeks as he arose with some difficulty and took Francette, who was now standing, in his arms. He cried out: "My little one!... My poor little one!" He could say nothing more. It was then that I noticed that, under her white dress, Francette was wearing a cross I had not seen before, and I realized that this meal had not been planned in my honor, but to allow Francette to announce her momentous decision, so as to cause the least grievance possible. When at last she was freed from father's arms, she came over to me and said:

"Believe me, Mayotte, I hold nothing against you. I don't understand your misdeed, but I shall pray to God all my life to make you happy."

Choked by my tears, I could not answer her.

So, I remained alone with my father and son. These two got along very well and they loved to play together. Father would tell horror stories about ghosts and phantoms, or about the Caribs. The child listened, opening wide his eyes, blue as the sea. And I, looking at him, would dream about the one I had loved. Ah! How I would have liked to see him there between my son and father, but I knew that even if he had not left me, this dream would have been unattainable. A naval officer can not live with a colored family, and perhaps, in his presence, I would have been a little ashamed of my father.

No longer was I jealous of the women in Father's past. To the contrary, I was rather pleased to know that he had made the most of his life. But the fact that these women and their children (who, after all, were my half-brothers and sisters) had deserted him, pleased me all the more. In any event, I was slightly compassionate, for there was no obstacle to my love. As for him, I knew that far from condemning me, he understood me better than he had ever understood Francette.

He was growing more and more fragile, however, and soon was no longer able to leave his room. To take his mind off his suffering, I sometimes read to him or told him about the projects I had undertaken. I had started to fix-up the house to make it more pleasant for him. I looked after the chickens and rabbits and even ended up by cashing Andres's check to buy a pig. Also, I did some embroidery work that I sold in Saint-Pierre. Thus, I was able to provide for the needs of my son and father.

From time to time, friends from Fort-de-France visited me, bringing me the latest news from the city that still interested me. After a while, I had renewed acquaintances among some women in Carbet who spoke so highly about a certain quimboiseur that I finally agreed to go see him. He was a very old black man. He gave me some drops that I was to have my father drink, and prescribed an incense mixed with holy water to be burned in father's room so as to chase away the Devil and evil spirits. I did what he ordered but could not see any improvement, and in the end, I persuaded my father to send for a doctor in Saint-Pierre.

The doctor, a métis, came. He took me aside to say that father was so seriously ill that he might die at any moment, and that I should send for my sister. Francette soon arrived and, weeping, threw herself in father's arms. I was distraught, for I thought he was going to die; nonetheless, I could not believe it.

The next day he was so ill, I took my son to his bedside. He gazed at my François for a long time, who, doubtlessly, reminded him of the children he had by the women who had deserted him. What was he thinking about? I could see quite well that death was about its task, and I no longer had strength to predict it. Suddenly, he opened his mouth, but no word came from his lips. Did he want to talk about the children? Did he want to say that he regretted his past life? He gave a final gasp, then closed his eyes forever. Francette immediately blessed him. Then I drew close and kissed him on the forehead at length until I felt his life pass into me. At that time, calm and strength was returned to me. I thought that I well might have sinned, but later when death visited me, the life which I had received from my father would in turn be passed on to my son. Even so, I was proud that he was white.

During the months that followed, I felt very much alone. I encountered the same hostility from the townspeople, and I could hardly bear their ignorance, their superstitions, their pretentious stupidity. If my child was separating me from my race, nonetheless, he did not give me another one. I no longer saw Francette who was achieving her novitiate, and, despite the blame she had heaped upon me, I missed her sorely.

I sold father's house, which didn't bring me much money because it was mortgaged, and I returned to Fort-de-France. But this city, where I had been so happy, offered me little pleasure. I remained indifferent to the officers who had known Andre and who courted me.

I wanted to get married, for I was not like Loulouze who used to say: "What good is a husband, if you have kids?" I would have liked so much to be a respectable woman. I would have liked to marry, but with a white man. Only, a colored woman is never quite respectable in the eyes of a white man — even if he loves her, I knew well.

So, in the end, after a few months of that delusive life, I boarded a freighter bound for Paris, France. I said goodbye forever to that island where I left only the dead. It is true that, for us, the dead are never altogether dead. In writing these pages, I have sensed that they were still lurking about me.

Notes

[1] Term used to designate those of different racial mixtures which rather than blending their characteristics, present them as in juxtaposition. For example, a black with blond, frizzy hair or with blue eyes.

[2] Mysterious and wandering evil spirits, most often in the form of wild or domestic animals.

[3] Spirits of the dead.

[4] or diablesse—a legendary diabolical creature appearing in the form of a seductive young black woman who preys upon hapless men and steals their souls. Also a Carnival figure.

[5] Quimboiseurs are consulted for sickness and on personal matters, such as love or revenge.

[6] Fine crystal manufactured since the 19th century in the city of Baccarat, 150 miles from Paris.

[7] In French there are two forms for you: tu and vous. A child would not use tu (the familiar form) as Mayotte did in speaking to an adult. That is why she apologizes.

[8] "Ba moin en ti bo! . . . Doudou!" a folksong associated with the Easter Monday holiday and sung to the beguine rhythm. (Leona Gabriel-Soime, *Ça c'est de la Martinique* Paris, 1966).

[9] métisse-a fair complexioned female of mixed blood.

[10] *Green Pastures*: the play by the American playwright, Marc Connally, appeared in 1930. The film, produced in 1936, with an all-black cast, featured Richard Harris as "De Lawd."

[11] 'A French Catholic priest (1663-1778) who pursued a severe policy of conversion among African slaves in Martinique.

[12] There were also eruptions in 1929-1930 in Saint-Pierre.

[13] Capécia refers to "Adieu foulard," a popular folk song in the Antilles usually sung in Creole. The young woman laments the departure of her sailor boyfriend who has been ordered to leave the island by his commander. The setting in the narrative suggests that the young woman in the riverboat is someone's "doudou"—sweetheart. The adolescent Mayotte sings fragments of the verses that she remembers.

[14] métis-a fair complexioned male of mixed blood.

[15] A large, impressive plaza in the heart of the city.

[16] Creole music and dance.

[17] A popular dance-hall in Fort-de-France.

[18] Carnival figures

[19] King of Carnival burned as a mannequin by revelers on Ash Wednesday.

[20] A sheltered place of anchorage offshore, but less sheltered than a harbor.

[21] After the defeat of France by Germany and the Armistice (June 1940), the local Martinican authorities and the legislatures, recognized the authority of Marshall Henri Petain who headed the collaborative Vichy government. A sizeable naval force was stationed in the Antilles, mainly in Fort-de-France. The *Emile-Bertin* was a cruiser.

[22] Capital city of Algeria in North Africa.

[23] In 1942, American forces debarked in Algeria. In 1944, the city became the seat for the provisional government of the French Republic.

[24] French aircraft carrier.

[25] Dragoons of Annan, a cavalry unit established in 1886 which became a colonial military unit in 1896. It was abolished in 1950.

[26] The economy in the Antilles suffered from disrupted relations with France and a naval blockade by the U.S. There was a scarcity of all commodities.

[27] Whites or "nearly white," refers to the descendants of early

European colonists born in the island. The French are known as "Metropolitains."

[28] Syria declared independence from colonial French rule in 1941. French rule ended in 1944.

[29] One in a series of propaganda events to promote a Marshal Pétain cult.

[30] See Chapter 6, Part 1.

[31] Representative of Vichy government from 1940-43 and the head of all military, political and economic operations in Martinique.

[32] The Atlantic coast

[33] The tree is of several varieties such as red dyewood. The name comes from a city in Mexico, Campêche.

[34] An earthenware pot; also the ingredients in it.

[35] Probably Freetown, Antigua

[36] Souls of the Dead Night.

[37] French cruiser.

[38] Hurrah for the *goal!* Used in sports and pronounced like the name [de] Gaulle.

[39] Pétain

THE WHITE NEGRESS

MAYOTTE CAPECIA

LA NÉGRESSE BLANCHE

roman

CORRÉA

I

The Whites and the Blacks

It must have been midnight and there was no one else in the bar other than Major Miquet and du Taillant. Suddenly, at the sound of racing footsteps in the street, the door was pushed open violently and a sailor dashed headlong into the room. Outdoors, a woman's scream rang out, then shrill voices in dispute. Isaure looked at the two officers who had risen.

"What's that all about?" asked the major in the severe tone he assumed when giving orders.

"Major, sir," began the sailor, both confused and breathless, "I was followed . . . by two blacks. . . . They took out their knives. . . . They wanted to kill me. . . ."

"Or cut your ass. . . . And that woman's scream? . . ."

"What scream sir? . . ."

"Just now. . . . You didn't hear it?"

"No, major, sir. . . ."

The officer threw a disdainful glance at the sailor.

"Don't play the fool. . . . You were with a woman?"

"Yes, major, sir. . . ."

"A black?"

"Yes, major, sir"

"Naturally. I know about this kind of business and I'm beginning to be fed up with it. Ok, we'll talk about it again tomorrow."

The sailor withdrew in a corner, seeking to make himself as

159

inconspicuous as possible, but the major turned abruptly toward him:

"So why don't you beat it?"

"You don't understand, major, sir," Isaure said, "They're keeping watch in front of the door."

She had a gentle voice with a slight lilt, the accent of the island's young girls, resembling the English accent. It wasn't altogether like that of the black girls who completely swallow their "rs." She barely articulated hers, lingering on the preceding vowels, but she pronounced them when she talked to békés.[1] So as to have her hair appear more sleek (which was frizzy only at the roots), she flattened it with care. She was one of those many mixed-bloods, so common in Martinique: her skin had a touch of banana, orange, coconut and coffee; her lips full, her teeth dazzling, but her face, highlighted with a bit of rose on the cheek bones, had the look of a white person. Lastly, everything about her, even her accent and her gestures, indicated that she was of mixed-blood.

Major Miquet and Lieutenant du Taillant were listening closely, for it was evident that the blacks, too excited to be still, were fidgeting on the other side of the door.

"How many were there?" asked the major.

"Two at first, but while chasing it's possible they took on others."

"Of course," affirmed Isaure.

"And as usual, they only had razors? No other weapons?"

"Yes, I think so," said the sailor.

Obviously, he did not want to leave.

"Even if they don't have their razors, they know how to throw rocks," said Isaure. "Ah, you have to see that, how they throw rocks!. . . ."

The major got up. He was now holding his revolver in his right hand and du Taillant had followed him.

"Let's go," he said.

But, more swiftly than a cat, Isaure bounded to the door. Arms crossed, she barricaded the path of the two officers.

"You must not leave, they'll kill you!"

The major smiled. He was fully aware of the tendency of the natives to exaggerate and dramatize. For him, a Breton, these Martinicans were worse than the people of Marseille. Nevertheless, the state of Isaure's fearfulness impressed him, for he knew her to be a courageous girl, but now she was trembling.

"I know them, major, believe me . . . I swear to you . . . I swear to you that these dirty niggers, when they are worked up, they're capable of anything. They don't know what they do. . . . They're savages . . . You don't know black blood, major. . . . If you kill a single one of them . . ."

"I don't want to kill anyone," said the major, "I just want to scare them."

"All the blacks will be on their side," Isaure continued, "That could be the signal for a revolt, for Liberation, as they say. You don't realize how excitable they are. They've understood nothing about this war . . . They're hungry and they think it's your fault, I mean Admiral Robert's, Marshal Petain's fault. When the *Emile Bertin*[2] arrived in Fort-de-France, they thought the boat was bringing them food. It was quite the contrary. The sailors took their women. That, above all, got to them. They've had no women since the ships were in the roadstead. And if you kill one at my door, they'll come back to get revenge."

"All right, let's wait a while," said the major.

He put his revolver back into its holster and sat down again at the table.

"Come, have a planter-punch with us."

Isaure filled three glasses with planter-punch, her specialty, and seated herself between the officers. But she was ill at ease; she could not calm down or keep herself from lending an ear to the door. The blacks were there, a few steps away; their whisperings and the nearness of their presence bothered her in a strange way. "The woman's not screaming now," said the major, "perhaps they took her away."

161

"What did they do to her?" asked du Taillant.

"Made love," answered Isaure in a terse voice.

"Then they're not so terrible."

"They can make love in a terrible way," Isaure declared gravely.

Since the two officers looked at her quizzically, she hastened to add:

"No, I've never slept with a black. They disgust me and I'm afraid of them."

That was true, she had never had a black lover. Perhaps, solely because the first one who had taken her at seventeen and who had given her that son with such a light complexion, was white. A first love orients one's life. Perhaps it would have been altogether different, perhaps she would have married . . . Wouldn't marriage with a black man be better that living with a white man? At least the children wouldn't be bastards. She shuddered, feeling extremely nervous. On the other side of the door, she still heard steps and voices. How many were they? Who were they? She cast a contemptuous look at the sailor, who, in his corner, was trying to remain unnoticed.

"In the past," she explained, "when a black man met a béké in Didier[3], he politely took off his hat and said 'Good-day, suh.'" (she imitated the black by lowering her eyes with a hypocritical smile). "The béké didn't answer. Now, the black no longer bows and it's the béké who runs after him, who taps him on the shoulder and asks: 'Say Pierre, how goes it,' and so on and so on."

Even though she was not yet twenty-five, she had not adapted to the upheaval in conditions. She was unable to rid herself of the respect for whites that her mother, abandoned by the sailor she had loved, nonetheless had instilled in her. It was not only to please the officers who frequented her bar and through pride that she did not want to accommodate blacks. When that dreadful Blanchard had dropped in on her and, idiot-like, perhaps to assert his rights, had awkwardly ordered a planter-punch, she had refused to serve him. When he insisted, she became angry and shouted:

"Get out! I don't want to see you anymore. What good is it that your name is 'Whitey,'[4] you're only a dirty nigger. . . ."

Blanchard had left midst the laughter and jeers. But one month after that incident, Isaure, terrified, had to appear in the court of law. Her white defender didn't shine in the presence of the glib mulatto whom Blanchard had chosen for his lawyer. The court found that a black is not to be treated like a "nigger," for Martinique is not a part of the United States. Isaure had said "dirty nigger," an insult that was against the law. Astounded, she heard herself condemned to six months in jail, and the postponement was of no consolation. However that dreadful Blanchard, blacker than ever, had left the court room swearing that there was no more justice and that things wouldn't stop there.

Once more, she told that story which still made her indignant. She was talking, perhaps, in order not to hear the steps, which, it seemed to her, were quickening. From the other side of the door, voices were mounting in anger, with desire. Having suddenly become silent in order to hear them, she thought she understood one sentence. They were speaking in that Martinican patois,[5] the language of her mother, of her childhood. Her eyes were fastened on the sailor and their fieriness died away. She detested that man with a vehemence that astonished her.

"They still haven't left," said the major, looking at his watch. "I wonder if we had best call the police . . ."

"Don't mix the police in this," Isaure retorted sharply.

Surprised, the two men looked at her. They didn't recognize that guttural tone, like that of the voices coming out of the night. Isaure scorned them for their amazement. She felt so terribly nervous and would have liked to become angry, for a row would have done her good. But could she get angry with white officers? In despair, she wrung her hands.

Outside, they seemed to be running in place without stopping. A tom-tom. Haunting voices rose feverishly. Was this a quimbois[6] the zombi[7]? She shivered, opened her mouth and, in order not to howl, she seized her temples in her hands; her body was on fire.

"The police mustn't be mixed up in this," she repeated indistinctly.

What business was it of these whites? What did they know about it? What did they understand? Why did they keep their eyes on her? Suddenly, without knowing what she was doing, she rose, and like a mongoose fascinated by the snake[8] she dashed toward the door, wrenching rather than opening it. Before the two officers had recovered from their stupefaction, she had flung herself into the night.

II
The Quimbois

"Now, Isaure," du Taillant asked timidly, "will you tell me what happened to you last night?"

On that day in Fort-de-France, an unaccustomed liveliness prevailed, especially in the port area. Sailors with red pompons and blue collars were leaving the Transat. Thick-lipped harlots, their faces grotesquely made up, awaited them. Their wooden heels, giving them height, clacked joyously on the pavement as they walked along, hips swaying in white, blue and yellow dresses, most often the background for huge red flowers, which added to this ambience of gaiety. The ill-famed cafes that were on a level with the clientele—the Venise, the Sourire de Paris, the Brest—were packed with sailors and strumpets of every color who let themselves be hugged and pawed in front of the white wood tables laden with punch glasses. Melodies of the beguine, swing and mazurka floated confusedly. Every other step, a street-walker was smiling and the few taxis on the island stuffed with officers moved at snail's pace.

"If we hadn't rushed out behind you, the major and me, if we hadn't made that rabble take off, I don't know what would have happened to you."

"I don't know either," said Isaure.

She shuddered on remembering the incident of the last evening: the two officers and the sailor who had taken refuge

165

in her bar after having fled from the blacks, the ones who had kept watch in front of her door. She could hear their tom-tom like footsteps that had driven her mad. Why had she opened the door? Why had she rushed toward those black brutes? Was it the revenge of that blood she had tried to suppress since childhood? She didn't want to know nor did she want to put the question to herself.

The market women who sold oranges, bananas, pineapple, apple-creepers, cinnamon-apples, and sugar cane were also smiling and behind fine displays of fruits, called out to the passers-by like street-walkers:

"Come here, my mistuh. Come see mama. Come sweetie."

The sailors laughed. The officers, more reserved, sought out the big cafes, the Coupole, the Europe, or went to find more respectable women in the Patisserie Suisse, in the Petit Belge.

"Do you mind if we don't talk about that anymore?" Isaure pleaded.

When the two officers had caught up with her in the street, she had burst into tears, for which she was now ashamed. "Leave me alone," she had said to them. "Leave me alone, I'm only a wretched negress, I'm not worth the trouble you're taking."

Firmly and gently, they had led her home. Isaure hadn't even thanked them. She really liked du Taillant. The timidity and friendship of the smooth-faced young officer appealed to her. She mended his socks; he told her about his fiance who lived in England. Never had there been a kiss or any such act between them. Isaure found that quite all right.

On the pavilion, groups of sailor were singing songs from every corner of France, and the children gathered around them, listened and laughed. There were still more vendors shouting: "Hot pistachio-nuts here! Hot pistachio-nuts!" Isaure recognized the odor and colors, all familiar to her. She needed them. She also needed du Taillant's presence, even though she sensed that, henceforth, something had changed between them. Above all, she must keep from thinking about that.

"Du Taillant," she asked, "have you ever been with a woman?"

The young man's face grew red.

"No," he finally responded.

"Well," she said, "don't try to understand."

She left the young officer at the Transat and quickened her pace. This was the fatal day of the full moon, she could wait no longer. She first went to the bank, where she asked for a thousand franc bill untouched by human hands; from this moment on, everything became serious. She next went back to the market, being careful not to return greetings from those who said hello. On that day, it seemed to her that her acquaintances were especially numerous. But they didn't insist, for they knew the meaning of Isaure's attitude and without always believing in it, they respected the quimbois enough, at least, not to make them fail. These women knew that whoever is carrying them out is not to utter one unnecessary word.

At the market, Isaure went straight to the canari vendor who sold those earthenware pots, locally known as "coconut-niggers." She made her purchase without bargaining, quite unusual in Fort-de-France, and left the vendor without a doubt of the use planned for the canari.

Then Isaure went into a jewelry store and asked for two silver rings. There too, without haggling, she accepted the price given by the salesman, all the while taking care to hand the bills with the right hand and to receive the rings with the left, murmuring: "Moin ka p'end ou, moin ka po'té ou" and then "Tant la té' ni soleil s'étend ou ka aimé moin." This means: "I take you, I feel you" and "As long as the earth is warmed by the sun, you will love me."

As she left the shop, the sky, heavily laden with clouds, burst forth, and the street, instantly transformed into a muddy torrent, soon held few pedestrians. Several men making their way with precaution, their skinny blacks legs hanging from white pants rolled up above the knees, looked like the spindle-leg cranes that haunt the marshes. Isaure hurried toward the pharmacy.

"I would like," she said, "some parchment-paper, oil of humming-bird, oil of roses, oil of 'bring-him-back,' oil-of-three-thieves and English honey."

The mulatto who was waiting on her smiled, saying:

"Nothin' like it to soothe the disposition like English honey. Sometimes they use it to tame bulls"

But Isaure, not saying a word, paid with her right hand and quickly checked the purchases that she had taken with her left hand. On the flask that held the oil-of-three-thieves was pasted a sticker representing the three crosses of the Golgotha.

Happily the shower was over, but torrents of water were still running into the gutters. A huge rat crossed the street almost at the same time as Isaure. She was accustomed to seeing and hearing them, the city being infested with them, but even so, she felt a revulsion. In the notions shop, she bought a pen, a new ink stand and a yard of white cotton cloth. Finally, in a grocery store, she ordered a pound of red beans and a half pound of corn.

"I would also like a quart of oil," she said.

"300 francs a quart," stated the clerk, after having glanced at the packages her client was holding. Isaure gave a start of indignation. Oil, like many other commodities, was rare during times of war, but even in the black market a quart ought not be over 100 francs.

At last, she was home. Lucia, her black maid, was waiting for her.

"Do you have supper ready?" Isaure asked.

"Yes, Miss Isaure, I fix supper. Two places, like always."

"François in bed?"

"Yes, Miss Isaure."

"Good. Ok, you can go help Ophelia. She'll surely need your help this evening. There's bound to be a crowd.

Every other evening (Daniel's evenings), Isaure's sister filled in for her at the bar. Lucia glanced with curiosity at the packages the young woman had brought back. Of course, she was fully aware of the male sheep's brain that had been marinating for three days in alcohol, even though her mistress had been careful to shut it up in a closet. She was also aware that four days prior, when the Gouverneur Moutet arrived at the Pirogues Wharf, Isaure had gone to buy a live sheep so as to be sure the brain was truly male. She had then muttered: "Daniel (this could be no one other than her Daniel), I bought you so that you'll be mine," and she had killed the sheep by hand. For three days they ate nothing but mutton. But Lucia also knew that a quimbois is done with the greatest secrecy and that, since acquiring the brand-new bank bill, her mistress was not to say anything superfluous. Hadn't she said too much already? Did she really need to ask whether the dinner was ready or François was in bed? She was devoted to her mistress and the best way to prove her devotion was to leave as discretely as possible.

So Isaure was alone at the opportune moment. She took the ink stand and the new pen and began to write diligently on the fine parchment-paper: "Isaure Thérésia, September 27, 1920— Daniel Duret, February 10, 1914." Then she brought the receptacle that held the brain into the bedroom, carefully spread the white cotton cloth over a little table and put the canari on top. She took the brain out of the alcohol and put it in the canari and, this time, said aloud: "Daniel, I set you down. I take your brain and it's you I take." Then, she grasped the two silver rings in her right hand and pushed them into the soft brain, while uttering these words: "In your brain, I thrust them so that you will be jealous no more," after which, she placed the red beans and corn in the earthenware pot and over them poured the oil of humming bird and all the others—rose, three thieves, "bring-him-back"—which she mixed with the English honey. Lastly, she poured out some oil and dipped a wick in it which she lighted, pronouncing with great solemnity: "Lamp, it is not you I light, but Daniel. May you be loving!"

Following all this, she contemplated her work with satisfaction. Not everyone can do a quimbois. She had not forgotten a movement, a word, and she felt rather proud of that. The lamp was to remain lighted for eight days. At that time, Isaure would bury the canari and its contents with the parchment paper, on which she had beautifully inscribed her name and her lover's, and all would go well.

She went into the ajoining room to look in on François. He was already asleep, his little hands resting on the edge of the sheet like birds. He was of a lighter complexion than his mother, but his hair frizzier than hers. The black race fades out less than the white. Gently, tenderly, Isaure placed a kiss on his small, stubborn forehead. She loved children and would have liked to have a host of them, but Daniel was indifferent toward that. She tiptoed back into her room. The night-light in the canari was burning gently, facing the other one on the shelf in front of the statuette of the Virgin, the one she had maintained as her mother had counseled since her first communion. The Virgin, however, despite her solicitude, had hardly protected her; she obviously disassociated herself from Isaure's relations with Daniel, who was becoming more and more jealous. He didn't understand how his lover, who happened to be around such a large number of men in her bar, could remain faithful to him. Nonetheless, Isaure admitted to herself: "It's true, I've never been unfaithful." The incident of the night before suddenly came to mind, but she instantly pushed it away. She was not herself; she must surely have been bewitched. But the new quimbois she had just performed, by restoring confidence to her lover, would set things right. It wouldn't be long before he arrived. Slowly, she took off her muddied shoes, put on red mules and changed to her Chinese house gown, the one Daniel liked best. And why not put on earrings? Those gold loops were heavy and sometimes gave her a headache, but Daniel liked them because they accented the exoticism in her face. Then too, they matched her necklace. She carefully put on make-up, wishing to be pret-

tier than ever. From time to time, she glanced over at the tiny
flame rising from the canari. Being very sentimental, she already imagined their dining tête-à-tête; it would be like their
first meal two years ago when he was gay, kind and in love.

She listened closely. Yes, it was his step that sounded in the
hallway on the planks covering the gutters that carried flowing waters. But that step did not forbode anything good. She
threw a supplicating look toward the canari. At last, the door
opened; Daniel banged it behind him. He was now in the
room, flushed, ruffled like a game-cock. He went toward the
young woman, who had risen, and tried to take her by the
shoulders, but she freed herself dexterously and managed to
get away. Then turning abruptly, he noticed the canari.

"What in the world is that? What's it for? he shouted.

He tried to grab the parchment-paper, but Isaure, more
agile, seized it and crumpled it in her hands into a ball.

"Why are you mincing about so?"

She didn't answer; she couldn't answer. Nothing on earth
could make her say: "It's for you, darling." With wide-eyed
indignation, she stared at the man for whom she had just gone
to so much trouble. She saw him as ugly, vulgar and odious.
He had gone over to the little table. With an unexpected
movement, he removed the cloth. The canari fell noisily, spill-
ing its contents, and around the brain, flattened on the floor,
the oil spread out.

"You brute!" cried Isaure.

She, too, was now trembling with rage, her eyes aflame, her
color darkening. Her head appeared to enlarge, her body to
thicken, and as she faced the man she seemed ready to spring.

She was beautiful. All at once, Daniel felt desire mingled with
anger. He took a step ahead and raised his right arm, not knowing whether he intended to strike or embrace his mistress.

"Don't touch me!" Isaure screamed. "I forbid you to touch
me!"

While the man hesitated, she grabbed a heavy ash tray and
brandished it above her head.

"I hate you, do you understand? If you come near me, I'll clobber you!"

She would have done it. Ordinarily so gentle, so submissive, when she was angry she was no longer in control. All the while, she knew that the simple threat sufficed because Daniel was cowardly. Indeed, he had stepped back. The quarrel, henceforth, continued with words, all the more violent because they had to replace actions.

"Give me that paper," he said reproachfully, pointing to the ball of parchment-paper that Isaure clasped in her hand.

"I won't give it to you."

"What is it? What's written on it?"

"That's my business."

"I know you're sleeping with du Taillant," he roared.

"With du Taillant? How do you know? So you're having me followed?"

"Everybody knows it. You are seen everywhere all the time with him. Three days ago you went to Morne Rouge. Today, you had the nerve to go walking with him on the docks."

Isaure could have explained, and no doubt proved, that there was nothing between her and the young man, but she absolutely had to get revenge.

"Ok, yes," she said in a quivering voice, "I have a lover."

"It's du Taillant?"

"No, it's not him."

"You have a lover? Do you dare repeat that?"

"I have a lover, I have a lover." she repeated.

"Who is he? I demand that you tell me."

Daniel's feature's were contorted, for he was visibly suffering. Isaure observed this with fierce jubilation while she kept a long silence.

"It's not true," he finally exclaimed.

"I'm lying? Do you think I'm not young or pretty enough to find a man who loves me? You think a man would turn me down?"

"You were willing?"

"Why not? I'm not married to you; I'm free to do as I please."

"I want to know who it is and when this happened."

"When this happened? You think we made love just once?"

"For how long?"

"For two months. No, three months. . . He's good at making love, you know."

Daniel grabbed a vase from the dressing table and threw it to the floor where it broke into smithers, but Isaure paid no attention.

"He makes love better than you," she explicated.

"Is it an officer who comes to your bar?"

"No."

"A white?"

She burst out laughing. My laugh is like the guiablesse's[9]; I am the guiablesse, she said to herself with real pleasure.

"It's a black." she finally admitted.

And since Daniel protested, saying that he didn't believe her, as if inebriated by her own words, she repeated: "A black, you understand? A black, a 'nigger.' One of those 'niggers' you detest and who will run you away one day, if they don't kill you."

"You're lying," he screamed.

"I'm lying?"

With a swift gesture like a smack, Isaure threw the ball of paper in his face; it struck him between the eyes before falling to his feet. He won't pick it up, she said to herself, he won't humiliate himself in front of me. Daniel waited a second, then the temptation won over his pride. He stooped quickly, picked up the paper, unfolded it and read: "Isaure Thérésia, September 27, 1920—Daniel Duret, February 10, 1914." At a loss, he raised his eyes.

"Isaure," he began.

She turned her back to him.

"Isaure, my little Isaure, forgive me."

"I won't forgive you," she said.

Her anger had also subsided, but her shoulders and thighs were still trembling.

"Come here," he said as he took a step forward, "Let me hold you, let's forget this silly business."

"No, I want nothing to do with you."

"Why did you tell me those lies.?"

"If you believed me, it's because you don't trust me."

"But how do you expect . . .?"

"You believed them. You were hurt, so good for you."

"I feel like making love."

"Not me, I don't want anything to do with you tonight. You'd better leave."

She motioned her head toward the crushed brain lying in the perfumed oils and the other oil.

"I've got to clean up all that mess. Don't you smell how that stinks?"

Her voice had softened, but she still wanted to punish him. Nonetheless, she let him draw close, open her dressing gown, lay bare her two small breasts which were pointed upwards provocatively. This she noticed with regret, but felt an excitement which he immediately took advantage of by pulling her against him. Then she closed her eyes, thinking that perhaps the quimbois had not been a complete failure.

III
Lucia's Love

Lucia, who had returned from the market, put her basket on the kitchen table and set about unwrapping her purchases: greens, about twenty gumbos, four green peppers, home-grown onions, thyme, ten huge crawfish that Martinicans call habitants, two pears, two pounds of couscouche, three pounds of red fish.

Isaure joined in helping her make a good calalou,[10] but Lucia paid her no attention. Ah! Today she wasn't idling! Already, while talking and singing, she had filled her stove with coal and dug a hole to stick in gummed wood. In honor of Lieutenant du Taillant, she had put on her best dress, red with large blue flowers, and since she was ashamed of her short wooly hair, she had hidden it under a canary yellow scarf. She looked liked a parrot, but surely she thought herself very pretty. Only her shoes were not quite to her liking: they were those rubber shoes made fashionable by the war, but she had no others. Moreover, Isaure claimed that she would be unable to wear real shoes, because, like many negresses, she had big heels, massililis, as they were called in local speech.

"Let me do it, Miss Isaure," Lucia insisted. "See, I already set the pot to boil."

The turmoil she was in didn't keep her from throwing herself into her work. After having cut the greens very fine, she put the whole lot in the pot and added a green pepper, a clove of garlic, pepper and salt. Finally, she mixed the contents with a beater so as to have a thick soup. In another pot, oil, butter, a bunch of onions and tomatoes simmered over a low fire. Lucia took out the red fish that she had dipped for several minutes in pickled brine made of garlic, pimentos, lemon and salt. She then squeezed a lemon into a cup in which she had put four large spoonsful of oil and finely chopped garlic, beat it together and poured that into the fish stock, the court-bouillon.

Isaure had taken advantage of the results of her quimbois to invite du Taillant to dine alone with her. There was no hidden motive, for she felt only a deep friendship for the young officer, perhaps a little pity. He was so correct, so timid, so lacking in experience, that he seemed to belong to another world and was truly like an exile among his naval comrades. Isaure was for him the only contact with the islanders. She liked it when he told her about his fiancee and about her distant, misty country. Perhaps, despite his constantly confirmed fidelity, the young man had a special feeling for the young Martinican woman; it was obvious that he was attracted by her charm. Isaure was not unaware of this and it did not fail to bring her pleasure. Lastly, the gentleness of du Taillant was a change from Daniel's brutality; no doubt this was why she took such pleasure in his company. The fact that du Taillant remained faithful to a woman he had not even slept with seemed to her worthy of unlimited admiration.

In his honor, she had put on her white sun dress and stuck a white flower in her black hair. She really looked much younger than Lucia who, nonetheless, was only twenty-two. Lucia was a pure African type: thick lips, flat nose, kinky hair and a glistening black skin. In her way, she was beautiful, standing out from the half-whites and half-blacks who were typical of the Martinican population. Since the far, far-off time of her ancestors, transported by slave ships during the time of Père Labbat, there must not have been one cross-breeding in her lineage. With her slave-like mentality, she was devoted body and soul to Isaure. Nevertheless, she didn't feel herself estranged from the latter as she would have if her "madam" were altogether white. If she felt more affectionate toward her, and, if for nothing in this world would she have stolen from her, she revered her less. There was a kind of familiarity between the negress and the mixed-blood woman. Isaure, secretive and reserved, was reluctant to confide, but Lucia did enough for two. The "madam" knew everything about her servant's affairs which were quite frequent. Lucia was a regular hussy. At certain periods she had, as she would say, "fire in her tail," and she would seek pleasure frenetically, worse than a cat in heat. Then amazed at what she had been able to do, and at great length, she described the sensations that she felt so deeply. Isaure listened to her with a strange smile. At times, she envied the black woman for not having more scruples than an animal. But, she would say to herself, one can experience love without being like Lucia. Since meeting du Taillant, however, Lucia had come to know the true meaning of love; this had been going on for about two weeks.

Isaure noticed that du Taillant's shirts and above all, his collars, were neither well ironed nor washed.

"Let me have your clothes," she suggested, " My maid has worked in a laundry and she can take care of them."

Du Taillant had gladly accepted and left a visitor's pass which would allow her or her maid to go aboard the Mékong. Isaure, wishing to avoid local gossip at any cost, sent Lucia with precise instructions and a note for du Taillant. Lucia had returned about four o'clock walking as if she were drunk, but Isaure knew she didn't drink. Falling on the kitchen tiles, her eyes bulging like a frog's, she wept bitterly. She must have cried all the way back, because her white cotton dress was drenched and bore long streaks of moistened dust. The sky, however, was cloudless.

"Well! Lucia what's the matter?" Isaure had asked. A deep sigh, wrung from the depths of the black woman, was the only answer. Her tears doubled in force.

"Did Napoleon steal again?"

Napoleon, Lucia's child, was capable of anything. Isaure had been able to have him placed in an orphanage, but, constantly, he escaped only to get in trouble.

Lucia shook her head to answer that it was not so.

"Is he dead?"

Again, no.

"Come now," continued Isaure who was becoming upset, "tell me what's wrong . . . I can't guess. You're impossible . . ."

"Mistuh de Taillant . . .," sobbed Lucia, "Mistuh du Taillant, Miss Isaure . . ."

"So! What about Mr. du Taillant?"

"He send this . . . for you . . ."

A letter and a package containing a pretty sarong that Isaure had admired a few days before while with the young officer, who had bought one for his fiancee.

"Good, Ok! Stop crying now, girl, and go do your work."

Nevertheless, Lucia had not moved and was still weeping. How could she hold so much water in her eyes? Isaure wondered. She was inundating the kitchen.

"Mistuh du Taillant . . . Mistuh du Taillant . . . ." she moaned.

"Tell me, once and for all what it is, so this can come to an end!" exclaimed Isaure with a hint of anger in her voice.

"Mistuh du Taillant," said the black woman, doubling her tears, "I loves him . . . I loves him . . ."

At the point of leaving the room, Isaure turned around, stupefied. She knew what "I love him" meant when uttered by Lucia.

"So," she said disdainfully, "you did it in his cabin."

"He do nothin' with me, and say nothin'. He not even look at me. He only talk about you . . ."

Lucia had to be sent home. This love that had caught her unaware made her ill. Isaure didn't over dramatize it, for she believed she knew her maid. This ought to be over as quickly as it had happened. Nonetheless, the next morning, Lucia arrived with a face more lined than if she had made love all night.

"You should have stayed home, girl, if you were tired," Isaure
told her.

Lucia shook her head.

"I come to wash Mistuh du Taillant's clothes."

Aside from this washing, she was incapable of any other
task. My! How she used soap! She never stopped rubbing and
never had there been cleaner clothes. She wanted to take them
to the officer herself. Before letting her go, Isaure took her
aside.

"After all, all you have to do is to tell Lieutenant du Taillant."

"Tell him what, Miss Isaure?"

"That you love him."

"But . . ."

"In any case, I have to tell you that there is nothing between me and the lieutenant other than a good friendship.
What he does with you or with another is not my business."

A smile lighted up Lucia's face and momentarily gave her
youth, but not for long.

"But him, I seen it, Miss Isaure, he love you."

"I've told you the truth and besides, I'm getting fed up with
your lovesick tales."

Lucia assumed a contrite pose.

"I always think you like him."

Then, after a silence:

"No, I can't tell him I loves him."

"You're not one to be timid with men."

"With him it's different. I'm only a simple negress, you know
what I mean, Miss Isaure. I only makes love with poor darkies
or poor whites who don't even count."

Lucia returned in just about the same state as the first time.
It wasn't over. She no longer worked. Isaure didn't know what
to do with her.

"Oh!" she said, "if he don't make love to me, that man be
the death of me. If he just touch me here, here . . ."

She uncovered her breasts, gripped the tips with frenzy.
"You're crazy, girl," said her "madam."

At last, Isuare resolved to speak to du Taiillant, doing so half laughing and half serious.

"You are a Don Juan in person, du Taillant. I would never have believed it, but you have kindled a powerful love in Lucia who neither works nor eats, and who says she's going to die if you don't make love to her. Could you possibly undo your vows to give me back a maid who works?"

"But . . ."

"Just for me," she continued. "I can't go on doing her work. Say, you have to begin sometime and, better still, with Lucia it shouldn't be unpleasant. She's a fine girl."

"I didn't even look at her," said poor du Taillant, who first blushing, then blanching, didn't know where to sit or stand.

"Well, look at her and if you want to make her real happy, touch her."

The next week when Lucia returned from the Mékong, she was quite composed.

"He look at me this time and he shake my hand!" she said proudly. "Oh! what a man! I never seen such a good looking and distinguished man."

At last, du Taillant came, carrying a rectangular package.

"That's for me?" Isaure asked with curiosity.

"No, it's for Lucia."

"That's good, du Taillant . . ."

"Yes, but believe me, I can't do more." the poor fellow stammered.

"What is it?"

"Shoes."

"Well," said Isaure, "I hope this will finally calm her down. Go present your gift right away."

Du Taillant asked his friend to accompany him to the kitchen. He then held out the package to Lucia, saying uneasily:

"Here is a little gift for you, now don't cry."

Lucia started to tremble, unable to utter a single word. Then she began repeating:

"Oh! Mistuh du Taillant . . .Oh! Mistuh du Taillant. . ."

"Well! Open the package, girl," exclaimed Isaure, "you're not curious . . ."

"Oh! Yes, I'm curious . . ."

When she saw the shoes, her enthusiasm knew no bounds; she wept, but this time for joy. She would have liked to prostrate herself before du Taillant, kiss his feet, but Isaure reminded her that it was time to serve dinner. The menu was comprised of calalou, that Lucia made every Monday but had given special attention to on that Monday, a lovely red halved pear, crawfish in cooking salt, red fish, and couscouche. A chocolate sorbet finished off the meal. Lucia had put on her shoes which doubtlessly hurt her heels, for she had difficulty in walking. Isaure was afraid she would fall over while carrying the dishes. The negress's lips went from ear to ear as he smiled, revealing gleaming white teeth. From time to time, she stopped and contemplated poor du Taillant with glowing eyes. Isaure, who was becoming provoked by all these wiles, had to reprimand her and send her back to the kitchen. After the meal, they could hear her singing: "Ba moin un ti bo, deux ti bos, trois ti bos, doudou"[11] No doubt, she was dancing too.

"There's going to be a big dance at the Lido in honor of the *Emile Bertin,*" du Taillant announced. "Would you give me the honor and pleasure of going with me?"

Isaure's countenance clouded over.

"At the Lido? Impossible. You know they don't allow blacks."

"But you're not black, Isaure. You're hardly métisse, your skin is almost white. In a few years when you have earned millons with your bar, you'll have a house built high in Didier and you'll pass for a Creole.

Isaure shook her head. "I don't want to be insulted."

"You'll be with me, you'll have nothing to lose . . ."

"No," she said. "I won't go. I'm from this country and I know them. Those béké goyaves are terrible snobs and even you, white as you are, if you settled on this island, they wouldn't let you go to the Lido if you were a millionaire. But you're here for a short time, so they invite you as a spectator to admire their wealth."

She added:

"Furthermore, I detest them. They're just good for eating, drinking and making babies. Oh! They're good for that alright."

"There are a lot of millionaires in Martinique?"

"There are enough of them who have gotten rich on rum and sugar cane by exploiting blacks and by ruining the country." said Isaure with an angry shudder.

Suddenly, hearing a footstep on the outside flooring that was not Daniel's, she listened closely.

"Excuse me," she murmured to du Taillant.

At the door, she found her herself face to face with her brother, Gustave. He was a handsome fellow, tall and muscular under his gray shorts made out of a flour sack. His face ressembled Isaure's, but he was white. Under his bacoué[12] was a tuft of flaming red hair. His accent, on the other hand, was that of a black; in his hand he carried a Carib basket.

"Hey, Isaure," he said in his high voice. It was strange to hear this woman's voice coming from such a male body.

"What are you here for?" Isaure responded in a hard tone, "I told you not to set foot in my house."

"Oh! your béké's here and you don't want him to see your brother."

"Get out of here," yelled Isaure, stomping her foot. "I tell you: get out of here!"

"I ain't going," Gustave calmly responded and added: "I got something in this basket for you."

Knowing him, Isaure realized she would not get rid of him easily.

"Ok, Come in here!"

She pushed him into her son's room.

"Wait for me. I won't be long."

She joined du Taillant in the next room.

"Who is that man?" he asked, "A sailor?"

"No, he's just a fisherman who brought me some fish."

All the while, du Taillant was aware of his friend's annoy-ance and, always tactful, he took leave. Isaure made no effort to keep him. When the officer had gone, she returned to the room where her brother was waiting. Having put his basket on the floor, Gustave had seated himself unceremoniously, and was looking askance at the little boy playing in a corner of the room.

"Ok, now tell what brings you here."

"I brought you some fish. See, all that for you."

Indeed, the basket was filled with fish, but Isaure cast only a brief glance at it.

"You didn't come to me to give me fish," she said. "I know you."

"Well no, I confess. I know I can be frank with you. Here's why I came: I need 300,000 francs."

Isaure was in shock.

"300,000 francs? For what?"

"A good business deal. You'll see, you won't be sorry. I bring you back your money with interest."

Gustave had always been the most resourceful and the least honest in the family—the two things usually go together. He had chosen the fishing trade because it would be profitable and also allow him the freedom he couldn't do without. Since the war, fish, replacing meat and becoming more and more scarce, had risen in price. It was also becoming a black market. Gustave didn't need to replenish his fishing boat as before, for ten pounds sufficed to make a rewarding day, but knowing him, Isaure felt that he would continue filling his boat.

"I can't lend you 300,000 francs," she said. "I'm not in the black market and not rich like you."

"Not so. You more rich than me right now. I'm sure you could if you wanted."

"No," Isaure affirmed, "I'm only a woman and I make an honest living."

"With your filthy whites you make an honest living."

"That's right. They're a whole lot better than you, my filthy whites. I forbid you to talk like that in my house and if you try blackmail, I'm the one who'll turn you in."

"I'm not scared 'cause I ain't in the black market."

"You're as much a liar as a thief. If you're not in the black market, what are you doing? Why aren't you in the war? That's what you'd better be doing."

"I can't go to war. France lost the war."

"The whites are still in it. They're braver than you and not so lazy. If they are here, it's not because they like it; they would rather go home. They're in Martinique due to force of circumstances."

"What force of circumstance?"

"If I explain, you wouldn't understand because you don't want to understand. Get out of here. Beat it, you've no business here."

Gustave began to roll his eyes like a real darkie.

"Ah! Isaure, if you wasn't my sister, I'd kill you like a fly."

"It's not worth the trouble, I don't have any money."

"And your white guy, don't he have money? That's what they all say."

"He doesn't give me any and I don't ask for any. I earn my living myself by working."

"Then you more stupid than I thought. So why you sleep with him?"

"I didn't say I sleep with him, but that's not your business. I'm free to do what I want with my private life, no? You come to kill me, to steal my money . . . Get out of here, assassin, or I'll call the police . . ."

"That don't scare me. I know the chief . . ."

"I know him too. Let's go. Get the hell out of here, you scum, and take these sorry fish with you."

Trembling with anger, she had started to shout. The little boy began to cry: "Mama! Mama!" and threw himself on his mother's dress. Gustave gave him a look filled with disdain.

"So that's your little mulatto? They'll get him one day. Your white folks won't be here much longer in Martinique and then things'll be bad for your son."

With that threat, he left carrying his basket. In the kitchen, Lucia, washing dishes, was still singing every love song she knew. Isaure felt compelled to vent her anger.

"You're crazy girl," she said. "Don't think because Lieutenant du Taillant gave you shoes that things are going your way. You've nothing to hope for. Anyway, let me tell you one thing: Lieutenant du Taillant hasn't yet slept with a woman."

"Not yet?" exclaimed the black woman. So he's . . ."

"Yes, he's a virgin," Isaure turning away her eyes.

Oh! If she could have seen her servant! She, who stood with open mouth, eyes starting out of her head, as if the word virgin had kicked her in the stomach.

Finally, she said:

"Miss Isaure! Miss Isaure! . . ."

"What?"

"Mistuh du Taillant, not a man like regular men?

"Of course he's not like regular men. He's not a dog. He's engaged and he wants to remain faithful to his fiancee, that's all."

Lucia looked confused:

"He engaged"

"Yes, and his fiancee is in England."

"Oh, good!" Lucia replied.

Isaure didn't succeed in shattering this rapture, this hope. However, that conversation had appeased her; she thought no more about her brother. Besides, these set-tos with him were not meaningful, for she knew that, in spite of his threats and tough talk, Gustave had no intention of killing her or her son.

One day, Lucia asked permission to take du Taillant's laundry home in order to wash it after work, on her own time. Consent was easily granted. But the next morning, she sent little Napoleon to tell Isaure that she had suddenly taken ill and asked that someone come by to pick up the laundry at her house. Isaure, who suspected a ruse, went herself.

Lucia lived in a shack, with a tin roof and wobbly floors, in the hollow of Terres Sainville. To make two rooms out of one, she had strung a rope from one wall to the other, and had suspended the laundry there. She hung her clothes on bare nails and slept on some rags that, each morning, she piled in a corner. Cockroaches, a kind of huge red bug, flew about here and there. How surprised Isaure was upson discovering, smack in the middle of this wretched dwelling that she knew well, a bed, a real bed, not very modern, to be sure, but whose mahogany wood was so highly polished that it glistened like a mirror. In this throne-like bed, completely nude, except for a yellow scarf placed coquettishly on her head, awaited Lucia.

It was evident that she had performed a quimbois. It was, however, her "madam" and not du Taillant who had come. She made quite a picture, seated in her bed looking out with her frog-like eyes, not even a blanket to cover her! Isaure couldn't refrain from laughing aloud.

"You're crazy to buy that! Does a poor girl like you sleep in a bed?"

"It's for Mistuh du Taillant," confessed Lucia, unabashed. "Do you think the Lieutenant will come to a shack like yours where people can see in from outside everything that goes on because the walls are like lattice work? You want to be paid by navy officers, now?"

Lucia lowered her head without answering.

"Let's go, girl. Get dressed," Isaure continued. "I've had enough of this farce."

To the great relief of du Taillant, Lucia didn't go aboard the Mékong again. Henceforth, Isaure arranged to see the young officer away from her home, and judging it best to leave Lucia with her black lovers, said nothing more to du Taillant. Thus, all was for the better. A few weeks later, Lucia confessed that she had made love with an especially ardent black man, using the bed. But she accompanied her confidences with a deep sigh:

"If only it was Mistuh du Taillant . . ."

"What!" Isaure exclaimed, "You still love him?"

"Still do. I don't know what he did to me, that man. I'll always love him. Yes, he's the only one I love, Miss Isaure, and if he make love to me, one time, I be faithful to him for life. Tell him that, Miss Isaure, I beg you. I never sleep with any other, and most of all, not one of those dirty niggers who's like mean cats. Tell him, Miss Isaure, I beg you."

This time, Isaure decided it best to leave Lucia to her blacks, and said nothing more to du Taillant.

IV
Signs of Rebellion

The radio was playing softly as usual. Isaure was half listening to Mozart as she gazed vacantly at the newly painted walls where the humidity had already left streaks, then at the light colored wood tables and chairs where some officers, accompanied by Loulou Carney, had settled. She had known this woman for a long time but didn't much like her. The daughter of a well-off family, not rich enough to be béké but white enough to have legitimately married an officer on tour of duty, she was boisterous and always ready to make a night of it. Now, Isaure's bar, located in the back of a small courtyard near the Savane and the naval base, was a quiet corner having nothing in common with le Central or the Coq Hardi. Loulou was out of place in this one.

Isaure glanced out the window at the basin, encircled by cactus pots, dwarf fern and flowers, where the fountain ran continuously. At her place everything was well kept and clean, not a speck of dust to be seen. Then, her attention was brought back to the group of officers. Loulou's presence had not succeeded in raising their spirits. In vain, one of them narrated a recent trip of the *Emile Bertin* to Saintes Island where the girls are blond and freckled and where he had eaten iguanas—huge lizards with hideous faces and bloated bodies, whose sole defense was their ugliness, but which when roasted, tasted like young partridges. They were not listening. Soon the consation turned to what was really on their minds: the landing of the Americans in North Africa. Admiral Robert, they said, expected Martinique to be attacked. This wasn't the first time; a few months before, when mobilization had been decreed, Isaure and her sister had to close their bar and leave for the countryside. The Americans were even expected to bomb Fort-de-France, but then, nothing happened; there was only great panic, a big farce. But this time, things appeared more serious.

Suddenly, the door was opened and Sallière entered. Isaure shuddered. Black and shiny, short-legged, pot-bellied, obsequious and garrulous, Sallière was instinctively repulsive to her. All the same. she could not forbid such an influential and dangerous person to enter her bar; he ran the newspaper, "The Trumpet" and exercised great political influence, even though he had lived on the island for only a short time. He claimed to have come from Paris where he was born. "I'm a Parisian," this black guy liked to say. Meantime, Isaure had heard that he had been deported from Puerto-Rico or Jamaica after some dirty business, and so had come to spread his poison in Martinique. He lived by means of blackmail, routing out black marketeers or the fisherman who carried deserters to Saint-Lucia[13] and, under threats of denunciation, extorted huge amounts of money from them. He knew everything, had his pockets filled with evidence and always had witnesses. He even dared to engage in another kind of blackmail. If, for example, he had the good luck to take an officer with a rich creole lady by surprise, he quickly took a photograph (his camera always at hand) and, if the woman or officer gave him trouble before paying, he didn't hesitate to show the infamous picture in the window of his newspaper office, where there was always a crowd gathered, Martinicans being fond of scandal.

"I greet you, the very beautiful and gracious Isaure," he said bombastically.

Then, turning toward the officers:

"And I greet our valiant defenders."

Though neither they nor Isaure returned the greeting, he seemed not at all perturbed. After having seated himself casually on a bar stool, he ordered a "planter."

"Listening to the radio? I bring you the latest news from 'La Trompette.' The landing was successful, right? Fighting going on, but our troops aren't their match, right? Many Gaullist soldiers in Africa. Land army as usual, right? Already in '40, not real smart. Admiral Batet has just joined them. Things look bad, ha,ha, ha!"

He was laughing as if the delivery of this news pleased him. The officers were scowling. Isaure sensed that they were fuming at not being able to throw the black out with a swift kick in the behind, but neither could she.

"And here it's clearing for action, right? Landing at Saint-Lucia, right? Or at Saint-Anne[14], where they'd find enough deserters to help them over there, ha, ha, ha . . .!"

He was in fine humor. In response, the officers signaled Isaure that they wanted the bill for their drinks. She went over to their table, but Sallière kept on as if he saw nothing.

"Four dead last night, right? Not so bad. After all, if the Americans land, we'll see a real massacre, so, ha, ha, ha! All these dirty niggers would benefit. They all for de Gaulle, ain't that so? Now it's still not so serious. Personal stories, simple news items, right? Know how that happens? A sailor meets a black who takes him to a cafe on the pier. After two or three glasses of punch they begin to quarrel, right? 'Dirty nigger,' the sailor says, 'What the hell you doin' here? Why ain't you in the war?' 'And you,' retorts the black, furious 'You came here just to hide, didn't you? So now!' The next day, they meet again, okay? The sailor, who went back to his ship drunk, has forgot the fight the night before and greets his friend: 'You coming to have a drink?' 'Me,' says the black, who hasn't forgot—you know a black man never, never forgets— 'Me, come take a drink with you? So I ain't a dirty nigger no mo'? Now let's see, am I yo' dirty nigger or I ain't yo' dirty nigger?'

'Oh,' says the sailor aghast, 'If you don't come on, I'll bust you in the mouth.' Then the black starts to yell: he's the one who'll bust the white in the mouth and so forth and so on. They come to blows, right? They start to fight. But since this takes place in one of those cafes where there are lots of doudous[15], the ones who take sides with the sailor 'cause his kind's their best paying customers, they help him beat the black, falling on top of him, one trying to yell louder than the other, ha, ha, ha! This guy manages to get away, okay, and a few days later, they find the sailor's body in an alley, his throat cut and his face slashed by a razor."

Isaure nodded. Yes, all that was quite true, that's what had been going on in Fort-de-France for some time. What was it coming to, dear God?

The officers had paid, but, nonetheless, did not leave. Sallière glanced slyly in their direction.

"I tell you these things because I believe you're interested in them," he said. "Other sailors return to the ship with awful belly-aches, right? Some die. Well, it's just because a black man or woman put bamboo hair in his rum, ha, ha, ha! There's nothing like a bamboo hair. You can't see it but it's very effective; it's used a lot here. Classic way to have your mother-in-law or father-in-law disappear! The trouble is, whatever the conclusions at the inquest by the Department of Investigation in these brawls with the sailors, the Martinican judges in the law-courts always side with the blacks, right?"

This time, the officers got up. Sallière was making fun of them in front of Isaure and Loulou Carney. Not being able to make Sallière leave, they left the place to him, and Loulou followed. Sallière made a deep bow.

"Honored to have met you, sirs, very honored, I assure you." As soon as they were outside the bar, his tone changed:

"Bunch of dirty-dogs, gang of thieves," he shouted, raising a menacing fist, "You'll soon have finished playing the swashbuckler in our land. We're going to avenge centuries of oppression that you imposed upon us."

He looked over at the young woman and said in honeyed tones: "You agree, dear, that you have to get even with them, don't you, Isaure?"

To be addressed in this tone of familiarity by such a person was an insult for the métisse but she dared not put him out. Heaven knows what aspersions Sallière would cast upon her, on her bar? What was he trying to do? Make her talk? Convince her? There was no shortage of bars where he would have made a better impression.

"I know," he continued, "that you only keep their company to earn a living, right? Me too, I have to make concessions. We're in the same fix, ha, ha, ha . . ."

He found glee in being odious.

"By the way," he asked, "have you seen Lieutenant du Taillant today?"

"No."

"Yesterday, maybe?"

"No," she repeated, giving him a look awry, for he was already making her uneasy.

"You know what happened to him?"

"What happened to him?"

This time she wanted to know.

"They're holding him prisoner on board one of their boats."

"Why?"

"They accuse him of having an underground wireless and of having helped desertions. Did you know about that? "

"No," Isaure said, shuddering, "I didn't."

Was it possible that this timid boy was a hero? Until now, Isaure had been perfectly indifferent to politics. She didn't even want to differentiate between Gaullists and Petainists, sailors and soldiers; the rivalries of whites and blacks, creoles and mulattos sufficed for her. She deplored these quarrels; she would have liked for people of different colors to get along once and for all. Couldn't happiness be found on an island as beautiful as Martinique? Did they need to quarrel with one another, despite the sun, despite the sea, despite the dance, despite love? The news about du Taillant was upsetting her.

"Maybe they're going to shoot him," added Sallière spite-fully. "In any case, Isaure, you must wait to be summoned by the Military Intelligence Office."

Isaure was not summoned to Military Intelligence, but the following day, after closing time, Captain Bassat, examining magistrate for the Navy, lingered at the bar. Isaure knew him well but that did not prevent her from being nervous and having a twisted smile.

"I'd like a few words with you," he began.

"You want to speak with me about Lieutenant du Taillant," she said pointedly.

Captain Bassat seemed surprised.

"Yes, rightly so. But how did you know?"

"Sallière told me you're holding him prisoner."

"That guy meddles in everything that's not his business," growled the captain. "I'll speak to you frankly, Isaure," he resumed, looking her in the eyes. "Du Taillant has been denounced. He had an underground transmitter and aided five men in deserting. I know he comes here often and that he even went to your home."

"He only came once to my house, but it's true that I saw him a lot as a good friend, believe me, Captain."

"I have no doubt of that," with a slight smile that annoyed Isaure. "Besides, there's no problem about that. Did he ever speak to you about politics?"

"Never."

"Why did he see you so often?"

"Probably because he liked my planter-punch. He's not the only one."

"But he saw you outside this bar. You were often seen together."

"You had us followed?"

"I could have had you followed, but I didn't. But you didn't hide and you know folks in Fort-de-France don't hold their tongues. Believe me, Isaure, if I have one piece of advice to give you, it's for you to tell me word for word what he told you. It's for your good and his."

"Why for his? Are you torturing him? Are you going to shoot him?"

"We have no intention of killing him."

"What do you plan to do with him?"

"Nothing, for the time being. We're waiting for him to tell us where the wireless is."

"If he had a wireless, he would have spoken to me about it. He trusted me."

"I'm sure of that. That's why I'm questioning you."

"Oh!" exclaimed Isaure, tapping her foot angrily, "Don't you have anything else to do than busy yourself with this nonsense? Haven't you heard that fishermen are bringing supplies to the German submarines that chase the boats supposed to bring us goods? For some time we've been without oil, butter, flour, shoes and cloth. Wouldn't you do better to get more of those things for us, than to arrest a brave young man like Lieutenant du Taillant? The people are discontented, Captain, they're going to rebel one of these days. Feed them, if you want to stop these tales about spies, smuggling and desertion . . ."

V
The Woman from Trinidad

Du Taillant's arrest had upset Isaure. She no longer had news about him. When she asked the officers who frequented her bar about him, they fell silent, annoyed. Had they killed him? With her mixed-blood's imagination, she supposed the worst.

It was during this time that she amazed herself by spurning Daniel, turning him away whenever she could. Daniel was only interested in his business, and paid no attention to politics.

"I don't give a damn about politics," he would say, "The war in Europe has nothing to do with us."

Isaure was beginning to find him vulgar, selfish and discovering in him a number of weaknesses and a large dose of dishonor. He took part in the black market, of course, and made a lot of money, but when he tried to give Isaure jewelry, she refused. It wasn't right for Daniel to make money while du Taillant sat in the depths of a dungeon or perhaps, who knows . . She was unhappy, in anguish. No longer did she smile at her clients, the officers, whom she had to continue serving because, more than ever, she clung to her independence. Her lone consolation was her son, François, that beautiful little boy, lighter than her, so gay and affectionate. She was proud to attend to his development. In by-gone days, she would say to herself: I am going to earn a lot of money for him, and when he's a man, he'll be like a béké goyave, he'll live in a

195

fine house high in Didier. But she was no longer certain of having the same ideals. So many things had changed in Fort-de-France, so many things were changing everyday. At the same time, it was as if something were awakening in her own blood—she didn't know what—but she, herself, was being transformed. She felt that soon the life she had led up to then would no longer satisfy her. Words like revolution and liberation, that formerly had left her indifferent when she heard them voiced by blacks, stirred up in her echoes of the past and disturbed her. She, too, had some black blood and when one has black blood, one is black. She could no longer limit herself to serve only whites.

Of course, still quite often she could not keep from being on their side. In the very house where she lived, things were going on that repulsed her. The house had been sold to a Mme Ramon, recently arrived on the island. Where had she come from? Some said from Mexico, others from Brazil or even Argentina. In the proper way, Mme Ramon, a pretty woman, still young, elegantly dressed, had paid Isaure a visit. She wanted, or so she said, to know the tenants and was, she said, delighted to find such a pretty one. For her part, Isaure found her charming, for Mrs. Ramon knew how to speak and to seduce. She announced her intention to change the house to a hotel, since there were two empty apartments, but of course, Isaure could remain in the one she now occupied.

Isaure asked for nothing more. Obviously, she could not guess Mme Ramon's real plans. Shortly after the latter's visit, she could not help but notice that the house had altogether altered in character. Sailors and street women entered and left constantly, which excited Lucia and exasperated Isaure. While passing by the half-closed doors of two apartments from which Mme Ramon had the locks removed, she caught sight of some lewd goings-on. There was not a doubt this had become a house of ill-repute, "a brothel," said Daniel, and he blamed it on his girl friend as if it were her fault. By no means was this type of rebuke necessary for this lady to be deeply offended. Women of mixed-blood are much more sensitive than white women; they value their self-respect all the more, since it's more easily suspect.

So Isaure, both shocked and curious, filed a complaint with the chief of police. Then, one day, her eye flattened against the flimsy boards that separated her dressing room from the room next door, she was amazed (it's true they were making a lot of noise on that day). From what she could make out, two half-naked women were struggling to beat up a sailor, more than a little drunk, and were trying to steal his wallet. True, this had nothing to do with her, but she could not refrain from yelling and knocking on the wall, which frightened the two women. She was ashamed to be the same color as they were.

The complaint brought no results; that is to say, the police chief, after having come to inspect the premises, came to an agreement with Mrs. Ramon. Perhaps he would even sleep with her, for the profligacy of this fat man was well known. A few days after, Mrs. Ramon again visited Isaure. More elegant than the first time, she did not appear in the least embarrassed. She had succeeded in frequenting the officer's club where Isaure had never been able to gain admittance, and she was often seen at the Lido. At first, the métisse was quite distant, but there was no way to disagree with Mme Ramon, she took everything pleasantly. Soon, Isaure forgot what was going on in that house and was mindful only of the intelligence, the distinction and the charm of her glamorous visitor.

When she told Daniel about this recent visit, he became angry. In turn, Isaure became angry and there followed one their finest scenes. Oh, if she had been able to do without men, a long time ago, she would have broken with Daniel! Did she love him? Had she loved him? She no longer knew. All that she knew was that her body wanted to be dominated. Perhaps this had its origin in her ancestors, slaves chosen in Africa and imported to Martinique like stud-horses. Oh, she had someone to take after! Even that white grandmother she had known in her childhood, that old lady, so distinguished in appearance, who had died among blacks, lost, déclassée, that grandmother who would say: "In love, there are neither blacks nor whites," was she not also victim of her sensuality? An illegitimate child, Isaure had not known her father. Her half-brother, Gustave, in spite of his eunuch's voice, had an incalculable number of mistresses of all colors. Théodosie, one of her half sisters, had been expelled from the convent while she was in novitiate training because it was discovered that she was pregnant. When questioned, she claimed she had never been with a man, but she was unable to persuade the Mother Superior that she had become pregnant through the Holy Spirit.

After all, Isaure was perhaps the most virtuous in her family. She had received a Catholic education and at the time of her First Communion was a true believer, very pure, very much in love with the Holy Virgin. Around her neck she still wore a small cross. If she had grown away from religion, wasn't it, above all, the priest's fault? She recalled with horror what had happened in the sacristy of the little church in Sainte-Anne. She had gone to ask the parish priest to be kind enough to baptize her baby.

"A baby," the latter had exclaimed, "you have a baby already?"

"Yes, sir."

"How old are you?"

"Eighteen, sir."

"And you're not married?"

"No, sir."

The priest said that was very bad, but a second after, he had made movements that made Isaure sick with disgust. After having admonished her, did he, in turn, want to make a baby with her? Luckily, she had yelled for help and the priest fled. However, since her son had been born out-of-wedlock, he was able to be baptized only on a Thursday, the day reserved for little bastards. On that day the church bells did not toll and the baptism, instead of being a celebration, had been an harassment. So, Isaure had to renounce confession, since she was not getting married and could not give up making love. She attended church more and more rarely.

Late one afternoon, while she was alone busily mending, a woman burst into her apartment. She was tall, good-looking with a white face and flashing black eyes, oddly set apart. With a suitcase in one hand, right away she began a glib explanation of her actions in English, from which Isaure caught only the word "Trinidad." Seeing that she was not making herself understood, the woman started to repeat "chambre" (bedroom), as if it were the only French word she knew. As luck would have it, Daniel arrived upon the scene. Since he spoke a passable English, he was able to explain to the woman from Trinidad that she was in a private suite and that the room she wanted to rent must be on the upper floor. Amiably, he offered to interpret and left with her.

It was half an hour later when he returned, and after eating, he declared that he had a lot of invoices to put in order and was going to work until midnight. Isaure was not too surprised at that, for indeed, although Daniel had a number of faults, he was not lazy. Alone, she was not long in becoming bored. Through the open window, the fresh night air invaded the room; in the distance, the sea glistened under the moonlight. She felt restlessness mount in her limbs and, after reassuring herself that the little one was sleeping peacefully, she wrapped a scarf around her head and left.

Under a star-studded sky, she walked with quick and lithe steps. As she passed before the police station and the jail, she thought about du Taillant. The nearly full moon highlighted the house tops, but above all, she had to look where she stepped because ankles were easily twisted in the gutters where the water flowed. Then she walked by the City Hall, encircled by palm trees that gently shook their fine dust at the mercy of the wind. From the smell of turpentine coming from mango trees, she knew she was approaching the Office of Intelligence. It seemed to her that she could have let herself be guided by odors, not always pleasant, because Fort-de-France had no modern sanitation. In the yard of each house, a stinking latrine sat until the blacks deigned to come empty it, which they did only twice a week. At last, she crossed the City Plaza, then Tamarinier's Lane, and stopped in front of Daniel's apartment, which was level with a small street. A weak light filtered through the drawn jalousies which were opened outwardly.

"I'm going to give him a scare," she said to herself and assuming a grimace, she readied her most frightening cry as she abruptly drew one of the panels toward her. Then she stood mute with stupefaction. Leaning over the bed, perhaps about to pull back the covers, was the woman from Trinidad, clad only in lace trimmed panties, like those in Paris. Daniel was quite close to her, still half dressed, it's true. At the sound from the jalouise, the two turned around sharply and Isaure had time to notice the woman's naked breasts, full and firm. Her heart came into her mouth. She rushed to the door, shook it and tried to kick it in, but since that didn't work, she went back to the window, jumped through it and fell into the room.

The woman had already covered herself and Daniel came forward, very distraught, but self-controlled and armed with an explanation:

"There was no room at the hotel. I couldn't let this lady sleep in the street..."

"This lady? Let's say this whore!"

"I just wanted to help her."

"And no doubt to help her undress too, while she's wriggling her fanny?"

Angry, Isaure was splendid. Daniel could not help but admire her.

"I was coming back to your place," he said in a conciliatory tone, "to explain what went on."

"Fine goings-on! Don't you ever put your foot in my house, do you understand? I don't want to see you anymore."

She slapped him. Then, going toward the woman who had taken refuge behind the bed, she grabbed her by the hair, dragged her to the window and threw her in the street. Finally, she, herself, managed to make a somewhat dignified exit by the door. But, alone in the street, she started to run and ran so fast that her heart was beating as she leaped over the gutters like a nanny goat. This exercise did her good and when she reached home she was more breathless than indignant. She felt elated by a new consciousness: freedom!

VI
The Attack

The presence of the *Emile Bertin* in the harbor of Fort-de-France caused a considerable growth in the male population. What Isaure observed in the house where she lived was insignificant compared to what went on in the mean streets of the port. There, the doudous lived in a perpetual carnival. There were those having affairs with sailors who, having nothing to spend their money on, provided for them magnificently. In their humble homes, straw mattresses had been replaced by box-mattresses and sometimes even real chests of drawers with mirrors, made by Lévitan, were to be seen.

The more involved women had broken off with their black husbands or lovers, and these men without women, furious at being deprived, went and joined the rabble that hung out by the cafes. Armed with razors that they handled skillfully, they stayed on the lookout for the departing sailors, followed them and with a nimble-fingered gesture, cut the back pocket holding the wallet. At times, the razor took a bite out of the hind parts and blood ran, but the sailor was too drunk to feel much.

Other women, however, didn't find it absolutely necessary to get rid of their husband or lover. All that was needed was to keep the place for the white from five in the evening to six in the morning, while he was off duty. And so, one day a week, when the sailor was on ship duty, the black had his night. If, as ill-luck would have it, the sailor arrived unexpectedly and found the black, naturally, he would be angry. But the doudou, playing innocent, would swear that the other man was her cousin who had just come from the country and had no place to stay, and so forth and so on. Sometimes the sailor went so far as to pay for the lodging of the so-called cousin who lost no time in taking advantage of everything. But if he were found a second time, things took a serious turn.

As a matter of fact, it was becoming dangerous to get around alone at night in the badly lit streets of Fort-de-France. Isaure had to learn that at her own expense.

Having gone past the legal time for closing the bar due to an influx of customers, having broken up with Daniel, and wanting to take her mind off him at any cost, she was walking home about two in the morning. The sky was black. It had just rained and noisy rats were wallowing in the muddy sewers; huge storm clouds covered the moon. Just as she came to the door of her house, she felt a violent blow between the eyes. She fell to the edge of the sidewalk, but before losing consciousness, she had time to hear a woman's cry and to notice a tall black man fleeing as fast as his legs could take him.

When she came to, she found herself at a neighbor's house, a nice woman but very talkative, who explained to her at length that if, by good fortune, she had not witnessed the incident and had not given fright by shouting to that riff-raff darkie, perhaps Isaure might be dead at that very hour. The young métisse felt very weak; wet cloths covered her face which was bleeding profusely. Her first thought was: don't let me be disfigured! The doctor reassured her: the black and blue spots would soon disappear; her nose was broken, but high enough that it wouldn't be too visible. All in all, she wouldn't come off so badly. She wondered just who had committed this terrible act. For sure, the hoodlum who had been seen in flight was only a flunky. For a relatively modest sum, men who hung around the port were quite ready to do all kinds of things.

The next day, the chief of police, as always, accompanied

by his dog, paid her a visit. She couldn't bear this huge man, ever since she had been witness to the following incident.

One evening about six, she was taking a walk on the Savane. Women, mostly from the respectable community, were seated on the benches, which at night were sometimes used as beds by the lepers when the asylum refused to give them shelter. This did not prevent the ladies from sitting comfortably on the benches while they complained: their husbands came home late or even not at all; they couldn't find maids, some of them were asking for two to three francs a month, others (who were satisfied with sensible wages) were truly too lazy. This chit-chat infuriated Isaure because she knew how those békés-goyaves treated their black servants, most often giving them hardly enough to live on.

On the pathways, groups of young girls leaving the convent or the boarding school were taking their daily walk. They favored the middle path where stood the monument to the dead of the Great War and which was dimly lit. There they met boys they knew and looked inquisitively at the newcomers. All this would end up with marriages or grief.

There were also some prostitutes, but the Savane was so poorly lit that they were hardly distinguishable from the nice ladies. On account of diseases that had broken out since the war, Admiral Robert had made them carry identity cards. As it happened, Isaure had just crossed in front of a group of women in the company of some sailors. She heard one of the women exclaim: 'There's the chief!' 'Oh no!' answered another, 'It ain't even six, not his time.' 'You wrong, ain't the chief, must be the big officer from the *Bertin.*' 'It's him, I swear. I saw his cap and his face.' 'He got his dog?' 'No, but he got his whip.'

The two women, leaving the sailors, began to run. In their state of crazed terror, they scaled the benches, jostling the people who were seated there. Children started following them, all in fun, shouting, but theirs was a quite different race, joyous and unafraid.

The chief had whistled for his dog and set it out to track

the two unfortunate girls. They tried to cut across a hedge of purple flowers with thorny stems, but the smallest one fell, having caught her dress in the thorns, and the dog ended by tearing the ill-fated dress bought at the Syrian's stalls.

The chief, waving his whip, arrived there double-quick.

"Chief, I won't do that no more." cried the wretched woman whose torn dress was splotched with blood.

"Shut up, you whore!" roared the huge man and he set the dog out for the one who was still running.

"Stop, or I'll shoot!" he howled.

Indeed, a bang sounded. He had shot his pistol into the air. The woman, terrified, stopped. The dog had caught her and led her to the police chief.

"We got our cards," the two women were yelling. "Have mercy, Chief, sir!"

But this man refused to see anything. Enraged, he had let his cigar fall, and, as if he held them responsible for that, he let loose a flood of curse words while lashing them severely with his whip until they were on the ground. Then, he made them get up, kicking them so as to whip them once more. At last, dishevelled, bloody, howling, they were allowed to scuttle off toward the Démosthène Bridge neighborhood.

To be sure, such incidents were protested, above all by the indigenous population. They must think they are in Venezuela, the people said, blacks from the Antilles wouldn't put up for long with these American customs.

They were going to make him understand this. One day, when the chief went strolling without his dog, a gang of Martinican men who were skilled in throwing stones had their fun by scaring him. On the third hit, his cap flew off. The blacks rushed upon the big man, grabbed his arms and legs, and midst bursts of laughter, threw him to the ground several times. Without his dog, the chief was not very brave, and he left that gang with head hung low.

When the chief came to her house to conduct his investigation, Isaure had had time to reflect.

205

"I remember," she said, "that guy Blanchard, who I treated like a dirty nigger, didn't think I had been punished enough. He left the courtroom swearing to get even. He must be the one."

"Have you seen him again?"

"Ah! he never came back to my bar, I assure you, sir. But I have passed him on the street and he doesn't speak any more."

The blacks rejected her for being in sympathy with the whites, at the very time she was beginning to be disgusted with those people. Would she always be alone, neither black nor white, hated by one, despised by the other?

She had seen Daniel only once. He had managed to get into her house, but she had put him out and had sworn that it was over between them. So, now it was not with him she was going to seek solace! To commemorate the break-up, she had burned Daniel's photograph and had replaced it in her bedroom with one of Emmanuel, François' father, which she had kept in the bottom of a drawer.

Isaure had decided to stay away from her bar as long as she had a bandage on her nose. Her sister, at times with Lucia's help, took her place. She did not even leave the house, but she was not bored, for she enjoyed being alone with her son, playing with him and making him work a little. François was learning to read and write. More than anything, he liked for his mother to tell him stories. Isaure remembered those she had listened to during her childhood: some must have come from France, others from America and others from the Caribbean. The latter were filled with tales of *moun-mos*, the souls of the dead. Several races, several religions were mingled in them, like the songs sung to her by her black mother and those that her white grandmother had taught her. All of this gave birth to a magic spectacle, like the mixture of races that had created this new race to which she belonged, because, all things considered, it was stupid to identify only two races: black and white.

Then, she had a visit that gave her the greatest joy—Pascal's. Some years ago, she had been in school with him in Saint-

Anne, but life itself had separated them. Pascal belonged to one of those poor white families set on the level with blacks. His brother had become a fisherman like the father, but he, by dint of hard work and intelligence, had succeeded in becoming educated. He ended up by being named overseer on a sugar cane plantation in Basse-Pointe[16] and had successfully settled in a good job. Pascal, in truth, was not handsome, but he had an open and energetic countenance. He hugged Isaure warmly as she, unconsciously, brought her hand to her nose.

"Oh, Pascal," she said, "you should have waited until this ugly thing in the middle of my face had gone away. I'm embarrassed to come before a man like this."

"Am I a man in your eyes?"

They laughed together like children, after which Isaure no longer felt bothered.

"Why didn't you come to see me sooner?" she asked. "Haven't you been at Basse-Pointe almost two years?"

"Almost, not quite. I didn't want to see you while you were . . ."

"With Daniel? You know, I left him . . ."

"Yes, I know . . ."

"And I'm sorry I ever knew him. But why didn't you come to my bar? We could have talked . . ."

"I don't like bars. I don't like officers," said Pascal.

They laughed again.

"Yes, I know," said Isaure, "You only like poor blacks. Well, your poor blacks, I call them 'dirty niggers.' See what they did to me?"

She pointed to the bandage covering her nose, no longer ashamed of it. In Pascal's presence, she no longer felt ashamed of anything. Never had she been so much at ease.

"If you hadn't treated them like dirty niggers, they wouldn't have done that dirty trick. You know how sensitive they are . . ."

"I'm a dirty negress too . . ."

"Let's talk about something else. Do you mind?"

They talked about many other things and Pascal stayed for dinner.

VII
The First Dance

After Pascal left, Isaure gazed at Emmanuel's photograph for a long time. Had she loved him? She had met him at her first dance; he had won her as a young girl and had abandoned her as a mother. He was a béké goyave and, for fear that he would be tempted to marry a métisse, his family, seizing upon the first pretext to keep him at a distance from her, had sent him to China. When he returned, he married a creole. This caused Isaure deep sorrow and, perhaps it was for spite that she then had submitted to Daniel's insistence, who, after all, was a French béké. Ah! What memories she had of that dance where she had met Emmanuel! She was sixteen then and, having lost her mother a year before, was earning her own living, such as it was, working in a chocolate factory in Fort-de-France. Her boss, a big, homely man but who was rich and kind, had arranged this dance at his home for all of his workers. With her sister's help, she made lengthy preparations. She wore the dress that she had dyed black after her mother's death, since she had no other; on those evenings when she washed and ironed it, she had to stay inside in her nightgown. She was still in mourning and could not display gold jewelry, and for that reason she covered her gold earrings with black cloth, but three silver bracelets brought out the soft brown flesh of her arms. She had carefully dressed her hair, through which the henna reflected reddish lights.

208

Not only did she redden her lips but she also highlighted her cheekbones with a bit of pink, which she thought made her color not so dark. But that was all, for she would not go to extremes like those disgustingly made-up negresses that were seen in the cafes. She didn't use eye make-up because her eyes had no need to be enlarged; men had always told her she had beautiful eyes. She had been one of the first at the meeting place on the Savane, where two trucks for the workers and a taxi for the musicians were waiting. The latter were resplendent in their well starched white pants and their red, blue and green bow-ties, vivid against their white shirts.

At last they loaded, the trucks started to move and soon entered a narrow and populous street. On each side, there were wooden shacks, wretched, covered with sheet iron or even tin cans. The people strolling in the middle of the street scarcely moved aside in this Terres Sainville district, and the drivers had to sound their horns constantly. Then they went onto a road lined on one side with flamboyant trees and on the other by a waterway giving off a nauseating smell. After having crossed a field teeming with bamboos, the trucks stopped in front of a house that looked like a chateau. This was Mr. Vidal's estate, the owner of the chocolate factory. Isaure had often heard about it, but she had imagined nothing so beautiful.

The taxi had arrived and the musicians had lost no time, because already could be heard the sounds of their instruments. In good spirits, everyone jumped to the ground from the trucks and rushed into the house. Isaure stopped on the threshold of the ballroom. The light, the bustle, the dressed-up people, the music, all of that together was too wonderful, too heady. But what caused her the most astonishment was the floor. She had not lived for long in Fort-de-France and hardly ever went out, and in her country town she had never seen the like. It shone like crystal-clear water, dazzling and formidable.

Gingerly, she put one foot forward, then withdrew it. The

pretty shoes that her sister had lent her were hurting, and it was due to them that she already had trouble standing up, so . . . Nonetheless, such desire to dash out like the others, to glide lightly, to float above that smooth sky-like floor . . .

Some of the people, unafraid, were entering. They jostled her, even pushed her in passing because she was obstructing the entrance. Through their laughter and noisy bustling, they heightened her timidity. This was so stupid! She had so looked forward to this dance . . . She was not going to leave, not with those shoes that were pinching . . . However, her silly heart was about to burst and kept her from moving forward. She remained immobile, eyes lowered, fixed on the shiny ground. It seemed to her that it must be as difficult to manoeuver out there as to skate, the way she had seen in a newsreel film.

Once again, she put one foot forward and withdrew it as if, already, she had slipped. She glanced around her anxiously. The big room where mirrors sparkled was filled with people. Dresses, hair, and complexions, themselves, were of every color. Never had Isaure seen such a mixture of races and classes.

After a while, Mr. Vidal noticed her and came toward her. Very red-faced, he walked with his legs somewhat wide apart due to his big belly.

"What are you doing here, Isaure," he exclaimed. "Why are you still in the doorway? Don't you see you're blocking the way?"

Isaure gave a ghost of a smile and threw out her arms in a desperate gesture.

"Are you afraid?"

Quickly, the young girl nodded yes.

"What are you afraid of? You're not a baby any more. Aren't you sixteen? Come on, let's dance!"

Before she could answer, there she was on that awesome floor. The huge man had grabbed her back and she placed her arms on his wide shoulders and lightly clasped her fingers behind the thick nape of his neck. It was in this manner, she knew, one should hold on. The orchestra was playing a beguine. Mr. Vidal was puffing, fidgeting and throwing himself about. His sweaty head, crimson, framed by Isaure's arms, looked as if it were cut off. The young girl following him, after a fashion, was held at bay by his protruding stomach. She had regained her confidence. After all, the floor wasn't so terrible; dancing on it was easier than on hard ground. How clever these whites are! Then she felt proud of having been sought out by her boss.

When the dance ended, she thanked him with a gracious nod. He took out a huge handkerchief from his pocket and wiped his forehead. He seemed to be worn out.

"Shall we go for refreshments?" he proposed.

He led Isaure to the buffet. In her town, every now and then she had attended political banquets given by the mayor, but she had never seen such abundance. Whole hens, turkeys, and ducks spread out on platters midst mounds of sandwiches, cold meats, little cakes and sweets of every kind.

"Help yourself, girlie . . ." Mr. Vidal kept saying.

Isaure stood confounded, not knowing how to choose. He served her iced champagne and laughed when she grimaced.

"You don't think it's good?"

"Oh, yes, it's good," she said politely.

"Eat, drink," he said once more.

He must be tired of me, thought Isaure, my timidity makes me look stupid. Suddenly, Mr. Vidal turned around.

"Say, there's my nephew. Come here Emmanuel, so I can introduce you to Isaure. But you know her already, I believe, it's not my place to introduce you to the pretty girls of Fort-de-France, huh? Well, have a good time, children!"

Emmanuel offered the young girl another glass of iced champagne, then he asked her to dance. Isaure always answered yes, for her mother had taught her that a woman ought to obey men and, above all, to be polite to white men. However, she wasn't long in feeling something other than respect for Emmanuel. He was white and even blond, with blue eyes,

211

and he danced well and laughed while paying lovely compliments to Isaure. From time to time, he abruptly pulled her to him, crushing her breasts against his manly chest. This was very nice. When the dance was over, he shouted: "More, more!" and Isaure clapped her hands, shouting too. They began dancing again. She had a natural rhythm and her body was shaken like an object floating on the clashing waves of a small creek. She responded to her partners movements and he guided her skillfully. Gestures took the place of words impossible to utter.

Then, Isaure was asked to dance by a young black, Pitate, who worked with her at the chocolate factory. She dared not refuse, but she felt ashamed to dance with him, all the more because he was inebriated from the alcohol he had drunk. He spoke patois, while dancing more and more intensely, faster and faster.

"Vini ti tac."

"Mettez a dans, mettez baille."

And each one of these strange verses ended with "Pan!" while he raised his leg and, indecently, gave her a nudge with his lower abdomen, bursting out with a savage laugh. Isaure felt Emmanuel's eyes fastened on her and her body no longer responded. He was growing taut before these movements that imitated copulation. However, she was not long in being overtaken by the rhythm and perhaps the fervor of Pitate; no longer did she think of him or Emmanuel. She was dancing.

When Emmanuel came to wrest her from the arms of the black, she looked at him, surprised, but said nothing. He left her no more. They drank, they danced, they laughed. He crushed her in his arms. She was proud to be with him and she liked him better than Pitate, but she had to admit that he didn't know how to dance the beguine like a black. She told him so, but confronted by Emmanuel's air of vexation, she added sincerely:

"It doesn't matter."

About one in the morning, the excitement was at its height.

A circle had formed around two colored men. Crouched, facing each other, advancing, withdrawing, half laughing, half threatening, constantly shouting in their guttural voices, they were trying to seize each other, all the while dancing. At last, one of them managed to grab hold of the thigh of the other, who, lamentably, hopping along, had to declare himself beaten.

Then, suddenly, the exhilaration quieted like the wind after a stormy night. In the corners, there were men and women who had drunk too much, eaten too much, dozing, squatting, heads on their knees. It was three in the morning when Mr. Vidal clapped his hands and announced loudly that the dance was over. Then, there was a rush toward the buffet, which in spite of numerous forays, was still quite well stocked. Mr. Vidal, laughing, encouraged the pillagers.

"Help yourselves," he said repeatedly. "All that is yours."

Isaure, who thanks to the champagne and dancing had lost all timidity, was successful in her struggle to get hold of two whole turkeys and as many cakes as she could carry.

The truck brought her home. As soon as she had pushed open the front door, she took off her shoes and stockings. Cautiously, on the tips of her bare feet, she mounted the wooden staircase. She couldn't keep it from creaking, which really upset her, because she had a horror of disturbing people. Sometimes, on Sundays, she and her sister stayed so quiet that the neighbors, believing them absent, would take the opportunity to talk about them. They could be heard through the thin floor partitions.

"I wonder," old Anna would say, "If those girls are still good . . ."

The two sisters would listen, stifling their laughter. In vain, another old lady expressed her doubts without the least proof. What would she say tomorrow, or rather today, if she heard Isaure return home so late, or rather so early?

Above all, Isaure didn't want to wake up her sister. She had made her plan. She would quickly undress; for once, she

213

wouldn't wash up; she would slip quietly into the double bed and go to sleep, turning her back to Ophelia. But she had not half opened the door when that girl was already raising her head. Isuare saw the surprise spread across her sister's face, who, no doubt, had just noticed the turkeys. Ophelia, however, promptly erased that expression from her face and, bounding out of bed, she snatched the shoes from Isaure's hands and started to examine them as if she had eyes only for them.

Those high-heeled gilded dance shoes represented her pride and luxury. For several months, she had worked in one of the big restaurants in the city and, thanks to the tips she received, she earned more than Isaure and had been able to buy them with her first savings. For a long time, she had noticed them in Honorato's window and they had become the topic of interminable conversations between the two sisters. At last, one day, the most eventful day in her life, she had bought them. She put them on for one whole evening during which she didn't take her eyes off them. Then, she put them on to go to mass. Ultimately, it became necessary, with other savings made on food (for the sisters were accustomed to hunger pangs at the end of the month), to go to the movies and buy reserve seats worthy of the shoes.

It should be said that, in Martinique, people are judged by their feet rather than their heads, so almost everyone owns at least one pair of shoes. Those shoes, which during the week remain hung above their beds, are worn by the peasants on Sunday, who carry them around their necks and put them on at the church entrance. Those feet are not comfortable in shoes and it's quite amusing to see those duck walks! But one must honor our Lord Jesus-Christ and the Holy Virgin, Mary. One must also show that one has what it takes to pay for shoes because churches are places of idle gossip.

Perhaps it was under such an impulse that one Sunday while Ophelia was still sleeping, Isaure had taken the precious shoes to go to mass. Ah! She remembered that day! She had hardly settled on her kneeler when Ophelia appeared, eyes gleaming and teeth clenched. Without a word, chest heaving, her sister had walked with jerky steps straight to her, and in two indignant gestures snatched her shoes.

All heads turned, and Isaure, who felt the smiles light on her like burns, was ashamed to the roots of her hair. She remained barefoot, kneeling, eyes lowered, anguished, wondering how she was going to leave. Luckily, Ophelia had not uttered a word. She had to make a majestic exit, shoes in hand and well in view, so that everyone knew that they belonged to her.

Isaure had struggled to stay to the end of the service. Of course, she had not escaped some teasing. All the same, she did not hold a grudge against her sister for that public humiliation and she had been all the more touched when, that evening, Ophelia, for her part, had offered to lend her the shoes for the dance.

So finally, Ophelia lifted her head and smiled. The shoes didn't have one scratch, even a grain of dust. They were exactly the same as the evening before.

"Well," she said, pointing to the turkeys and other food that Isaure had put on the table, "where did you steal all that?"

This was their way of speaking. In talking to her sister, Ophelia even adopted a guttural voice that Martinicans use when speaking the local patois, which is in contrast to the soft, sing-song inflections that they reserve for foreigners.

Isaure stretched and yawned.

"I'm sleepy . . ."

Already, she was undressing. Carefully, she hung her black dress on a rope. Ah! she knew the price of things in those times!

VIII
Sainte-Anne

Isaure had returned to work, no longer wearing the bandages on her nose and face, all traces of the attack having disappeared. So, as before, she went to her bar every other evening. The work, however, had become drudgery; she no longer smiled at the officers and gladly raised the price of drinks. In short, she was working only to earn money.

One evening, a strange thing happened to her. As customary, she had remained after closing to straighten up the place. Just as she was locking the door, a man who seemed to have waited for her in the street came toward her. He had the bulk and gait of a sailor, although he was in civilian dress. At first, Isaure recoiled. Was this a trap? Was this man going to strike her again, kill her?

Without hesitating, he said:

"I'm here on behalf of Lieutenant du Taillant."

"Lieutenant du Taillant?" she repeated.

"He gave me this for you."

"Have you seen him?" asked Isaure, taking the letter mechanically. She felt stupid.

"I was under orders to take him food. Good-bye."

Isaure ran after him.

"How is he? Have they hurt him?"

"He's ok," the man answered tersely.

Then he went off into the night.

Isaure opened the envelope that had just been placed in her hands. It held another envelope and a small piece of paper, but the streets were too poorly lighted for her to read, so she ran all the way home.

A few words were scribbled on the paper: "I'm asking you to deliver the enclosed envelope as fast as possible to your brother. I'm depending on you." No address, no signature and not a friendly word. It was certainly du Taillant's handwriting, but Isaure wondered, at first, if he had really planned to appeal to her. When all was said and done, this was a special mission, nothing more, nothing less. And what did du Taillant have to do with Gustave? The fact that these two men knew each other and, without a doubt, were accomplices, to her was rather unsavory.

She slept badly. In the morning, she gave Pascal a call, asking him to come by immediately. When the young man came to lunch, as promised, she told him exactly what had just happened to her. This was not indiscreet, for she knew Pascal was incapable of betrayal, no matter what. Moreover, he seemed to be rather lighthearted, amused.

"Ok," he said. "This paper has to be taken to Gustave."

"But he's in Saint-Anne. Can't I send it by mail?"

"That above all, no."

Suddenly, Pascal looked at her oddly.

"I'll go with you and we'll go together in my car. Tomorrow's Friday, so I can be away until Monday. How about you?"

"I'll make arrangements with my sister. Ophelia's nice," Isaure replied.

And so, she was to leave the next day on a trip with Pascal! She would see Sainte-Anne where they both had spent their childhood. She was excited all day long; repacked her suitcase three times, tried on all her dresses and remembered to take her swim suit. No longer was she thinking about du Taillant.

It was six in the morning when Pascal drove up in front of her door. He had bought some food and seemed to be jovial and in a hurry.

"But I haven't taken a shower yet." she cried.

"Just for once . . ."

"Oh, no!" she exclaimed. "Wait there. I'll be quick . . ."

For nothing in the world would she have given up her shower. Nimble as a cat, she leaped to the foot of the stairway and was, indeed, in the backyard standing before the big tub of clear running water. She filled a pan and emptied it over her body. That cool, fresh water in the early morning hours made her shiver delightfully and gave her skin a bronze patina.

"Does the water feel good?" shouted Pascal.

"Fine. Come join me . . ."

"No, hurry up, Isaure. I want to be in Sainte-Anne before noon. Don't you feel like eating a good blafe[17]?"

"Take it easy. We'll be in Sainte-Anne to eat your blafe. I'd like some too, along with the fish you'll catch at the Table du Diable. Oh, how good that'll be!"

"At any rate, I won't have time to fish before lunch," Pascal replied with a laugh.

But in the course of the conversation, Isaure had dressed and fixed her hair. She was now before him, dressed in navy blue slacks and a white sports blouse bought at the Syrian's black market.

"We go," she said, purposely using an expression from their childhood. She sat down beside Pascal in the open car and they took off at once.

Near Démosthène Bridge, they came upon huge cars, called taxis, that served the southern coast. On their side panels wide strips of unbleached muslin indicated their destinations: Diamant, Saint-Luce, Marin, Rivière-Salée, Petit-Bourg, Lamentin. The sharp turns made the baskets of vegetables fastened to the roofs dance, and threw the men and women seated inside one against the other.

"I believe God is seated in those taxis," Isaure commented, "But I wouldn't take one without first going to confession."

Pascal was going fast, but he knew each turn. He could have

rolled along with eyes closed. After quickly driving through the section of Sainte-Thérèse where the odors of drainage mingled with the scent of flowers and fruits, he pointed out the Dillon factory. Once in the countryside, they crossed over a small hill, on the other side of which, dozed the plains of Lamentin, cane fields dancing under the wind. Pascal explained to Isaure why certain ones lay fallow.

"They are resting in order to be grown next year."

"It's marvelous," said Isaure. "I'd like to stop here and stay all my life."

On another hill was outlined the silhouette of a chateau.

"It belongs to an old béké," said Isaure.

"Do you know him?"

"No, but they say he was very rich. He had a lot of children on the island and endowed all before dying. They say he had a pact with the devil."

"I don't believe with the devil," replied Pascal. "If it was as easy as that, everybody would have his castle. I rather think that he did good business by placing his money in foreign banks."

At the banks of the Lézarde River, they were forced to stop. A severe rain must have fallen in the mountains and the river had overflowed. Mangoustes and all kinds of little animals were floating on the water. Barges were already ensuring a crossing to pedestrians, who, in order to board them, had to wallow a bit. Men rolled up their pant legs and women folded back their dresses, all of that done in high spirits, with outbursts of laughter. Finally, the heavy clouds covering the sky dispersed and a radiant sun warmed the fields. Little by little, the water disappeared in the cane fields and Pascal was able to start his car again and pass by the river.

They climbed the hill where the town of Ducos was perched. A narrow sidewalk edged the small wood houses with tin roofs. Oxen, dragging carts of cane, were headed for Petit-Bourg. In the distant green fields, an engine was pulling a dozen wagons filled with sugar cane, and from time to time its whistle tore through the serene ambiance.

It was about eleven when they reached Sainte-Anne. The fishermen had already returned, but on the beach there were still many women waiting the arrival of the boats from Sainte-Lucie and Rivière-Pilote that would bring them vegetables, manioc flour and bread-fruits.

The market was located at the church entrance, so conveniently that the housewives—all the while dickering over a penny—could hear mass. To avoid this haggling, Admiral Robert had tried to impose fees on the vendors. The police intervened once, but since there was nothing at all in the market place the following week, the mayor had decided to close his eyes to it.

Gustave had moved and was now living in one of the finest houses in Sainte-Anne, just outside the town. He greeted his sister and Pascal very pleasantly. Pascal accepted the drink made with tafia[18] and absinthe leaves soaked in white rum for several days; Isaure preferred good green coconut juice. She gave du Taillant's message to her brother, which he read at once but showed no surprise and made no comment. Then, he led his guests to a large table, laden with big pots of babaroise[19] and splendid dishes of fried cod, bread snacks, blood sausage and lamb covered with a layer of onions and spices. Other plates held bananas and pilibos. All these foods emitted odors that recalled Pascal's and Isaure's childhood. Nothing like this existed in Fort-de-France.

"You came at the right time," said Gustave. "You lucky to find me. I'm leaving early tomorrow morning on the sailboat, but the house is yours."

"Where are you going?" Isaure asked.

"That's my secret . . ." he answered, smiling.

Evidently, Gustave took only Gaullists across. Perhaps he even used this as a pretext to hide a more lucrative traffic. In spite of everything, even though she readily touted a disdain for money, so much wealth impressed Isaure and even prompted respect. "You don't fish anymore?" asked Pascal.

"I don't have much time."

"Can you lend us the fishing boat tomorrow?"

"Sure, make yourselves at home," Gustave said graciously.

In the afternoon, he had a chance to have a conversation with his sister.

"I'm glad you're with Pascal. He's a nice guy."

"I'm not with him, he just drove me here."

"He's a nice guy, " Gustave repeated. "He's the only béké goyave who is ok."

Toward five in the evening, Pascal and Isaure went down to the beach where a noisy crowd awaited the fishermen's return. Their appearance caused a stir as cries and greetings arose from all around.

"Isaure! How you are, dearie?"

The women admired her dress. The men talked congenially with Pascal, pleased to see him again. But already, rectangular sails had appeared on the horizon and soon the boats were there. Motor boats were waiting to take the fresh fish to Fort-de-France.

They climbed back to the town square and walked along, chatting under the double row of magnificent trees. Then, they admired the view: to the right, beyond the beach that led to Pointe[20] Marin, they saw the black, solid mountain mass ending with the Pointe Borgnesse; behind this cape stretched the entire southern coast, which from Sainte-Luce to Pointe du Diamond strung out from point to point, each one a more delicate grey; above stretched the crest of hills, dominated by Morne Constant; still more to the left, detached from the coast, the huge Rocher Fidèle. The sea, in changing hues of pink, was glimmering underneath clouds floating gently in the evening sky.

On the front steps of the city hall, the town clerk, bloated with fat and importance, taunted his enemy, the priest, whose church was next door, by lolling about in pajamas. Nothing had changed since Isaure's departure, everything was still the same as in her childhood. The war itself had in no way modified the ways of the people of Saint-Anne. Their little grudges, their minute hatreds remained intact.

"Let's go to Yvonne's," Pascal suggested.

He was already crossing the square; Isaure followed. They went into a narrow street that separated the city hall from the church. There were still the same stones that had torn their feet as children. Perhaps, it was due to these stones that Isaure began to hum a tune of yesteryear, a song that her heart cradled like a mama cradles her child. She saw the young Pascal, holding a linen headband in his hand that was used by all the girls.

Vonvon jetez, jetez li d'iè moin ché gadez
Vonvon qui ka fait la belle ba moin, ché.

In the clear night air, laughter mounted with the songs. Ah! she loved that! But she was no longer a little girl, she was a woman. Heavens, how life, how Daniel, had transformed her! Now, she told herself, I want to think only of Pascal; he's the one near me now, and I don't want those other memories anymore.

At last, they entered a frame house with two rooms and a porch. Yvonne, a negress, still good-looking at forty, welcomed them with joyful shouts. One of the rooms was a cafe where several fishermen, seated at tables and facing their rum punch drinks, were boasting about their feats. Yvonne, who was very religious, first showed them the new statuettes of saints bought during the numerous pilgrimages she had undertaken. In a bowl set before the Holy Virgin, a small flame was quivering.

"But you ain't seen everything, my children. I got a room that looks out on the courtyard. Oh! how sorry I am not to show you that room, but it's locked. A sailor papered it for me and I now have running water."

"I'm not surprised," Isaure said laughingly, "that the mayor has given you running water. They told me, my dear Yvonne, that you have become his right arm and you help him to marry people."

"Of course. I'd like to marry you two off."

"We didn't come to Sainte-Anne for that. We came to these parts to see my brother."

Mme Yvonne began to roll her eyes tragically.

"Ah! Isaure, you do well to come to him. That boy's lost."

"Lost?"

"Yes, lost. The devil's in him. He's baptized . . ."

"I don't understand. He's lost because he's baptized?"

"Oh child, no doubt his godfather didn't do a good job of praying for him."

"Baptized or not," said Isaure testily, "the devil can't do anything. If a pig doesn't eat bananas, is it his master's fault?"

"Oh, child, the city ruined you."

"I remember the story of two people, who I won't name: one was a church cockroach, the other never went to church— he preferred going to the churchyard. Well, he was the one who lived best and had the best life."

Pascal was smiling as he listened. He knew that Isaure had her view on priests and that all the explanations he might have given her would change nothing.

Mme Yvonne held the métisse's hands and squeezed them hard. Isaure felt that she had something important to tell her, but that she was holding back.

"I have no secrets from Pascal," she said. "Speak, be quick."

"Oh well my child, your brother become Adventist. He got himself baptized in the sea like Jesus in the Jordan. He don't work on Saturday and he go out on his boat and nobody know why."

"Gustave's goings-on are not my business, my dear Yvonne. He's big enough to do what he thinks best. Oh! I can see that Sainte-Anne hasn't changed!"

Isaure stopped suddenly. In the open door, a tall, attractive woman had just stepped within the door frame and the bright light behind her kept her features indistinguishable, but by the silhouette alone, it was obvious that she was not from the region.

Yvonne said: "Good-day, Mme Andrée," and the fishermen raised their heads without seeming too surprised. Evidently, this wasn't the first time the foreigner had come into the cafe;

she must have been at Sainte-Anne for some time. Isaure recognized her as the woman from Trinidad, the one she had
dragged by the hair in Daniel's bedroom, the one she had
thrown out through the window. The woman, no longer hesitating, came forward, her hand extended.

"What a surprise to see you here."

Isaure did not take the hand offered to her. She asked in a
forceful tone:

"You speak French now?"

The métisse was at the point of getting up and slapping
her. She rose, but when she stood, she turned to Pascal.

"It's time for us to leave. Gustave doesn't know where we
are."

Pascal drank the rest of the corrosol[21] in his glass and went
out. He had noticed his friend's agitation and once outside,
he asked:

"You know this woman?"

"Oh, I saw her once in Fort-de-France. It's not important;
she's not worth our while."

She was lying. This was important to her, at least. Why was
her past cropping up suddenly in her path?

Luckily, a little farther on, they were stopped by old Mayotte
who had just carried her pigs their feed. Right away, she began to complain, as in the past.

"Isaure, my sweet, these animals so much work, believe me.
I got to pay somebody to bring water from the marsh, one
franc for ten liters. It rain so little around here! Last year the
sun dry out the marshes and grass go in the ground. The sheep
die hungry and I lose two cows . . ."

Isaure, nonetheless, lingered with her and it was Pascal who
had to remind her that Gustave was waiting for them. But she
had known Mayotte when she was a little girl, and she enjoyed rediscovering a past older than the one she had just
evoked.

IX
The Sea

At six in the morning, Pascal and Isaure were already on the beach, bordered with mancenilliers, whose sap and leaves and the shadow itself, according to certain folk, are filled with evil spirits. Gustave had left two or three hours earlier with his sailboat while the village was still sleeping.

There was quite a bustle on the beach. Bare chested fishermen, wearing *bacouas*[22] to protect their heads from the sun, paddled their boats in a circle in order to lay down huge nets that other fishermen on the beach were pulling back with ropes. Once this was done, they went on shore to help their fellow workers to haul. Then the children rushed into the sea and, screaming, beat the water with their hands. The women waited with their *couis*.[23] Slowly, the net drew tighter and the fish jumped, scared. Finally, after an hour's work, they were beached on the sand. The silver fish were wriggling, others were beating the sand with their powerful tails. A small grey shark was put aside and killed right away. The catch had been good. The noisy crowd drew near; the distribution and selling began.

"Man Hector, ou lé deux kilogs."

"Ça ka fait cent f'ancs."

"Missié Eugène, ba moin un kilog." [24]

Finally, shouting all the while, they ended up coming to an agreement. The nets were washed and stretched out, the rigging rolled up, the fishing boats refloated.

Pascal and Isaure had not seen Gustave leave at dawn. They didn't know that on the doorstep of his house he had found a large red pepper, completely charred. But Gustave knew what that meant: if he had stepped on it, he was lost. However, he had little fear of his enemies. He had taken his precaution according to a Hindu recipe that he alone in Saint-Anne knew, and which had always been successful for him. It was rather complicated. First, using charcoal on a sheet of white paper, he would take an impression of his good foot, that is, of the foot he first put on the ground that morning. Then, he would wrap the piece of charcoal and three pennies in the paper and keep all of it for three days under this bed. The night before, being very careful to take out the package at the same hour that he put it there, he had taken the three pennies and had thrown them over his left shoulder, without turning around, at three different crossroads. Finally, he had thrown the remains—that is, the paper and the charcoal—into the sea. Thus, he was quite calm, and of course, he had not said a word about all of that to Pascal and Isaure.

Those two put the fishing boat in the water and got on board. Pascal started off by rowing while Isaure was at the helm, but soon they left the calm waters of the Sainte-Anne roadstead and, with the wind blowing more forcefully, they could hoist the sail.

Putting out to sea, they had a general view of the peninsula. On one side, the ocean surged and lapped a steep and almost deserted coast, growing thin toward the headland's deep crag—called English Bay—almost closed by a reef and some islets. Just before the southern headland stood a plateau, one hundred meters high where no vegetation grew. Isaure knew it well. It was called the Savane des Pétrifications because the objects left there through the years were covered with a coat of limestone that gave them a stone-like appearance without taking away their original shape, and which caused visitors to believe that they risked being changed into stones. Off this plateau loomed several rocky islets, among which was the Table du Diable, facing the headland of Enfer[25] which ended the Savanne des Pétrifications. The sea became rough and the boat, listing toward the shiny waters, struggled courageously against the currents. Around them, quick as silver arrows, flying fish darted from the waves, rising some sixty centimeters and, after having traveled about ten meters, alighted on the water like a seaplane. Isaure knew that, at night, they flew high enough to fall all by themselves into the boats; the fishermen had only to cook them for their breakfast. It was an easy catch, less heroic than catching tuna. That fish had to be snared "en Miquelon" which doesn't mean that it was necessary to go all the way to Saint-Pierre and Miquelon,[26] but one had to go far enough out to sea to lose sight of the coastline. When the tuna was hooked, it was roped until it choked, for it was brought to the boat only when dead. This was not without danger, for if caught in the currents, the fisherman risked being carried off instead of bringing in the fish. The stories of Miquelon were worthy of Tartarin.[27] Isaure had heard about them from the very mouth of her brother, Gustave!

At last, Pascal guided the boat to an oblong islet on which, among the herbage, stood a lighthouse. It was the islet at Cabrit. They grounded the boat and chose a shady spot to unpack their supplies. The open air had given them an appetite; they, however, were not thinking about eating.

"Let's go in the water," suggested Pascal.

The water was calm and transparent in the creek they had chosen. Pascal delighted in diving, and swimming under water he passed under Isaure's body, sometimes catching her by one foot trying to make her swallow water, as in by-gone days when, as children, they swam together. But hardly had he surfaced when Isaure caught him and, laughing, tried to dunk his head under water. Their supple bodies moved slowly and gracefully. They grappled with each other until, out of breath, they had to separate to get a breath of air. It was wonderful play.

When they finally left the water to dry off on the sand, they were not as much at ease. They remained for a moment seated very close to each other. They were alone with the sea and the sky, somewhat at a loss, having neither game to play nor movement to make, and finding themselves on solid earth, sheltered from the wind. Suddenly, Pascal placed his hand on Isaure's bare leg. She shuddered. This gesture, however, which perhaps was one more of possession than desire, seemed natural to her. She was not at all shocked by it, the shudder she felt was even strangely pleasurable. She wished that the hand had felt bolder. But Pascal didn't move; it even seemed that he dared not look at her. He was silent; he remained silent. In the end, it was Isaure who was the first to speak.

"It's good to be here," she said.

She would liked to have said: "I like for you to touch me," but a kind of timidity which astonished her more than anything else, didn't allow it. He was the one who asked finally:

"You like for me to touch you?"

She signaled yes, precipitously, with her head, her eyes glowing with gratitude, and drew a little nearer. She was not accustomed to that hand placed upon her, and it seemed that for the first time in her life she was in the presence of a man, while knowing that she belonged to that man.

On the way back, the wind rose, swelling the sail and causing the boat to list as it left a deep trace behind, ploughing the sea. It romped like a huge dog in the waves and the sun. Isaure, seated on the side, at times felt sprays on her face, and she licked her lips with delight. When they arrived in the well sheltered bay of Sainte-Anne, Pascal lowered the sail and pulled the fishing boat onto the bank.

They were alone in Gustave's house and that night the young man could not do otherwise than to stay in Isaure's room.

X
Liberation

"You ought to let your bar go," Pascal said a few days after they returned to Fort-de-France. "It's not wise to be around sailors at this time."

"I want to earn my living," Isaure answered. "Even if I had enough money, I would like to keep on working. Work is a woman's dignity."

"A married woman . . ."

"I'm not a married woman."

"Even if I married you?"

Isaure looked at her lover with terrified eyes, dry eyes where, nonetheless, there burned an immeasurable flame of hope. But right away she lowered her head in order to extinguish this look and murmured in a tone of resignation:

"That's not possible . . ."

Nevertheless, Pascal knew what he wanted and when had an idea in his head, he didn't have it in his feet, as the island people say. He sought to convince Isaure, but as time went on she no longer responded. Then he took advantage of this silence to talk about his plans to his own family. A few days after, he found his sweetheart in an angry mood.

"Why didn't Isabelle say hello to me?" she exclaimed.

Pascal shrugged his shoulders.

"When I met her she rudely turned her head. Why didn't she look at me on purpose?"

Isabelle was the youngest of Pascal's sisters whom he had provided for as well as their mother since the father's death. Didn't that give him the right to give orders? Even if he had not done his duty as conscientiously, he was the only man in the family.

The announcement of his plan to marry Isaure, however, had created a tempest. Being creole, Pascal's family was much more prejudiced against colored people than the more recently arrived settlers on the island. Even though they were not rich, they considered the length of time their family had lived there a title of nobility.

Ah! That had been a spirited chorus!

"A girl who owns a bar," exclaimed one of the sister.

"Who's had a string of lovers," another added.

"A negress . . ."

"This brings shame to all of us," said the fourth.

In vain, Pascal affirmed that Isaure had always lead a decent life, that he had known her for a long time, that he couldn't find a better woman. His sisters had known Isaure since childhood and they knew Pascal's reasoning was justified, but that didn't change the skin color of the one he wanted to marry. Pascal, at last, had reddened in anger.

"She could be ebony colored, I'd marry her anyway," he cried out, stomping his foot. "I don't give a damn about your prejudices, do you understand? Who's earning the living for everybody here? Who's head of the family? I'm telling you to shut up, I've had enough of your nonsense."

There was no need to relate this scene to Isaure, no need to answer her questions, to explain why Isabelle had not greeted her. Already the métisse was lowering her head.

"You shouldn't marry me, darling," she said. "You know that a white man doesn't marry a negress."

"You're not a negress."

"I'm a mixed-blood, it's all the same."

"So you don't love me?"

"You know that I love you."

She tried to repress her ardor, to let go of her wonderful hope. The humility of colored people mounted to replace her susceptibility.

"I'll live with you, if you want," she said. "I'll do what you want. I'll obey you like a dog. You don't need to marry me."

Pascal took one hand and slowly, patiently, he began to explain that these prejudices came from past history.

"My sisters are idiots. They don't understand that the Allied victory, the success of Communism is definitely going to abolish this stupid racism. Yes, yes, even on our island. I'll say even more: the future is for the blacks and in five or six years— all question of love aside—perhaps I'll be more than happy as one of the first to have married a colored woman."

Isaure smiled sadly. She didn't believe in Pascal's hopes, she couldn't reject all at once what she had been told, all that she had seen. It was true, however, that blacks, in the face of the growing defeat of the Germans and the discrediting of Vichy, were lifting their sights, already welcoming General de Gaulle as their liberator. That year, the planters had not planted even though (or because) Admiral Robert had asked them to in November. The fishermen no longer wanted to fish because transporting deserters brought them more. Moreover, there was no place to spend their money, since all the city stores were empty. Limitations allowed a quasi-official black market to flourish so much so that the highlands of Didier were stuffed with goods while the city below was beginning to suffer severely.

Discontent was widespread; the Navy was openly criticized by the békés goyaves, békés goyaves by the mulattoes, mulattoes by blacks. The latter were becoming unbelievably insolent. They spoke openly about revolution, encouraged each evening by the voice of Henri Gallantière sent to them by radio from Boston.[28]

It was on a Saturday evening that a frenzied crowd shouting "Long live de Gaulle, down with the whites!" marched in the streets of Fort-de-France, without the police or the naval force being able to stop it. The next day, Sunday, on the occasion of the opening of the bay where the *Emile-Bertin* lay careening, Admiral Robert appealed to the masses for calm and work. He had arrested the ringleaders but was forced to release them immediately. There were new demonstrations; the black population, again and again, was bellowing threats.

Pascal couldn't hide his enthusiasm, while his sisters lived in terror. Isaure wished for the revolution with all her heart; she felt herself ready to side with the blacks. It seemed to her that her happiness, her life, depended on this.

The whites, themselves, were divided. Suddenly, it was learned that the white regiment stationed at Balata had just rebelled and that General Tourtet, at its head, was threatening to open fire on the city if the Admiral didn't give himself up.

Then panic was mingled with enthusiasm. All the while shouting, "Long live Tourtet! Down with the Nazis! Down with Admiral Robert!" women, childen and even men fled to the countryside, while others, however, brandishing their razors, acting like cut-throats, swore to butcher all the békés.

At last, Admiral Robert capitulated. He published a communique in which he declared that "to avoid the flow of blood between French people," and forced to give in as a result of the inhumane blockade by the United States, he had asked the latter to dispatch a plenipotentiary who would discuss with him the transfer of new French authorities to the islands.

On the 14th of July, the cruiser, *Le Terrible*, having entered the Fort-de-France harbor, disembarked Mr. Hoppenot. Three weeks later, Pascal married Isaure.

According to the wishes of the woman of mixed-blood, the marriage was very simple. No doubt it would have occurred unnoticed in the midst of such serious events, if Sallière hadn't thought it his duty to write an article in his newspaper, praising Pascal for no longer having color prejudice. There was, however, no compliment for Isaure, and Sallière of course ended with a few insults addressed to Admiral Robert whom he called nothing more than Admiral Poyo.

XI
Farewell Du Taillant

Abruptly, everything started happening inversely. Those who had been despised were glorified, those who had been in hiding were in power, those who had wielded authority had taken flight. Admiral Robert had fled to Puerto-Rico and the infamous chief of police, persecutor of the prostitutes on the Savane, managed to follow him. Gustave, Isaure's brother, formerly a fisherman, was now mayor of Sainte-Anne. On reading Sallière's newspaper, no longer *The Trumpet* but now *Liberty*, the mouthpiece of the Communist party, Isaure learned that Gustave, who had transported numerous deserters and aided countless escapees, had been decorated and was looked upon as one of the greatest heros of the island. Sallière had of course been decorated; he took advantage of the occasion by printing his picture on the first page of *Liberty*.

From the newspaper, Isaure also found out that the woman from Trinidad, whom she had thrown out of Daniel's bedroom and had met in Sainte-Anne not too long ago, was a spy for the Admiral. The black Gaullists recognized her as she prowled the environs of Sainte-Anne, and had her head clean shaven. After having been amply beaten, she was put on board alone in a fishing boat and abandoned in the open sea, but two or three days later, she landed ashore. It appeared that she had not yet recovered from her adventure.

Amidst all these events, Isaure's marriage had not caused

the scandal that she feared. Pascal's sisters, themselves, terrified by what was taking place on the island, didn't perform too badly. One day, however, Isabelle, who harbored the tongue of a snake, insinuated that Pascal had always favored negresses. Obviously, she used the word to hurt Isaure who had sworn, once and for all, to remain calm and polite with her sisters-in-law, which was not easy. One day, after a visit from Isabelle, she burst into tears. Another time, she performed a jealous scene as she had done with Daniel. She questioned him about his past, asked him if were true about his taste for black women as ascribed by Isabelle. Pascal gently answered that he'd always liked blacks, men and women, that he preferred them to whites, above all to békés goyaves, that he had had other affairs, but now he was too much in love with Isaure to think about any other woman. His gentleness and tenderness succeeded in soothing the hot tempered métisse. She ended up by blaming herself, asking his forgiveness. Pascal responded:

"You don't have to ask me to forgive you. All I ask is for you to have confidence in me."

"You are so strong and good," she said. " I don't know why I don't let myself be happy. I don't know what gets into my blood."

She dared not speak about her black blood.

There were times, however, when she let herself go and was truly happy, happier than she had ever dreamed of being.

They lived in a pretty, one-story white house, modern colonial style, at the edge of the plantation where Pascal worked. From the windows, Isaure could see the blacks, with their cutlasses, cutting sugar cane into three pieces, and the mules slowly gathering the stubs that would be used for making rum. Pascal arrived each evening at punch time. Everything was prepared for him. He was in good humor and loved to have fun with little François, taking him on his knees, telling him stories.

"Soon we'll give him a little brother," he would say.

Isaure would smile. She felt like another woman since being married. At last, she had the right to love a man, to go out with him, to kiss him in public if she wanted (but she didn't want to). Even if she had not cherished Pascal as much, even if she didn't get along so well with him, doubtlessly, she would have loved him for the simple fact that he had become her husband. She had always aspired for legitimacy and permanency, she who had been illegitimate, then an unwed mother, she who was neither white nor black. Emmanuel had abandoned her with child; Daniel had not given her a child, but hadn't married her. One day, she said to Pascal:

"He saw me only as flesh."

But she no longer wanted to think either about Emmanuel or Daniel; she wanted to think only about Pascal and their happiness. For her, life was becoming a fairy story, it was like a scene in those movies where young millionaires married beautiful, poor girls. Unconsciously, she had started to sing again as in the carefree days of her youth. She even went to confession, which had not occurred for three years.

They lived privately, never tiring of each other and not caring about being with the wealthy békés, their neighbors; they despised those so-called aristocratic creoles who with a sure hand had led their families to opulence and their island to ruin. They scarcely had need for amusement. Isaure did the housework along with her faithful Lucia who had followed her and Pascal.

Since the incidents of Liberation, quarrels frequently broke out among the blacks on the plantation, but Pascal, who knew each one, knew how to settle them fairly.

Two or three times they went to dance at the Madiana, an outdoor dance hall on Schoelcher road, less snobbish than the Lido and less common than Select-Tango. Isaure dearly loved to dance with Pascal, but she still preferred to stay at home alone with him. One day in the late afternoon, Lucia burst into the room where her "madam" was.

"Ma'm Isau'! Ma'm Isau'! You know who's here? Couldn't

believe my eyes. I swear to you! Bet my life you can't guess who! "

"Well, tell me and let's see!"

"Mistuh du Taillant. He's here and in a fine captain's uniform."

"Du Taillant?" exclaimed Isaure. "So, where is he?"

"I had him sit in a chair on the veranda. Oh, Ma'm Isau'," the black woman repeated, crossing her hands over her heart. "It's not possible Mistuh du Taillant come back?"

Du Taillant had not sat down; he was pacing the veranda somewhat nervously. On seeing Isaure, he walked over to meet her.

"Du Taillant," she cried out, "how pleased I am to see you! What a handsome uniform! Are those your captain's stripes? You've truly earned them. If only you knew how I've worried about you. Did you know that I've been asking about you?"

"I know, Isaure. I also know how faithfully you took the message I entrusted you with and I've come to thank you."

"Oh," said Isaure, "it was my husband who took charge of the message. He went with me to Sainte-Anne. It was there, you know, that we became engaged."

"So, perhaps you owe your marriage a little to me."

"Why, of course," Isaure said laughingly. "Life is funny, eh! All in all, it's rather my part to thank you. But I'm forgetting my duties as a hostess. Would you like a little punch? Do you still like the 'planter'?"

"Yes, that's right, a 'planter'," said the young officer in a melancholy voice.

Isaure didn't need to call Lucia for her to bring the best rum. With dexterity, Isaure made the mixtures: sugar syrup, two-thirds rum, lemon and something else that was her secret. She held out the glass to du Taillant.

"How long have you been here?"

She was surprised at not having anything else to ask him.

"I returned from the United States day before yesterday with the *Emile-Berlin*. I had a hard time finding you. I went to

236

your former apartment and then to the bar. There, I met your sister who informed me of your marriage and gave me your address, and then I couldn't come to see you sooner after all that happened . . ."

"Oh," Isaure said. "Why all these brawls? Can't people live happily, now that the war's over?"

"Our sailors don't have good memories of Fort-de-France," the officer explained. "They realized that their doudous had tricked them with the blacks and they're determined to get revenge. On the first evening, they landed armed with kitchen knives and knucklebusters. Coming upon their former mistresses unexpectedly, they broke up the furniture they had given them. Of course, news of their behavior spread quickly from house to house."

"I see that from here. The frantic doudous had to knock on their neighbor's door: 'It's awful, dearie, they break everything; they'll kill everybody, what a mess!'"

"As a matter of fact, they didn't touch the women, they were satisfied to fight with the black men. I was on duty that evening. There was a real commotion. A lot of the black households, in panic, moved away in a few minutes. I saw trucks passing with all kinds of things piled helter-skelter, going at fast pace toward the countryside."

"Yes, I saw that too."

She remembered having gone down to Fort-de-France with Pascal. Not far from the port, they met a huge black man dressed in white, in such a way that the new red ribbon he wore in his boutonniere burst out like a flower. It was Sallière. In spite of his fancy dress, he had stopped to shake Pascal's hand. "Unbelievable things are happening, aren't they? A state of siege should be declared, shouldn't it?" A truck laden with furniture hastily piled on, with a black man perched on top holding on perilously, cut off his words while jostling him.

"Brawls have been many and serious, such that yesterday sailors were confined to the ship. But they were outraged. Some managed to get dinghies, others jumped in the water

and swam as a gang to shore. Last night, five sailors were killed
and forty wounded, some seriously."

"How many blacks were killed?"

"I don't know," du Taillant confessed. He rose.

"And you, du Taillant," asked Isaure, "aren't you going to
get married soon?"

"I don't know."

"You're not leaving yet?"

"I have to get back on ship before it's too late."

"My husband will be here shortly. I'd like for you to meet
him. You know that it was because of him, I was able to deliver
your message."

"Yes, without a doubt, I ought to thank him too," said the
young officer. "But you will give him my excuses. I'm forced
to return on board early this evening."

"Then come back another time."

"Certainly, if I can," said du Taillant. "I don't believe that
the Emile-Bertin will remain much longer in Fort-de-France
harbor. Its presence here causes too many disturbances. And
then . . ."

He seemed to hesitate a moment, still timid despite his
captain's stripes and his heroic deeds. Abruptly he extended
his hand.

"I'll say good-bye, Isaure. Thank you for what you've done
for me."

Isaure was surprised not to feel any emotion. When Pascal
returned, she told him:

"I had a visit from du Taillant. He was very sorry not to see
you, but he had to get back to the Emile-Bertin."

"I hope he'll come back," said Pascal rather indifferently.
"I don't know," Isaure answered.

Deep down, she had no desire to see du Taillant again; she
had never even thought about inviting him to dinner.

XII
The Catastrophe

"Once upon a time there was a little girl whose mother and sisters didn't love her," Isaure began. Since being married, she had told François many stories. He listened silently, looking at his mother with large, attentive eyes.

"The little girl was often beaten and she had much work to do. Each morning, she had to fill jars at the river. Now one day, she noticed a tiny fish in the river, who, because he was little, was always beaten up by the others. Feeling very sorry for him, she dug a hole beside the river, filled it with water and placed the little fish in it. From that day on, everyday at exactly eleven o'clock, she would bring him food, and to have him come to the top she would sing:

> *Solino, Solino, bel Solino*
> *Soli, mon coeur*
> *Soli de io . . .*

And the little fish answered, wriggling:

> *Kai man io*
> *Kai man io*
> *Kai man de io*

"At home, they kept on beating the little girl. Only at the river was she happy. One day, however, her sisters followed her and heard her singing and they told their mother what they had seen and heard. The mother forbade the little girl to go to the river. The next day, the little fish had nothing to eat. On the day following, the wicked sisters went down themselves and, imitating the little girl's voice, they sang:

> *Solino, Solino, bel Solino*
> . . . .
> *Kai man io.*

Then the wicked sisters threw bits of poisoned bread to him and the little fish ate them."

"Is that true, mama?" asked François.

"Wait now. The sisters returned home and said:

'The fish is dead.'

The little girl wept but she said: 'It's not true, the fish can't come to the top, he couldn't have died.'

So the mother said: 'Alright, go get some water.'

When she arrived at the river, the little girl sang:

> *Solino, Solino, beautiful Solino . . .*

There was no answer so she threw herself into the hole which was now a pond because it had grown along with the fish, and she drowned. The pond closed up and lovely flowers grew on the spot. One day, the mother went to cut them, but she heard a voice singing:

> *Mother, oh, mother*
> *Don't cut my beautiful hair...*

Frightened, the mother ran to the King and told him what she had heard. The King decided to dig up the spot and he sent a courtier to uproot the ground. But just as the man was brandishing his sickle, he heard:

> *Headsman, oh, headsman*

Don't cut my beautiful hair,
Because it's mother who put me here.

The courier was afraid. He ran away and went to tell the King
that he had heard a woman's voice singing. The King decided to
go himself. As soon as he arrived, the voice rang out:

My King, oh, my King.
Don't let that gentleman do it,
Because it's mother who put me here.

The King got down from his horse, brushed aside the grass
and flowers and uncovered the little girl who had grown up
and become very beautiful. He took her to his palace and
married her. The little girl invited her mother and her sisters
to the wedding, but, filled with jealousy, they told the king
that she was a sorceress and that she should be killed. Then
the little girl told the King the story of the fish.

'If you don't find him in the spot where I was,' she added,
'Then kill me.'

Once again, the King went down to the river. On the spot
where he had found the little girl, there was a pond and suddenly, he saw the fish. Then the king wanted to kill the mother
and the sisters, but the little girl persuaded him to do the
opposite, to build them a house next to the palace and they
lived happily ever after."

Isaure loved to tell these kinds of stories. Perhaps she told
them as much to reassure herself as to amuse François. Indeed, around her there reigned an atmosphere, at times, odious to her. Despite Pascal's optimism, it appeared that Liberation had not settled matters. The Emile-Bertin affair had
enraged the blacks who before had fled from the sailors, but
now clenched their fists, shouted, railed against every kind of
béké, swearing to kill them all. They created dreadful scenes
with their reconquered women. Isaure heard reports through
Lucia who had lived for a while with a sailor, but who since
had taken up with a black.

"Sometime he put himself in front of me and yell, showing you-know-what: 'You kin do for me what you done for those old whites.' And sometime he get mad and want to beat me. He's dying from jealousy. He yell that I'm a traitor. Ah, what a life, Ma'am Isau'!"

As for Isaure, she had to undergo countless harassments, not only from her in-laws but from the blacks themselves. Since her childhood days, when whites were all-powerful, they treated the mixed-bloods like blacks. Now that a reverse racism had developed, in the eyes of the blacks they were almost as unpopular as the whites. In the same family, there were visible signs of terrible hatreds: a black boy detested his brother whose color was lighter than his. It was better to be either white or black, not between the two, like Isaure and her son. She had managed to marry a white, a béké goyave, but for all that, she had not become white and her in-laws made her feel this keenly.

The love that she felt for Pascal didn't blind her. Deep down, she was not as happy as she had expected. She feared bringing harm to him and differences that perhaps were not really important, in her eyes, assumed exaggerated proportions. It seemed to her that the plantations's black laborers looked at her askance, and, at times, it even seemed to her that she was the cause of these rivalries, these jealousies, these hatreds, which were springing up. Without a doubt, Pascal would have convinced her otherwise, but she dared not speak to him of such things.

One day, they had a visit from the manager of the Macouba plantation, also owned by the proprietor of Basse-Pointe. He was a large man, by the name of Perret, who had a kidney ailment and seemed to be more yellowish and weary than usual. While serving the traditional punch, Isaure listened in on the conversation of the two men.

"The workers at Macouba are on strike," Perret was saying. "They're clamoring for a salary raise; the Communist leaders have egged them on. I've never seen blacks in such a state.

They're mouthing threats while they go about waving their cutlasses. I haven't been able to go near them."

Pascal smiled. Perhaps it was Perret's cowardice that made him smile.

"It's only their words that are terrible. I know them well. They shout real loud, they swear they're going to kill everybody, but in the end they do nothing."

"It's not like before, now that politics are mixed up in it."

Pascal shrugged.

"Do you want me to go over there?"

Perret was waiting for this offer.

"To tell the truth," he said, "I think you alone can make them listen to reason."

Isaure wanted to cry out to her husband: "Don't go!" But Pascal had risen. When he made a resolution, he never lost time. She consoled herself by murmuring:

"Take your gun, Pascal."

Pascal's face became stern.

"Are you mad, Isaure? How can I take my gun against my black friends? That's not my way, you know that. I've other ways to calm them down."

He was so sure of himself that, at first, Isaure was not truly frightened. She let him leave in Perret's car. When alone, nonetheless, she reassumed her uneasiness. Time passed so slowly that she found it impossible to remain in front of the living room clock. She went outside and, mechanically, walked toward the plantation.

That day was one of torrid heat; not a single breeze to move the long stalks of sugar cane. As usual, the laborers, men and women, were busy cutting, gathering and loading. Their shacks, scattered on the plantation, for the most part, were empty. Things, however, were not as usual. As Isaure went by, there were stares: burning, quick, furtive, askance; stares that frightened her because they were not those she was accustomed to. They were not only flashes of desire or envy, but they seemed to gleam with an evil delight, a kind of triumph, like arrows devised to wound her, precisely reaching their mark. Was Pascal encountering these same stares? Did the blacks already know what was going on over there, what was going to happen? She began to be afraid, even though she still heard the regular slashes of the cutlasses on the stalks and the sound of the mules' hooves striking the ground, and though she saw nothing more than bare backs, dark, bowed and glistening from sweat.

Then she came to the end of the field where there was a kind of storehouse which, in by-gone days, had been used as a jail cell for slaves. They would stay there several days, feet in irons, in a miserable position, beaten and deprived of food. Isaure was not unaware that the cell existed but she had never had the curiosity to go inside. The heat inside was unbearable. On the walls, she noticed two thick iron rings. Her grandfather and great-grandfather had, perhaps, been chained to such rings, had suffered such torture, had died under whiplashes. She hastened to leave, for she was afraid of her own thoughts. What was Pascal doing? Oh, surely, he wasn't going to beat the blacks, he who loved them so much! He had left without a weapon, confident only in the force of his presence, his word. But he was white, nothing prevented him from being white and he still might think like a white. For a moment, she stood immobile, contemplating her shadow, a slight, very dark shadow. Then only, did she realize that it was for his life that she was fearful. For generations, so much hatred had accumulated àmong blacks! How could they forsake seeking vengeance, now that the opportunity presented itself? Oh, for sure, they knew how to disguise their thoughts, they had learned to do that at length, in the course of centuries of oppression, but every now and then all of this exploded, and so ended their submissiveness, and they became raving, wild beasts who neither recognized anyone nor knew what they were doing. Why hadn't she understood that this anger of the blacks was mounting, overflowing? Had not she witnessed enough incidents these latter days to have had her eyes opened?

Ah! She no longer wanted to think! She started walking, retracing the path she had just covered, at a slow pace, nonchalantly, with that swaying of the hips characteristic of the island women, and which she accentuated, perhaps unconsciously. No longer was she stared at. As she went by, she saw only black, brown and yellow backs, more and more bent over. It was the way they bent over before their former masters, but with a different meaning. She went forward in solitude and sadness, even her well-fitted sun-dress gave her an uneasy feeling. She would have liked to be wearing a simple black dress like that of the old negress that she had just passed, a black checked scarf wrapped around her head. At last, she came to the place in the field where she could see the house. Perret had come back. She saw his car there almost at the same time that she noticed him standing on the veranda, head bowed, seemingly hesitant, while near him, Lucia was wildly gesticulating.

At that moment, her sadness and fear became panic. She began to run, no matter the suffocating heat. Her heart leaped in her chest like an animal Oh, let it explode, she cried inside, so that everything will be over, so that I, too, will be dead.

XIII
The Visit

Isaure had lived through the funeral services, neither seeing nor hearing. It seemed to her that all nature, even the sunlight had become indifferent. She barely endured Lucia's lamentations and rebuffed François whenever he tried to come near her. She could not, however, remain forever in that state, for everyday life was not so tolerant. The owner of the plantation already had let it be known that he needed the house for the new overseer.

One week after Pascal's death she went to see her sister. She felt a need to confide her suffering and to talk about her plans, because it was crucial that she make plans. But, since Ophelia greeted her with such obvious empathy, she decided that it would have been cowardly to complain.

"I came to see you so that you can find me a house," she stated simply. "I plan to settle in Fort-de-France."

"Find a house? You know perfectly well that's like asking me to find a darkie with blue eyes!"

"Nevertheless, I have to leave the plantation," Isaure persisted, "I can't stay there . . ."

Her sister gazed at her steadily. How much she has changed in a few days, she said to herself. But Isaure found that Ophelia too had changed. Why doesn't she offer to take me in with her? Of course, she would prefer Clément to her! She would also like to keep the bar for herself, since she knew that she was now able to run it alone. Ophelia was still looking at her, hesitantly.

"Isaure," she said finally, "I know I'm going to hurt you, but I have to speak frankly and tell you what I've heard. Pascal's mother would like for you to leave the island."

"For me to leave the island? Why?"

"Because you've had a child by Emmanuel, because you kept a bar in Fort-de-France, because you served Gaullists and, above all, because you have been the wife of Pascal who was killed by blacks. She says that you have ruined her daughters' chances to get married."

Isaure had the feeling that she ought to have cried, but she experienced a sort of joy on learning that Pascal's family worried themselves about her to such an extent.

"Is she claiming that I'm responsible for the death of my husband?"

"No, no, I don't think so . . . But she has been to a lawyer and says she'll come to you to lay claim to what belonged to her son."

"Who told you all that, may I ask?"

"Sure. Well, can you imagine, it's Emmanuel . . ."

Isaure gave her sister a suspicious look.

"Emmanuel? He's here?"

"Yes, he's here, imagine that. He arrived on one of the latest boats and even came to have a 'planter-punch' at the bar. He came looking for you and was real disappointed not to see you."

"I have no desire to see him," Isaure said violently.

She returned home, very annoyed with her sister. Ophelia, then, no longer understood her? For nothing in the world would she see Emmanuel again. What right did he have to meddle in her business? She was indeed outraged.

Only when the sun vanished behind the mountain, did she regain calm. This was the hour when the birds, rejoicing in the coolness, came out of the shady woods and began to sing. From the marshes, the toads answered them. Insects slowly ascended toward the darkening sky, and entering through open windows a thousand multicolored, tiny butterflies were fluttering around the lamps. On the terrace, François entertained himself by pushing june-bugs inside match boxes, while Lucia brought in the chicks and fed the rabbits.

Isaure put the little boy to bed and came back to settle down on the terrace to enjoy, once again, the cool air. Lucia soon joined her for, once night fell, she was not courageous and, even in the kitchen, she saw ghosts. Isaure willingly kept her company, for, in all honesty, she didn't mind that Lucia was so fearful because that kept her from going out at night.

Lucia tried to work like her mistress, for she was not lazy, but her thick fingers were hardly accustomed to holding a needle. "Oh, Ma'am Isau'," she sighed, "you work like a fairy!"

"You've seen fairies before?"

"No, Ma'am Isau', it's mama moin ka dit ça."

She began to yawn and soon lay down on a mat at her mistress's feet and fell asleep. From time to time, as Isaure looked at her, a trembling shook the black woman's body, as if she were still afraid in her sleep.

Suddenly, Isaure raised her head, believing that she had heard a slow, hesitant step alongside the hedge. No, she was not mistaken. The dogs had already bounded in the direction of the sound. She called out to them:

"Patrick, Caco!"

Lucia was still sleeping. Did she need to awaken her? She looked at her watch; it was nine o'clock. It's probably a worker, she said to herself, who has come to ask for a little ether for someone sick. She had always been helpful to them. Since Pascal's death, however, the blacks no longer came to see her. The noise stopped. No, it was not a worker; he wouldn't have stopped since he would know the dogs and wouldn't be afraid. A thief, then? It's too early for a thief. It's probably Gustave who's coming by after a trip. All the same, the dogs were still barking. Now more anxious, she went to get Pascal's gun, the one Pascal ought to have taken to defend himself against his black assassins, and came back to the terrace. If it's a thief, I'll kill him! Yes, I'll kill him. No longer afraid since holding the weapon in her hand, she went down the steps and glided silently like a bird toward the hedge. Suddenly, she was faced by a black shadow in the night.

"Who are you?" she demanded in a loud voice.

The shadow answered without delay.

"I'm Mrs. Guymet."

Isaure dropped her hand holding the gun.

"So it's Pascal's mother who comes to see me at this hour?"

"It's Pascal's mother," the shadow replied.

"Well, come, madam, do come into my house."

Her heart beat quickened. When her visitor was on the terrace, she looked at her. That milk-colored face made a striking contrast between the black dress and the hat covered by a veil; even the earrings were covered with black crepe. Isaure, who had changed to a white satin dressing gown, felt a twinge of jealousy.

"You don't dare visit me in daylight, that's so, isn't it?"

"I didn't come here for us to quarrel," Mrs. Guymet said with an air she was straining to keep genteel.

"So, why did you come?"

"Can't you guess?"

"No, madam, unfortunately, I have no gift for reading other people's minds."

"Here," said Mrs Guymet, not abandoning her lofty demeanor, "I have received a document from Pascal's lawyer. That's why I've come to see you. I would like to come to an agreement about certain matters."

It soon became evident that the old woman had come only out of self-interest, in order to recuperate things belonging to her son and to settle money matters. Isaure was so disgusted with this, that she yielded on almost all points. Nevertheless, toward the end of the visit, Mrs. Guymet pretended to be concerned about the future of the métisse.

"And now, what are you going to do, my dear?"

"Leave," answered Isaure, in a unresponsive tone.

Eyes flashing, she had to govern a frightful anger. Ah, if she could throw this old woman out the door, how much she would enjoy that!

"Yes," Mrs Guymet asserted in her most lady-like voice, "I believe that's what best for you to do. You have to realize that your situation has become most difficult."

"I don't want my child to be born in this island," Isaure declared.

"What? Your child?"

"Oh yes, I guess he's not only Pascal's."

"Pascal's?" repeated the old woman, speechless.

"Pascal didn't tell you we were expecting a child?"

"But . . . you were only married since . . ."

"What does that prove?" Isaure asked, ruthlessly, and then added: "That's why he married me, because he was a good man. Really, you didn't know?"

Ah! How Isaure enjoyed lying! This was a black vengeance, a vengeance from the days blacks had only these rather servile weapons, the lie, the ruse, in order to struggle against the power and the intelligence of the whites. Standing before this creole who was her mother-in-law, in whatever she did, in whatever she said, she was asserting herself as a negress. This was becoming sheer pleasure. She added:

"How little you knew your son!"

Mrs. Guymet had dropped her air of false gentility. She no longer knew what to say and, at last, defeated, wretched, she departed.

XIV
Adieu Martinique

When all the household belongings and the furniture were set out on the lawn, Isaure began to read the list aloud:

"One bed, one armoire, one dressing-table, one night-table."

Each time, Lucia, pouring forth a flood of tears, touched the object named as if giving it a good-bye caress and answered in a choked voice:

"Yes, ma'am. That's right, ma'am."

"Three paintings, a large snake skin bedside rug (the plantation blacks had given it to Pascal for his wedding gift), a walnut armoire, five leather chairs, three bedside lamps . . ."

Isaure caught her breath; she needed courage to continue. She had needed some on going to the auctioneer and asking him to arrange the sale of all these household furnishings.

"It's quite easy," the auctioneer had said. "All you need to do is make a detailed list of what you want to sell. That list must be made public eight days before the sale, just when the goods will be shown."

"You know under what conditions I lost my husband. I insist that the sale take place quietly, sir."

"Of course, but I'm obligated to conform to the rules."

A date had been set. A truck would come to pick up the furnishings. The day had arrived; the truck would be there in two hours and there was no time to lose. Isaure grew taut.

251

"One dining-room, comprising a table that seats twenty-four, eighteen chairs in home-grown mahogany, one large bench, a small table, a Limoges dinner-service, twenty-eight crystal cups. . . "

Those cups were her mother's, who was very proud of them. She, too, had been proud of being able to bring them to Pascal.

"One box containing rum, port and liqueur glasses . . ."

"You got to say how many, ma'am, those auction folk, they all thieves," sniveled Lucia.

Isaure had to count the glasses.

"One tea service of varied colors."

"You got to say the color, Ma'am Isau', how many red cups, and how many green, please."

Once again, Isaure had to comply. She was forced to admit that her maid was right, but it seemed to her that her heart, her life, was frittering away in little pieces.

"A set of unused saucepans and a set of used saucepans."

"Five unused saucepans and eleven used," sniveled Lucia. "After all," she added, "them two that ain't hardly been used, so you could say seven unused saucepans."

"We must tell the truth."

"Tell the truth to them robbers!"

Isaure told her to hush, for she was impatient to finish.

But when she came to little François' room, she found herself incapable of ennumerating, notwithstanding Lucia's reproaches.

She simply said:

"One child's room, completely furnished."

Better to be robbed than to tear apart her heart.

A few days later, in her empty house, Isaure had a visit from Gustave. He had written her a nice letter, so nice, in fact, that he must have received help from his secretary. She had not seen him since Pascal's funeral. He was dressed in a handsome black suit, wearing two ribbons in his boutonniere and had just bought a car.

"You see how empty it is," Isaure said. "I've decided to sell all my things at auction."

"Yes," Gustave replied, "I saw that in the paper and that's why I came to see you."

"I've decided to leave the island and go live with my son in a more civilized country."

"I think you're doing the right thing," he said.

"Since Pascal's death, my situation has become very trying. The blacks don't forgive me for having married a béké and the békés . . ."

"Yes," Gustave said, "but where are you going, if you don't mind my asking?"

"To France, to Paris."

"Paris? It could be that I'll see you there soon."

"Really?, Isaure exclaimed in surprise. "So you want to leave too? You're having problems?"

"It's possible that I'll be named as Representative," Gustave stated plainly.

Isaure almost smiled, but nothing surprised her anymore.

"The sale will be the day after tomorrow at nine-thirty."

"What does Pascal's family think of that?"

"Oh, don't speak to me about those people!"

"Even so, they're your in-laws."

"Pascal was my husband, the others mean nothing to me. Let's talk about something else, please . . ."

"If I can help you at all, just let me know . . . "

"I would like for you to attend to Pascal's vault."

"Your wishes will be carried out," Gustave said gravely.

Isaure thanked him.. This was the first time she had engaged in such a long conversation since the death of Pascal. Even though Gustave didn't ask, she began telling him about that death, at least what she knew about it. A black himself had described the scene, Perret also, but he had remained at a discreet distance. Isaure hated him.

At Macouba, Pascal had walked alone toward the threatening crowd of blacks, smiling, waving his arms to signal friendliness. Arriving in their midst, he got up on a large rock and shouted: "My friends!" There was no doubt that he had intended to give a short speech, but his voice had been drowned out by yells. He was quiet for a moment, waiting for them to calm down; still smiling, it seems. He must have recognized some of the blacks in the crowd of strikers and, if he had been able to get to each one privately, he would have easily succeeded in convincing them. Was he not their friend? He had gestured to them, but on that day, under the burning sun and in the inward heat of anger, everyone was deaf and blind. All of a sudden, a stone had whizzed by his ears, then a second, a third . . . He had reassumed a louder voice:

"My friends . . . "

A tall black man had pulled him by the legs, he fell back violently and his head struck the ground. Then came the onrush, like a football melee. Blows rained down from everywhere and the sight of blood, which was not long in flowing, only served to incite those savage brutes more. Miraculously, he finally succeeded in getting away and in lying down in a thicket of bamboo. There he stayed for such a long while that Perret, at last, became worried and went to see what was going on. He arrived on the scene at the very moment when Pascal was moving back toward his friends, imploring their help, making a last appeal to their better judgement. He was dragging himself on his hands and knees, leaving behind him a bloody trace. But the blacks, pitiless, whose leaders had willfully fostered hatred, jumped on him and, in an instant, had finished him off with cutlass blows.

Perret had finally called the police. But it was too late. The blacks, terrified at what they had done, fled, scattered, leaving Pascal's mutilated body at that place.

The inquest followed. It appeared that they were tracking down the guilty ones. There would be a law suit and sentencing, Isaure had been assured.

"More the reason," she concluded, "for me to leave."

Gustave agreed with his sister who was a little disappointed by that. She would have liked to be contradicted.

"At this point," continued the young woman, hesitating, "I would like to ask you a question. In spite of your hope of coming to Paris, this is perhaps the last time I'll see you, you know. Promise me that you'll answer frankly."

Gustave raised his hand as if he were taking an oath.

"I swear," he said.

"Do you believe that . . . that I'm in some way responsible for Pascal's death?"

Gustave averted his eyes.

"All Pascal had to do was not get mixed up in that business!"

"That's not what I asked you. Didn't he hurt himself by marrying me? In the minds of békés, I know so, but with blacks . . ."

"Things have sure changed," said Gustave.

She was feeling so, for since Pascal's death, her situation had become impossible. The blacks who had killed him held a grudge against her; they did not forgive her for their misdeeds. During the law suit, it would be intolerable; she wouldn't even be safe.

Without a doubt, Gustave understood, more or less clearly. "After all," she said, "your skin is lighter than mine."

Her brother grimaced in anger.

"You know good and well that don't matter. I'm a nigger."

He uttered that word, shameful as of yesterday, with pride.

Isaure let him leave. She had thought she could talk freely with him, but there was little doubt that he wished for her departure, even for her disappearance. She could be an obstacle to his political career. She would leave, that was certain. But would she find a country where she could finally escape the curse of being neither black nor white?

XV
Too Late

Isaure received the following letter from Mrs. Guymet:

My Dear Child,
I come to you to ask your forgiveness. I did not know that you were carrying Pascal's child; that changes everything. A mother's heart is begging you to forget the things that I said to you yesterday. Just tell me what I must do to atone for my offense. When I told Isabelle that you are expecting a child, she wanted to go see at once, but I had to restrain her since I didn't know how you would have received her. I cannot tell you how much I regret having caused you so much distress, how much I deplore the misunderstanding that separates us. Isn't it possible to forget the past? You can't imagine how moved I was when you announced that you were pregnant. I yearned to take you in my arms. Let the heart of a mother, of a grandmother, entreat you not to leave the island. Let me see Pascal's child, let him be born here at home, I implore you, Isaure.

And then came the rain, the first rain since Pascal's death. The sky was overcast, a violent wind started to blow in from behind the mountain where the rumbling of the storm could be heard. The river had already become a brick-red torrent. And then the rain rushed in. The drops first sank into the sandy earth, but it took a quarter of an hour for lakes to form everywhere. Lucia was wading in three feet of water trying to give a hand to the frantic chickens. Water was now flowing over the first step and the house was like an island. Now, Lucia was arranging the rain-pipes in an effort to save a bit of that rain water, blessed because it came from the heavens and eagerly used as a cure. Only when the storm had ceased did she take off her soaked clothing. The sun shone brighter than ever and quickly drank up all that water. The house tops were smoking like chimneys and the earth like a volcano; birds were singing, animals voiced their joy. Isaure went out on the terrace to breathe the smells rising from the warm, damp earth. The chickens had already come out again to look for worms in the soggy ground. A gentle breeze lightly waved the branches, causing small drops of water to fall. Isaure was regaining a bit more zest for life, and for the first time, she felt responsive to the exuberant nature of her country. At that moment, Lucia appeared to announce that there was a woman "ki ka mandé pou ou."

"What woman?"

"I think it Mr. Pascal's mama."

Isaure leaped to her feet without noticing that she was barefoot; she had an uneasy conscience because she had not answered the letter. Actually, she would not have known what to say. There she was, all at once, facing Mrs. Guymet.

"Be so kind as to enter, madam."

"I afraid of soiling your living-room, I think we'll be better here."

She pointed to the kitchen. Then only did Isaure notice that she was drenched. So she had come out in the rain? Still so as not to be seen?

"No matter," said Isaure, "You see, I have no more furniture."

"Yes, I was told that you were going to put it all up for auction. So you have really decided to leave?"

Pascal's mother sat down in one of the two remaining kitchen chairs.

"You'll excuse me, madam," Isaure said, "but I'm in the middle of moving. I leave tomorrow morning."

"You received my letter?"

Mrs Guymet's voice was distressed.

"Yes, madam, and I thank you, but I haven't had time to answer. I'm sorry."

"So my letter didn't change your decision?"

Isaure indicated the empty room with a nod:

"You see, everything is already gone far away. I would be too, myself . . ."

"But you're pregnant, Isaure. If the waters are rough, will you endure the trip?"

"I have to."

The old woman closed her eyes as if uttering a prayer. Suddenly, she rose and placed her two hands on the shoulders of the woman of mixed-blood.

"Isaure, my girl," she murmured, "Once again, I beg you to forgive me and to forgive Isabelle. Perhaps she has been a little jealous of her brother, the only man in the family, can't you understand?"

"God alone can forgive you, madam. He will forgive you, if your sins are not mortal."

Once again, Mrs. Guymet closed her eyes and reopened them to say:

"For the love of Pascal, stay with us. For the love of this child who will bear his name, the name of my husband."

"I am a negress."

"But that's not true. Your skin is almost as white as mine."

"A white negress, if you wish, but a negress all the same. My ancestors were slaves, and now that we are no longer slaves, we are lepers. And also, I kept a bar, had lovers, had a child who's not Pascal's. Excuse me, as a matter of fact, he's calling me now."

Indeed, having just awakened, François was calling his mother and Isaure was happy to have this pretext for leaving Mrs. Guymet for a while. Unconsciously, she took a small picture of a saint from a suitcase and pinned it under her dress, next to her heart. Almost immediately, she was calmed. She then went back to talk to Mrs. Guymet.

"He isn't sick?" asked the latter.

"No, madam, he was asleep and just woke up."

"There's nothing like rain to make children sleep," said the old woman.

Isaure was touched by these words.

"You know, madam, I ran a bar only to earn my living and my son's."

"I know, I know," said Mrs.Guymet, confusedly.

"You must not believe what people say. You know that Martinicans often have sharp tongues. I am a woman of color, but I have lived respectably. I have not been unworthy of Pascal. He knew me and understood me; we loved each other and, wherever I go, I'll remain faithful to his memory."

She was intoxicated by her own words, but stopped, however, when she saw Mrs. Guymet take out a handkerchief and dab her eyes.

"I didn't intend to grieve you, madam," she said.

She accompanied her mother-in-law a little farther than the plantation gateway. Fresh greenery seemed to have sprung up since the rain, and in the foliage, flowers — now brighter — spread out with new aromas. Nonetheless, slowly making her way back toward that house she was going to leave, Isaure felt very sad.

If she had accepted to go live under the same roof as Mrs. Guymet, would that have really changed the situation? The proposal of the proud creole had really touched her, but she was under no illusion, for it was not for her that these women were being so considerate of the child they hoped would be white and male ... Once he was born ... Ah, Isaure, was a true Martinican, it was easier for her to believe in what she imagined than to persuade others of it.

"I'm not expecting a child," she said to herself harshly. "I'll never have a child by Pascal."

She stopped for a moment near a shack. A black was singing a beguine while accompanying himself awkwardly on his guitar. The tune — which she knew well — was melancholy, and the voice was sensual.

This is, perhaps, the last time I'll hear that, she told herself. She didn't want to linger. She now understood that her stupid lie was forcing her to leave, more so than the hostility of the blacks, or Emmanuels's presence in Fort-de-France, or the attitude of her own family, or the pending law-suit. Everything was arranged; her cabin reserved on the boat which was to leave on the 23rd; today was the 22nd. A little while ago, she had told that to Mrs. Guymet, and so it was that on the eve of her departure it was too late to change her decision. Too late. And that way was best, no more hesitation was possible.

Slowly approaching her empty house, she was thinking that not much remained to do. Oh yes, her good-byes to Lucia, which foretold a lot of tears, and they would last a long time. So it would be best, she decided, to begin them as of this evening, since my sister, of course, will come to get me tomorrow morning.

Notes

[1] -or béké goyave—designate whites who are descendants of European colonists and born in the island of Martinique.

[2] The French cruiser that brought gold from the Bank of France to Martinique.

[3] Residential district in Fort de-France where, traditionally, only upper class whites or very rich gens de couleur lived.

[4] Isaure associates Blanchard with blanc/blanche meaning *white* in English.

[5] The Creole language

[6] A kind of evil spell with esoteric proceedings, or witch-craft, by which means it is claimed to harm people, to cure the sick, to chase away or conjure evil spirits in a predetermined place.

[7] An apparition, phantom or spector, a wandering soul which terrifies the one who sees it. Almost always in black.

[8] Reference to a favorite sport in the Antilles in which the mongoose and the snake, enclosed in a cage, engage in a battle.

[9] A legendary diabolical creature who appears in the form of a seductive young black woman and who preys upon hapless men and steals their souls.

[10] A soup made of cabbage, gumbo (okra), ham bits, roast cod and spices.

[11] Taken from a popular song in Martinican folklore, sung and danced to beguine rhythms. "Give me one little kiss, two little kisses, three little kisses, sweetie."

[12] -or bacoua/bacoué. A woven, wide brimmed hat with a conical crown, worn by Antillean fishermen.

[13] An island to the south of Martinique and the principal connection for the Resistance in Martinique. The fisherman were the main agents for the pro-Gaullists faction.

[14] A town at the southern tip of Martinique.

[15] As used here, the word denotes a seductive Antillean woman.

[16] City on north-west coast of Martinique.

[17] Or blaff — fish cleaned, scalded, cooked in a spicy sauce and seasoned with red pepper, lemon.

[18] Popular word for brandy; also for white rum in the French Antilles.

[19] or babaroise — a drink made with milk, ice and rum, or gin.

[20] A cliff projecting into the water.

[21] Drink made from a plant grown in the Antilles.

[22] See note 13.

[23] Half of a calebasse, a large non-edible fruit which when emptied of its pulp can be used as a bowl.

[24] Creole, rather than French, would be the language spoken by Martinicans during such transactions.

[25] Table du Diable= Devil's Table; Enfer=Hell

[26] Francophone islands off the southern coast of Newfoundland.

[27] *Tartarin de Tarascon,* by Alphonse Daudet (1840-97), is a lightly ironical tale of a boastful southern Frenchman.

[28] The Boston radio, affiliated with the BBC network, broadcast derogatory comments about Admiral Robert who issued increasingly severe regulations prohibiting Martinicans to listen in either public or private. (Claude Chauvet, "La Dissidence sous Vichy." *Cahiers* . . . 134) See Endnote # 41 *Introduction.*